NEW YORK REVIEW BOOKS
CLASSICS

SCHLUMP

HANS HERBERT GRIMM (1896–1950) was born in the town of Markneukirchen and fought in World War I. After the war he taught Spanish, French, and English in Altenburg, and published *Schlump* anonymously in 1928 to avoid drawing his employer's attention to his pacificist beliefs. *Schlump* was not the commercial or popular success Grimm had hoped it would be, but his anonymity protected him when the book was burned by the Nazis in 1933. To avoid suspicion, Grimm joined the Nazi Party and worked as an interpreter in France during World War II. After the war, however, he was barred from teaching because of his party membership and began working in the theater and, later, in a sand mine. In 1950, two days after meeting with East German authorities, Grimm committed suicide; it is not known what was discussed at the meeting.

JAMIE BULLOCH is a historian and translator of German literature. His most recent translations include *Look Who's Back* by Timur Vermes and *Raw Material* by Jörg Fauser.

VOLKER WEIDERMANN is the former director and editor of the Sunday edition of *Frankfurter Allgemeine Zeitung* and is currently a contributor to *Der Spiegel*. His most recent book is *Ostend: Stefan Zweig, Joseph Roth, and the Summer Before the Dark*.

THIS IS A NEW YORK REVIEW BOOK
PUBLISHED BY THE NEW YORK REVIEW OF BOOKS
435 Hudson Street, New York, NY 10014
www.nyrb.com

First published anonymously in Germany in 1928

The translation of this work was supported by a grant from the
Goethe-Institut which is funded by the German Ministry of Foreign Affairs

Library of Congress Cataloging-in-Publication Data
Names: Grimm, Hans Herbert, 1896–1950, author. | Bulloch, Jamie, translator.
    | Weidermann, Volker, 1969– writer of supplementary content.
Title: Schlump / Hans Herbert Grimm ; afterword by Volker Weidermann ;
    translated by Jamie Bulloch.
Other titles: Schlump. English
Description: New York : NYRB Classics, 2016. | Series: New York Review of
    Books Classics
Identifiers: LCCN 2016019773 | ISBN 9781681370262 (paperback)
Subjects: LCSH: World War, 1914–1918—Fiction. | Pacifism—Fiction. |
    Soldiers—Germany—Fiction. | Psychological fiction. | BISAC: FICTION
    / War & Military. | FICTION / Psychological. | FICTION / Literary. |
    GSAFD: War stories. | LCGFT: Autobiographical fiction.
Classification: LCC PT2613.R52125 S3513 2016 | DDC 833/.912—dc23
LC record available at https://lccn.loc.gov/2016019773

ISBN 978-1-68137-026-2
Available as an electronic book; ISBN 978-1-68137-027-9

Printed in the United States of America on acid-free paper.
10 9 8 7 6 5 4 3 2 1

SCHLUMP

*Tales and adventures from the life of the anonymous
soldier Emil Schulz, known as "Schlump." Narrated
by himself.*

HANS HERBERT GRIMM

Translated from the German by

JAMIE BULLOCH

Afterword by

VOLKER WEIDERMANN

NEW YORK REVIEW BOOKS

New York

BOOK ONE

Schlump had just turned sixteen when war broke out in 1914.

That evening there was a dance in the Reichsadler – the final one, as the soldiers were due to mobilise the following morning. After sunset Schlump stole into the gallery with his friend; they didn't dare enter the dance hall itself. The big lads, the twenty-year-old turners and metalworkers, would not allow them to share in the treasure; they needed all the girls for themselves. These older boys couldn't take a joke, and were often quite rough. Up above, the two friends leaned over the banisters and gazed down ravenously into the hall.

At midnight the band played a fanfare and the trumpeter announced a break of fifteen minutes to allow the girls to cool down. Schlump and his friend slipped out into the pleasant summer night, beneath the stately old maple trees.

When the quarter of an hour was up, they headed back and came across a long line of giggling girls who were blocking the entire street. They were no older than Schlump and had been in his class at school, but of course they were already invited to attend the dance. Indeed, the elder boys prized these girls above all the others. One of the girls called out to Schlump, 'Hey, you, come over here.' Schlump could see the lamplight playing on her blonde locks, which shone almost white. He didn't trust her. But she broke free, the others called out to him, and his friend said, 'Go on, you've got a good chance with her!'

As Schlump went over, he was grabbed by a pair of hands that guided him on to a narrow path set beneath dense foliage, at the end of which a lantern cast a weak light. His courage boosted, he put an arm around the girl's waist and pulled her towards him. When they reached the lantern he took her chin in his hand and looked at her face. 'You're a pretty girl,' he said. 'What's your name?' 'Johanna,' she said softly. Then he moved her into the shadows and gave her a long, ecstatic kiss on the lips. She whispered into his ear that he should come and dance with her, and then he could take her home; she'd put off the other lads.

He crept back up into the gallery, keen to point out the girl to his friend. But he couldn't find her. The two boys went home. Schlump was blissfully happy. He could hardly believe his luck and was convinced that there could be nothing more beautiful on this earth than the girl.

A few days later he'd forgotten Johanna.

Young people are so profligate; they live in paradise and yet fail to notice when they come face to face with fortune personified.

Schlump lived up in the attic. His father was a tailor by the name of Ferdinand Schulz. Whenever he looked up from his needle his gaze glided across the colourful roofs of the old town and greeted the watchman in his little tower room. Schlump's mother still had the playful nose and bright eyes of her childhood, when she used to leap over the fences with the boys and nick strawberries. On Shrove Tuesday and at Whitsun she'd put on boys' trousers, join the singers in the street, and amass a sack full of pretzels and cakes. But when her tiny breasts began to swell beneath her blouse and she realised that she was a girl, she stayed quietly at home, dreaming of pretty clothes and beautiful shoes, although at big celebrations her liveliness and sense of fun would be once more on display. Back then all the boys would give anything to get a good gawp at her.

At seventeen she began her courtship with the earnest tailor, and at nineteen she married him because his serious and honest nature appealed to her. They celebrated a christening almost immediately, but the little girl died soon after the birth. The couple remained childless for ten years. The tailor went into business for himself and stitched for people at the window in his little room. He aged quickly; his short hair turned grey and his voice sounded weary and anxious. They had a boy who they christened Emil, because this was the name of the mother's brother, a soldier. People said that Emil was the spitting image of his mother. He went to school and was soon the top dog amongst his fellow pupils as well as the class joker. If Emil Schulz was part of the group you could hear the racket from miles away.

On one occasion some stalls had been put up in the marketplace for that Sunday's shooting competition. Emil threw the knapsack off his back and clambered up the first stall he came to. Making a hellish din, the young louts hurled into the street anything they could lay their hands on. But trouble was just around the corner: a policeman grabbed Emil by the scruff of the neck and bawled at him, 'You mischievous little Schlump!' He may have been thinking of shrimp, scamp, scallywag and lump – a muddled concoction of all of these. At any rate, Emil was given a good thrashing and ran home howling.

The marketplace was populated by terribly hard-working people who spent the entire day outside their shops, smoking cigars. They'd witnessed the whole episode. And when our little hero skulked gingerly across the square the following day, they all asked him, 'Hey, Schlump, you got a proper hiding yesterday, didn't you?' From then on they all called him Schlump, and the name stuck for the rest of his life.

Schlump's parents sent him to secondary school, which was a great sacrifice as the school was expensive and the tailor had no money. At Easter, Schlump took his final exam.

His certificate was of little use, but he did have a talent for drawing. He became an apprentice in a weaving mill, and learned how to draw patterns and designs. But as he worked, he could think of nothing but girls and the war. A few of his friends were soldiers and he wanted to volunteer too. He could picture himself in a field-grey uniform, the girls eyeing him up and offering him cigarettes. Then he would go to war. He pictured the sun shining, the grey uniforms charging, one man falling, the others surging forward further with their cries and cheers, and pair after pair of red trousers vanishing beneath green hedges. In the evenings the soldiers would sit around a campfire and chat about life at home. One would sing a melancholy song. Out in the darkness the double sentries would stand at their posts, leaning on the muzzles of their rifles, dreaming of home and being reunited with loved ones. In the morning they'd break camp and march singing into battle, where some would fall and others be wounded. Eventually the war would be won and they'd return home victorious. Girls would throw flowers from windows and the celebrations would never end.

Schlump became anxious that he was missing out on all of this, and was desperate to sign up. But his parents forbade him. On his seventeenth birthday he went in secret to the barracks and volunteered. They examined him and deemed him fit for the infantry. He returned home bursting with pride and his parents abandoned their opposition. Schlump's mother wept. On 1 August 1915 he took his trunk and moved into the barracks, very pleased with himself.

Schlump had grown into a lean and strong young man, and the recruits' training was child's play for him. He moved as nimbly as a weasel and handled a rifle with skill. But to begin with his limbs ached and he felt like crawling up the five steps to the latrine on all fours.

In his second week Schlump had barrack-room duty, which is to say he had to keep the barrack room clean and fetch coffee. On the Tuesday, he'd just finished the washing, and was hurrying back into the barracks with the basin, and the stool under his elbow. As he passed the non-commissioned officers' quarters a hand grabbed his arm tightly. 'Hey, son, here's five pfennigs – go and get me some coffee from the mess.' The five-pfennig coin was in

Schlump's hand and the corporal had vanished. If you go now, he thought, you'll have to wait ages in the mess. The older soldiers will be at the counter and they don't let recruits push in. Which means you'll be too late to fetch coffee for the platoon, and so they'll all be angry at you, while you'll be in the corporal's bad books for ever. Everyone will think you're an idiot.

Suddenly Schlump had an idea. Tossing the five-pfennig coin into the corporal's mug, he put this behind the door to the barracks, shot past the NCOs' quarters, picked up the large coffee pot, threw on the spectacles belonging to the man in the bed beside his, and sped back out to fetch the coffee. On the way back he bumped into the corporal, who was shaking his fist and cursing like a sailor. Behind the spectacles Schlump pulled a silly face and slipped past him.

It was time for their lecture in the drill hall. They filed in wearing fatigue dress and carrying their stools. The hall was empty save for ashes and filthy windows. It was freezing cold; the sun was just coming up. Schlump thought about the war. What if life was equally dull there, and just as frightfully cold?

They set off on their route march. In good spirits again, Schlump marched out into the morning and sang with the larks that warbled as they rose from the sods in the ploughed fields.

Deputy Officer Kieselhart, who was in charge of training the recruits, was a man of peculiar habits. He would often creep up behind one of the poor recruits and grab the seat of his trousers with relish. Woe betide the soldier who provided Kieselhart with a mere handful of slack; his anger knew no boundaries. One day he was standing behind Schlump, whose trousers were baggy because they were a metre too long. But when his hand met a bottom as hard as steel, the deputy officer praised Schlump in front of all the non-commissioned officers. He never forgot this fine recruit and showed him favour at every opportunity. Thus Schlump had taken the first step forward in his career (although it was to be his last, too).

The only thing he didn't like was the blue peacetime uniform they wore, with shiny buttons. Schlump didn't have the patience to polish all these buttons until they shone like white-hot iron. When the company fell in, he'd lift up his coat tails, vigorously rub the buttons of his sleeves on his trousers, then use the inner side of his sleeve to work on his coat buttons. He would stand to attention as erect as he could, and when the sergeant approached sternly, he'd flash him a glance with the brightest eyes in the world, forcing the sergeant's gaze to shift to his neighbour, Private Speck. Speck was a shoemaker, who cleaned and polished with a touching zealousness in every spare moment he had. But whenever he fastened his coat, his thumb would rub against the gleaming buttons and extinguish their lustre. Then the sergeant would come and hurl a torrent of abuse at the poor shoemaker.

Schlump thus freed up plenty of time to spend in the mess, where two pretty girls worked. One was curvaceous, blonde and blue-eyed; the other slim, with brown eyes and a brown plait. Every morning the curvaceous one set aside a roll and a hunk of salami for him, which he'd nip in and grab before setting off on a march. The slim one fed him chocolate during their time off in the afternoons. When the two of them were alone in the mess, she'd place the piece of chocolate between her own white teeth and Schlump had to take it devotionally into his mouth, a ritual he very much enjoyed.

Once, when it was getting quite dark beneath the chestnut trees, Schlump saw the blonde one fetching water. He hurried over to her and gallantly worked the pump handle back and forth. He offered to carry the pail for her too, but she refused, upon which a friendly scuffle ended up in a very lengthy kiss. At that very moment, the elderly Sergeant Bauch came out of the barracks and walked past them. Schlump had not been a soldier long enough to know how to deal with every situation. In a panic he clicked his heels together loudly, pressing the poor girl to his chest with such force that her glowing face sank on to his shoulder, and thrusting his right arm smartly alongside the seam of his trousers.

A reasonable man, who had two sons of his own in the war, the sergeant smiled kindly and went on his way.

Time passed quickly. Their training in Germany was to last eight weeks, six of which were now up. The recruits were transferred to the military training camp at Altengrabow. Sergeant Major Bobermin, who on Sundays had made them circle the barrack yard for three hours, barking the same commands over and over again – 'Lie down! Up! March, march!' while the soldiers' sweethearts watched from the benches in tears – this same Sergeant Major Bobermin addressed them prior to their departure: 'Attention! You will now proceed to Altengrabow! The military training camp. You'll be billeted in barracks. Be sure to tie up your arse every evening so it doesn't get nicked while you're asleep! Forward, march!'

Every morning, early, horribly early, they set out on a march, their backpacks filled with sand, and live cartridges in their ammunition pouches. It was cold and grey, and the barracks stood there ruthlessly. Everything was colourless; the world looked like an empty factory. The artillery regiment next door was still asleep and nothing stirred. On and on they marched until the mist eventually cleared and the sun rose high in the sky. The recruits started to swelter, the sand stuck their eyes together, and sweat ran down their cheeks, leaving behind channels as it dripped on to their ammo pouches. The tight belt chafed against your waist, and the spade clanked against your legs, and the mess tins knocked your head whenever you shifted your kitbag. Schlump had a full weight of sand on his back because he'd been caught out that morning. Corporal Mückenheim had lifted the flap of his kitbag – Schlump had forgotten to fasten the strap – and discovered an empty sandbag. Schlump was ordered to fill it and to report at lunchtime to the NCOs' quarters in spotless marching gear to perform one hundred about-turns. Schlump was sweating and seething with anger. Eventually they were allowed to assemble their rifles and shoot at moving targets. Schlump enjoyed shooting at the dark heads that popped up. It was great fun and filled him with enthusiasm for going to war.

On the way back, they had company exercises. The captain sat on his horse, issuing commands. The NCOs sweated and looked thoroughly annoyed, even though they weren't carrying kitbags themselves. They took out their anger on the recruits, who had to wheel round and were forced to run through the sand like hares. The recruits were boiling with heat and rage. They met the artillery regiment, who were slumped drowsily on their caissons on their way out to target practice. Behind the copse by the sandhill they had to lie down, take their rifles in both hands, and then haul themselves up through the sand on their elbows. This was the worst thing of all. Some were so furious that tears came to their eyes. At last they reached the top. The captain ordered the company to fall in and issued commands on the march: 'Load blanks and lock! Cavalry approaching from the right! Aim! Fire!' The salvo resounded, the captain's horse staggered, and the captain leapt down. His steed had taken a shot to the neck. The company marched back to the barracks. The man responsible was never found. Schlump was happy. The march had not been too much of an effort as he was a strong young man, but he was happy all the same. For he was hoping that they might be permitted a few days' rest.

They formed a long line for food: sauerkraut with belly of pork. Schlump took his full piping-hot bowl to the mess hall and was about to sit at the nearest table when a towering cavalryman stood up and sneered, 'What? Does this snivelling young recruit think he can eat with us?' Sensing the contempt and derision in these words, Schlump picked up his dish and hurled it at the tall man's gob. The cavalryman reeled and screamed; the hot sauerkraut was burning his face and running down his neck. His comrades leapt up and fell on the infantrymen, who were coming in with their full bowls. In a trice a battle was being waged with sauerkraut and dishes. There were casualties on both sides and it needed a strong detachment of infantry to restore peace. Schlump had slipped away. The cavalrymen sat in detention, nursing their sore heads.

The following evening there was an outbreak of dysentery amongst the recruits. A red trail marked the path from the barracks to the latrines. The recruits were segregated and ate apart from the others. Schlump was pleased about this as he feared the cavalrymen might exact revenge.

A week later, they returned to the garrison.

On 4 October, they entrained. The band that played at the station sounded as if it were howling with intense pain, and the people on the platform sobbed as if their hearts were being ripped apart. The soldiers were excited and full of curiosity; the future stood before them like a terrible monster they had to overcome. The journey lasted five or six days. They disembarked in Libercourt, after which they marched through grubby villages, staring in wonder at the sober houses and joyless farms of the French. Nowhere did they see the tidy gardens you'd find in front of farms back home, nor the homely timber frameworks on gables nestling beneath huge lime trees. The windows looked like dirty holes, and filthy steps led from the street straight into kitchens. So, was this France? They came across old women with black moustaches and snuff in their nostrils. The sky hung low, heavy as lead, and it started to drizzle.

The road never ended. The recruits were fully laden; still in their hands were packages from loved ones they'd been given just before the train departed. Some men were already falling out of line; they sat in the gutters, panting.

Finally they came to a stop. The soldiers assembled their rifles and, after the counting off, which seemed to take for ever, entered their quarters, an empty factory with broken windows through which the rain blew in. Some damp straw was on the floor. It was dark, and the soldiers tripped up on the holes in the floor where the machinery had been. Those fortunate enough to have candles were the envy of the rest. Everyone was given bread and coffee, after which the men slept.

Duty began the very next day. It was worse than in Altengrabow. The soldiers rolled around on the wet, sticky fields and returned as filthy as swine. This was followed by muster, by which stage they could no longer think straight.

After a few days Schlump was summoned to the orderly room. 'You've got a school leaver's certificate; can you speak French?' the sergeant asked. 'Report to local occupation headquarters right away. Off you go, march!'

Schlump took to his heels and reported for duty. He was released from military duties and assigned office work. He made every conceivable effort to make it look as if he knew what he was doing, and indeed it didn't take long before he found he could understand the French people he had to deal with. He had to act as interpreter, which was no easy task as the Frenchies spoke an appalling local dialect. A few weeks later the communication came through that the headquarters in Loffrande needed a replacement for the service corps, who were moving on from there. Schlump was the only person they could think of sending there.

Feeling very proud, he set off that evening. He wandered slowly, his thoughts focused on his new job. By himself he would be responsible for the administration of three villages – him, a seventeen-year-old recruit. He ambled through Deux Villes, where the recruits were making a din in their factory. They'd just returned from a march, and Schlump was glad not to have been with them. Then the path continued through open fields. Dispersed beneath him, and partially hidden in the mist, were the houses of Loffrande; to the right a few houses in Martinval, where he'd not yet been; and to the left, Drumez. He stopped by a road sign. On one side it read *Occupation Headquarters Mons-en-P*; on the other *Occupation Headquarters Loffrande*. This was to be his realm.

The village seemed friendlier than the others. It had tall, majestic trees, and the houses were hidden behind dense green hedges, between which narrow little paths snaked. In front of the headquarters – an *estaminet*, one of those cafés typical of the region – babbled a small, clear, welcoming stream. Jumping over it, Schlump went inside. On the left was the office, a large room with a table, a number of chairs and a small stove. On the right was the bar and a big kitchen. At work in the office were men from the service corps – three clerks, a sergeant and a corporal. They handed him a cigar box and explained that this was the coffer. Then, having showed him a mountain of documents and books, they gathered their bags and left. The men were from Holstein, and Schlump had great difficulty understanding when they chatted amongst themselves. Now he was alone in the headquarters and he felt slightly uneasy.

As he left the office, Schlump noticed that night had fallen. Opening the door opposite, he was assaulted by clouds of smoke and a clamour of voices. The bar was stuffed with French peasants. He could see nothing but the dim light of a petroleum lamp by the far wall. Finally he found an empty chair, but it was terribly gloomy in that part of the room. The landlady came up to him; she seemed to know who he was. He told her he had no billet for the night and asked whether she could be of any help. At that point a girl stood up, threw a scarf over her shoulders and said something to him before slipping out the door. All he'd been able to make out was the word '*monsieur*'. From the billows of smoke a voice announced that Estelle had gone to find him a billet, but that it wouldn't be easy as the soldiers weren't leaving until tomorrow.

Schlump's eyes gradually became accustomed to his surroundings. Young lads and powerfully built men sat at small tables playing cards. They were all smoking and nursing tiny glasses of beer. At the back, by the lamp, a woman and her daughter were serving food and drinks. Nobody paid the slightest attention to Schlump any more. He'd brought with him a couple of eggs, which he was keen to have cooked. Eventually he found the landlord and asked him the favour. The landlord was happy to oblige, and a few minutes later his wife came out with a plate, a knife and the eggs. She wanted to stay and chat, but Schlump found it terribly hard to understand her. But he realised that she was anxious and meant well.

Estelle returned half an hour later, with red cheeks and out of breath. She appeared to be blonde and blue-eyed like the curvaceous girl from the mess. Taking him by the hand she led him out of the *estaminet* and to his quarters. Schlump was surprised, but very happy to go along with her. The stars were twinkling in the sky; it was a cold night. He asked her whether she was called Estelle. She nodded and said it was the name of a star. He pointed out the star to her – Stella – and she gave it a lengthy gaze. She seemed proud of it, but also amazed that this foreign soldier should know her star. Then the two young people walked side by side in silence, and Schlump thought of his mother. He felt as if he were being guided by his guardian angel.

All of a sudden Estelle stopped, pointed out his billet and disappeared. He could still feel the warmth of her hand. Then he turned around slowly and entered the house.

Schlump got a real shock when he set off for his head-quarters the following morning. From a distance he was met by a cacophony of voices, and as he approached the building all the heads turned towards him and fell silent. On the right were the men with their horses; on the left the women and children of the village. Schlump realised that they were waiting for him to allocate them their tasks. He started to sweat as he tried to summon up everything he'd learned at school and frantically prepared what he was going to say. He was wearing his field cap and was embarrassed by his trousers, which were far too big.

Plucking up courage, he stepped amongst the crowd and first approached the women, who he was most afraid of.

He asked them, '*Qu'est-ce que vous avez fait hier?*' – 'What did you do yesterday?' They all replied at once, the girls gawping at him with mischievous, teasing and scornful eyes, and the women talking at him incessantly, their voices a mixture of amusement and contempt. Unable to understand a word, he said, '*Eh bien, faites la même chose aujourd'hui!*' – 'Well, do the same today, then!' They turned around as one and left, seemingly on the verge of hysterics.

Schlump was about to turn his attention to the men when he saw an odd-looking soldier coming down the road. The girls greeted him from a distance and Schlump heard that they called him Carolouis. He had unbelievably bandy legs and his hat was perched on his head at an angle, but beneath this was an extremely amicable-looking face. 'Comrade, I'm part of the occupation authority here; I'm practically a native in Loffrande and I'm in charge of the locals,' he said in his Palatinate dialect. Then he went away with the men.

Schlump entered his headquarters and was about to get down to work when the landlady stuck her head around the door and said, '*Monsieur ne veut pas déjeuner?*' – 'Would you like some breakfast?' Schlump went over to the bar and sat at a table with the landlord, Monsieur Doby, where he had a cup of hot milk and some lovely white bread. Monsieur Doby treated him with great respect and was keen to talk, but Schlump could barely understand the man. He returned to his office, behind which was a small room with a bed, where he would sleep from now on. As he held his hands up to the stove, Schlump wondered why the French had no doors on their stoves, and why you had to remove all the pots first and take off the rings before refilling it with coal.

Then he leafed through the files and books, in an attempt to acquaint himself with everything, telephoned all the authorities he knew, and politely asked the clerks to help by reminding him of all his duties and engagements. For he knew that there were many reports to be made. Once this was accomplished, he sat at the table, held his head in his hands, and listened to the gruesome melody that droned from the Front. The cannons fired incessantly and the window panes rattled in the nails holding them in place, for the putty had long since fallen out. As he listened to the wicked music, Schlump thought of his mother. He found it astonishing that he was now on his own in France, running the local administration.

Then he went outside, whistling cheerfully as he took a tour of the village.

The grey sky stretched dismally and tensely over the countryside. As he walked through the fields, Schlump looked over at the forest and saw the leaves falling from the trees. He felt happy to be alive. He could no longer hear the song that the cannons drummed into his ears day in, day out. The young lads were ploughing and the horses whinnying; breath puffed from their nostrils, billowing into the bright autumn air. The men were digging to channel the water that collected in the meadows, and scooping out the sludge from the trenches. Carolouis toppled from one furrow to another, and the freshly ploughed sods smiled up at the sun, which had just forced its way through the mist.

Schlump walked over to Martinval, where the women were working. He'd installed them in two barns; the women in one, the girls in the other. The women were nattering as they picked over potatoes, and didn't say much to him. But as he headed for the girls' barn, he spotted one of them vanishing from beside the door. She must have been looking out for him, for the barn was in the middle of a farm and you couldn't see anybody approaching. He heard their singing break off abruptly and it went absolutely silent. Schlump entered to find the girls busily at work. One was lighting a spirit stove and offered him a cup of coffee. He was astounded to see that the barn floor had been swept so clean it was virtually gleaming. Another girl showed him the potatoes that had been sorted through and those that were still to do. Then they started singing again. Marie, a pretty girl, stood up and danced, and Schlump had to sit on a chair they'd fetched for him. The girl, whose black hair coiled round her small head like snakes, sang as she danced, flashing sideways glances at Schlump with her dark eyes. Then she gave way to Céline, who invited Schlump to dance with her while the others sang. He realised that the girls liked him, and he pulled them close to him, dancing with each one in turn, all except Estelle, who stayed in the corner, gazing at him with her large, silent eyes.

Schlump went back out into the autumn air, the girls still singing behind him. In his mind he could see Marie's head of black hair and Estelle's large eyes. He was enchanted by all the beautiful girls, but he had no idea that he could also pick many of these roses that offered up their blooms to him so endearingly. This happy young man was content to enjoy their sweet perfume, rather than lusting after their nectar.

That evening, pretty Marie scurried into the bar, swept past Schlump, and cast him a number of furtive glances with her black eyes, before looking over at Estelle, who did not raise her eyes and kept her hands quietly in her lap.

On Sunday, Schlump had serious duties to perform. At nine o'clock he had to distribute the oats for the horses. The peasants sent their girls, who were waiting for him at the barn door. When he opened up, they stormed up the steep stairs in a mad rush, their skirts flapping this way and that, allowing Schlump a glimpse of the dimples in their knees. Once in the loft, they frolicked and cavorted and romped about, diving into the oats, jumping on the scales and fixing their eyes on Schlump in an attempt to extract a few more kilos for their poor horses. For the rations were meagre and strictly prescribed.

At eleven o'clock, the young lads and men between sixteen and sixty gathered for roll call. Schlump read out their names and they answered '*présent*' before filing into the *estaminet*. Monsieur Fleury, a rich grain dealer, always insisted on buying Schlump a beer. He was an elderly giant of a man, whose broad back ran in a straight line past the neck up to his head, like a bull. His lively blue eyes were set deep beneath thick white brows, and when he laughed, his full lips parted to reveal two rows of white teeth between red cheeks. His voice droned as if he were speaking from within a wine barrel. He said to Schlump, 'Only seventeen years old and you're in charge of the old men and the young women – quite an achievement, eh?'

When the grain dealer left, the landlord, Monsieur Doby, sat next to Schlump and said, 'I want to tell you a little story about Monsieur Fleury; he's an old rogue, you know. He's the richest man in the area. Well, one day he was going with his horses – they were famous throughout the country; he always had the finest horses around – as I said, he was going with his horses over to Contigny. As he passed the ironmonger's he was surprised to see the shop closed and the hallway draped in black. He stopped, and as he was well acquainted with the young woman there, he got out and climbed the steps to enquire about the bereavement. Upstairs he found the widow weeping beside her husband's coffin. He removed his hat, made the sign of the cross, and offered up a prayer, as is only right and proper. Then he sat next to the widow and waited in silence, out of tactful respect for her grief. After half an hour he stroked her hand, gently took the handkerchief from her fingers and dried the tears on her cheeks. But the widow would not be consoled; she just continued to sob, unable to utter a single word.

'Monsieur Fleury had limitless patience. Talking to her as softly as might a pastor, he found stirring words of praise for her husband, causing the woman to burst into tears once more. He dried her cheeks again and now put his arm gently around her waist, for it seemed to him that in her distress she was on the verge of passing out. Her head sought security on his chest and she kept weeping, still unable to speak. Monsieur Fleury softly stroked her hair away from her face, held her chin, patted her cheeks, planted a kiss on her forehead and offered some heartfelt words of comfort.

'And just as another sigh was about to escape from her lips, he kissed it back into her mouth.

'They were sitting very uncomfortably, for their knees were up against the hard coffin. He asked whether they might move it a little to one side, to allow them to be more at ease on the sofa. With a sigh she agreed. Taking one of the handles each, they dragged the coffin into the corner. Then they sat back down, and the horses outside had to wait till the following morning before seeing their master again.

'As he rode off at daybreak, he waved gently at the house with his whip, and behind the curtain the widow waved back with a smile, until he vanished into the distance. Then she wiped away the two big tears on either cheek and let the curtain fall back.'

Madame Doby, the landlady, had caught the end of the story. She seemed to know it and was not at all pleased with her husband. 'Don't believe a word of what Monsieur Doby says,' she told Schlump. 'He's such a big liar.'

Schlump was now settled in Loffrande and he'd almost forgotten that he was a soldier. He was punctual with his reports and made it a point of pride not to miss an appointment. He let Monsieur Doby advise him on agricultural matters, and all his decisions showed an astonishing technical knowledge. Nobody had reason to be dissatisfied with him. Order prevailed and, apart from the cannons thundering at the Front, everything was peaceful in his three villages. In

Loffrande there were only peasants and a blacksmith; no shoemaker, no tailor, no grocer, nothing. The wives bought their soap, their pots and pans, and their odds and ends in Mons-en-P. Every Tuesday they'd assemble for this purpose, for they were not allowed to leave the occupation district without military authorisation. Then they would set off, with Carolouis lurching behind, faithfully escorting the women and protecting them from gendarmes and other authorities. On one occasion, however, Carolouis came back in a rage, cursing like a trooper. One of the women had called him a '*tête de baudet*'. He knew exactly what that meant, which was curious for, in general, his acquaintance with French was rather poor. For example, he found it bizarre that they said '*chair*' when they meant 'flesh', because everyone knew that a chair was something you sat in. But from then on he no longer accompanied the peasant women on their trips to Mons-en-P. Besides, he had work to do in the fields.

Schlump requested soldiers, comrades of his, from the barracks to supervise the women. They were good fellows, nice boys who carried out their duties impeccably. One day a soldier arrived wearing his hat on his head as straight as a candle. A trainee civil servant, he was twenty years old and a very proper fellow. He knew well that only the smartest were selected for such tasks, so he was full of pride as he reported for duty to Schlump, whom he looked up and down with slight disdain, for Schlump's hat was at an angle and the seat of his trousers was still baggy. The women assembled outside the headquarters, and Schlump gave the recruit succinct instructions. He was to divide the women into groups of four, preferably in columns, take them from shop to shop in Mons-en-P., and then duly deliver them back home. The recruit left the office with his head held high.

When they saw him coming, the peasant women set off and some were already a considerable distance ahead. But our recruit ran after these women, grabbed them by the arm, and pulled them back. The peasant women were in shock; they looked at each other, at a loss as to what to say. The first four did stop, but the fifth put up resistance and rushed back to the others. '*Mais il est fou, ce Prussien! Il est maboule, hein?*' They clucked excitedly and angrily, brandishing their thick umbrellas. But the recruit refused to back down. He went purple in the face, he huffed and puffed and issued orders, and finally he had them all together, more or less. He marched beside them as platoon leader. On the way he met his captain. 'Platoon, march!' he commanded, thrusting up his legs in the goose-step. The captain was struck dumb with astonishment; he stood there on the street, unable to stop staring at the recruit as he marched on his way. Schlump had been standing behind a curtain with Monsieur Doby, the two of them killing themselves with laughter.

The Amazons reached the market square in Mons-en-P. without any mishaps – then all of a sudden they vanished out of sight. One ran this way, another that way, and the recruit was just able to grab the last one by the skirt. She put up a fight, however; absolutely livid, she bashed his hand with her umbrella and ran away cackling. The poor young lad stood there distraught. Alone in the middle of the market square, he didn't know what to do. He didn't dare go back to his company, for he couldn't report that he'd carried out the command, and he didn't fancy returning to Loffrande either. So for a while he stayed where he was. Then he turned around slowly and slunk pensively into the mess. He was fearing the worst; he was terrified he might be court-martialled. He sat in the mess for ages, his elbows on the table, wearing an anxious expression.

But at five o'clock in the afternoon he saw a few familiar skirts crossing the market square to wait outside the mess. A few minutes later, they had all assembled again and they went home serenely, though not in formation this time.

Schlump gave his comrade a few hard-boiled eggs to make up for the scare he'd had. He praised the recruit and affirmed that it wasn't such a simple business after all.

The week came to an end and there was a mountain of reports to compile. One for each individual question. For our wonderful German army was organised down to the minutest detail, and legions of Schlump's superiors were performing administrative duties behind the lines. One wanted to know every week how much hay was available; another the quantity of grain, potatoes and seed; a third how many shovels, spades and sacks; a fourth how much land had been ploughed and harrowed and sown that week, how much had been done already and how much was still to do; and a fifth enquired about population numbers and the quantity of Russian prisoners-of-war at work in his district. Under the last heading Schlump was able to write 'nil' every week. He worked hard and made a duplicate of every report, which he filed away in a special folder. For questions were often referred back to him, and it was awkward if you couldn't remember what you'd put in your report the first time.

Then Monsieur Bartholomé came in, who was the best seed sower in the village. He took the key to the seed store, and every day he'd leave the door open behind him. And every day Schlump would curse like a peasant and shout after him, '*Clos chl'huis, nom di Diou!*' Bartholomé would turn around, smile, and say in good French, '*Pardon, monsieur, je n'y pensais pas.*' Then he'd set off with the key, rattling the huge chunk of wood it was attached to.

Scarcely had he left than the door opened again. This time it was a wild little devil with black hair and the darkest eyes: Marie. She skipped over to Schlump, took him by both hands, and dragged him behind his desk into a corner where they couldn't be seen. There she threw her arms around him and kissed him so forcefully that he couldn't breathe. But Schlump knew what to do. He grabbed her even more tightly and kissed her more passionately. She thrashed around in his arms like a cat, trying to escape his grasp. Lifting her up, he carried her to his tiny chamber, in which was nothing save for his bed and an old cupboard. He could feel her small, firm breasts and pressed her closer. She kicked with her legs and a fierce struggle ensued, that beautiful, age-old battle in which submission is just as sweet as victory.

Schlump was on the verge of claiming his victory, and Marie was close to submitting with wanton pleasure, when the telephone rang. Well, Schlump was still a recruit. Obeying like a good soldier, he went over to the telephone, picked up the receiver, and listened. 'Enemy planes approaching from the north-west. Pass on the message!' It was a warning that came almost every day, and often at night. But it was not pointless, for on one occasion the English flyers had dropped their filthy bombs on the women and girls of Loffrande, killing one and seriously injuring several more. There was no factory siren in the village and Schlump could not warn the inhabitants because by the time he'd had a chance to get out to the fields or make it to the women in the barns, everything would already be over.

Angrily he hung up the receiver and stormed back to his nest. But the bird had flown and Schlump realised he'd been a blockhead.

Marie didn't come back, and whenever Schlump met her she barely glanced at him, letting him know how much she despised him. Now there was no mistaking what an utter fool he'd been.

Years later, when the war ended, Schlump was chatting to an old reservist about life. The latter said to him, 'Look, young man, there's only one thing I regret, and that's all those times when I could have had a good time with a pretty girl but missed my chance.' Schlump immediately thought of Loffrande.

Whenever the peasants wanted to go to the city or another village, to visit a friend or a sister, or buy linen or a new hat, they had to obtain a yellow pass. Schlump had set aside Fridays for this task; they would arrive with their groschen to fetch their yellow laissez-passers. And when the peasants took the pen to write their signature, they'd draw three crooked crosses that looked like broken tombstones. Schlump was shocked by this, and he told them that back in Germany not only the peasants but the cattle too could read and write.

The girls used to come in the afternoon, often a dozen or more. Amongst them was blonde Céline with her sparkling eyes and nose like a tiny mouse. She had fine, soft skin that shimmered gently in the sunlight, and she was constantly sniffing with her fine slender nostrils. Then there was bronzed Suzanne with her large brown eyes and brown locks that danced down over her forehead, concealing the most wicked thoughts. She had a body like a gazelle and long, slim, predatory fingers. Then pale Jeanne with the black hair. She stood upright, had a soft, gentle step, and she'd put her head on one side and push forward her thighs, which curved beneath her soft hips. There were other beautiful girls whose eyes shone with mischief. Tall Marianne, with her luscious red cheeks, high, wholesome breasts and lovely teeth. And beside her, little Anna. She had eyes that were a perfect sea blue, two tiny breasts, and soft skin with a bluish shimmer. She hardly ever said a word, but she always gazed, and she was often breathing deeply. Then her eyes would glow like diamonds in the moonlight. On Sunday they all wanted to go to church to see Monsieur Cabot, the handsome, sincere pastor.

It was evening by the time he was finished with them. For the girls were high-spirited and made life difficult for poor Schlump. Crowding around him, they all spoke at the same time, talking so quickly and saying such crazy things that he couldn't understand them. Then they laughed and nudged each other, and all twinkled their eyes at Schlump. They dictated nonsense when he was writing and picked up the wrong passes. At last they were gone, and Schlump could hear them trotting off.

Then he swiftly tidied his desk, because he was hungry, and headed over to the bar. He'd just closed the door behind him and was standing in the dark groping for the other handle when two strong, soft arms grabbed and pulled him, and two warm lips kissed him and then disappeared, and two small, slender arms took him, and two soft, cool lips kissed him and disappeared – and then they were gone. Schlump could just about make out the rustling of a couple of skirts. But he knew who it was: tall Marianne, and little fifteen-year-old Anna.

Madame Doby never laughed at her husband's jokes. She was worried sick. She had two unmarried daughters at home, two strong sons in the fields, and it was wartime. You never knew what was around the corner. What if the Germans retreated and dug their trenches right through the village? What if the boys were marched away to compulsory labour service or a prisoner-of-war camp? She suffered, and her husband's jokes were pure torture. She was good to Schlump, well aware that he could have made her life even more difficult if he'd been a wicked man. She also knew that he had a mother who fretted like she did. She asked him to send her regards from Madame Doby; the women were united in their suffering. Schlump had no idea how clearly his mother realised what was in store for him. But when he saw the anxious face of Madame Doby, he grasped something of the anguish that war could inflict on those who didn't bear arms themselves but who knew the lives of their loved ones were in danger.

For the time being, however, life was good. Once a week he'd wander over to his company in Mons-en-P. and get some tinned meat from the kitchen in lieu of the rations due to him. This he'd give to Madame Doby, who'd take a bundle of haricot beans from the supplies hanging beneath the eaves and make a purée, which she'd add to the meat once it was cooked. They all ate together at a table, and from one dish. Estelle would serve and always gave Schlump the best bits. Once he was alone with her and five-year-old Hélène. Flore, the big sister, and the others were busy at work. The three of them ran around chasing each other. Schlump caught Estelle; grabbing her firm arms, he pressed her against the wall and gave her a kiss. Taking his head in her hands, she pulled him towards her and whispered in his ear, '*Je vous aime*' – 'I love you.' In shock, Schlump let go. He was taken aback and blushed. For in his eyes she was worth more than all the others put together. But she had watched his reaction and knew at once that he didn't love her back. She left the room and didn't show her face again for a while. A few days later she moved in with her *marraine*, her godmother, where she helped tend the cows and separate the milk. Only when Schlump had to leave Loffrande did she return and help him roll up his coat and pack his kitbag.

The peasants were unhappy as well. For unlike the Dobys they didn't have an *estaminet*. And many of their fields lay fallow; only the ones close to the road were farmed. There were no longer enough horses in the village, and the number of cattle was dwindling, too. Buying and selling had ground to a halt, and there was nothing to buy even if you'd had any money. In fact, private property had ceased to exist; there were no rich and poor any more. Everyone had to work, provided they were strong and healthy enough. The fields were cultivated by all, no matter who they belonged to.

On Mondays, Gaston, the black-eyed foreman, went to the town hall in Mons to fetch money. And Friday was pay day. They all gathered outside the door to Schlump's headquarters: the peasants with lots of land and those with smallholdings, the women, the girls. They made such a racket by his window that Schlump had great difficulty counting out the money. To keep the girls quiet, he summoned Carolouis and gave him an old carbine without a lock, which the cavalrymen had thrown out and which Schlump had found in the arsenal behind his bed. With his bandy legs, Carolouis paraded haughtily up and down the assembly of girls, the carbine over his shoulder. He rolled his eyes and wore a stern expression. But the mischievous girls were not in the least afraid. They crowded around him, then scattered with an ear-piercing scream. And little Bertha stuck out her leg, tripping him up. As he stumbled, he brandished his carbine wildly in the air before falling flat on his face. When he got up again, the gun had vanished. This upright soul from the Palatinate was seething with rage. He waved his fists around and cursed so indecently that the moon hid behind the clouds. The girls took fright;

they fell totally silent and stood obediently by the door to the headquarters like chickens outside a henhouse. After a while Carolouis stopped swearing; when he saw them all waiting there so dutifully, his anger took flight, and the moon re-emerged from behind the clouds. Carolouis was smiling again, and the girls breathed a sigh of relief.

Schlump could now count out the money in peace. First the men, then the women, and finally the girls. Then he went into the bar, where he smoked cigarettes and played cards with some young lads. He'd have forgotten it was wartime if the cannon fire didn't regularly make the windows rattle so loudly that they all jumped.

It was morning. Schlump was sitting at his desk, writing a letter to his mother. Suddenly the door opened and a field gendarme entered with his brass breastplate and clicked his heels. He went over to the desk, opened a notebook and had Schlump sign. Then he tore out a sheet of paper and placed it on the desk.

'Is there a Madeleine Thouart living in this district?'

'Yes,' Schlump replied. 'In Martinval, in the very first house you come to.'

'Yesterday she was stopped on the road to Thumeries without a pass.' The field gendarme saluted and went out, his spurs jangling.

Schlump examined the piece of paper more closely and scratched his head. He knew he had to punish the woman to maintain discipline. He knew, too, that he could fine or imprison her. But she was poor, and he didn't know where to lock her up, for there were no cells in the village, nor anything similar. Schlump was in a considerable dilemma and he thought long and hard about this problematic case.

Then he had an idea. He remembered a nice little house that had been abandoned by its owners. Its windows were set so high that you couldn't jump out of them. He went to take a closer look. One room was in good condition. The stove seemed to be in working order and the windows shut properly. He had the house cleaned and put in order. He locked the back door and kept the key to the front door in his pocket. He had wood and some coal delivered, as well as a table, a chair and a bed. Then he called for Madeleine. She appeared shortly afterwards and stood anxiously at the door. She had reddish hair and honest blue eyes.

'Madeleine,' Schlump said, 'I hear you were caught by a field gendarme.'

'Yes, monsieur,' she said. 'I wanted to get a new skirt for my little sister Lolotte. That's all, monsieur, please believe me. The old one is so tatty, and my sister's such a wild girl.'

'I do believe you,' Schlump said with concern in his voice, 'but I have to punish you all the same. For if I were to let you off then I'd have the entire village running away as it pleases them and I'd be the laughing stock of the district!'

'What do you plan to do with me, then?'

'I have to lock you up for a day, Madeleine.'

'*Mon Dieu*, but where? We don't have a prison here.'

'There's no reason to be afraid, Madeleine. I'll see to it that you don't freeze and it won't be that bad.'

She fell silent, then all of a sudden gave him a look of

proud defiance. 'You do whatever you like, monsieur,' she said, before going out.

Schlump instructed her to come to headquarters at five o'clock on Wednesday afternoon. She was to bring bed linen and food for a day. Monsieur Doby laughed and asked whether Schlump was intending to go and check on her every two hours. But Schlump wasn't in a mood for his jokes as he found the matter a trifle embarrassing.

Madeleine arrived punctually with a basket on her arm and a package in her hand. She was extremely patronising towards Schlump and barely deigned to look at him. Schlump took the huge key and headed out with her, Monsieur Doby giggling behind them. He'd asked Madame Doby to put a pot of coffee on the stove to make life in the prison a little more bearable. Madeleine set her basket on the table and inspected her quarters. She sat down and took a needle and thread from the basket.

'Madame Doby will bring you a warm meal at noon tomorrow,' Schlump said, 'and I'll come to fetch you at six in the evening.'

Madeleine didn't reply. But all of a sudden she stood up, looked at the bed and then stared at Schlump. She shifted her gaze back to the bed, then looked at Schlump once more before blushing; she was deeply embarrassed. Schlump didn't understand. They continued to stare at each other for a while, both of them too embarrassed to know what to do or say next.

'But monsieur,' she said finally, 'I cannot...' She paused helplessly, peered under the bed, then looked at him with ever more anxiety and embarrassment written on her face.

Now the penny dropped. 'I'll be right back,' Schlump called out as he vanished. He hurried to the fence separating the *estaminet* from the neighbouring house and took down one of the many chamber pots that adorned the grey posts like helmets. They were all carefully arranged with their handles facing front, like a platoon standing to attention. Beside them was a second platoon, the neighbour's chamber pots, their handles facing in the opposite direction and exhibiting their backs. Schlump grabbed the first one: a white pot, which may have been a corporal, as all the others wore blue uniforms.

He marched through the entire village with this faintly ridiculous vessel, greeting the people returning from the fields. Astounded by what they saw, they asked him whether someone was on their deathbed, for he was carrying the chamber pot as solemnly as a priest.

But Madeleine was very grateful to Schlump and no longer angry at him.

Monsieur Rohaut stood at Schlump's door, twirling his hat between his large fingers. He had three gorgeous daughters, the eldest of whom was Jeanne with the curvy thighs. Rohaut begged Schlump for his fields to be cultivated, which were now lying fallow for the second year in succession. 'I do understand, Monsieur Rohaut,' Schlump said, 'but as you're well aware, we have too few horses and yokes and we have to work the fields by the road. For when the major drives here from Thumeries for an inspection, he wants to see people at work.' Schlump felt sorry for the man, because he looked so sad, and because Monsieur Doby was forever pulling his leg, as he was slow on the uptake and invariably acquiescent. Rohaut always took off his boots outside the *estaminet* so he could greet the landlady in his clean clogs. On one occasion recently, Monsieur Doby had filled these boots with slops. As it was dark when he left, Rohaut thrust one foot unsuspectingly into his boot, and although his face was squirted with sewage he tried with the other foot to see whether the miracle would be repeated.

Monsieur Rohaut thus left the office an unhappy man. No sooner had he entered the bar to greet Madame Doby than a terrible accident occurred out in the street. The boys were playing soldiers and robbers, for which they'd crafted wooden swords and taken the chamber pots they'd found on the fence as helmets. Little Erneste, son of Widow Foulard, whose husband had died in Maubeuge in 1914, bravely went for the wretched robber. But the latter was no coward; tossing away his sword, he bashed the pot with his bare fist on his foe's head, slamming it so hard that it sank over the boy's ears. Erneste grabbed the pot with both hands and tried to yank it off, but in vain! It merely got stuck over his ears. The boy started to howl as if he were being roasted on a spit. Unable to find a way out from the chamber pot, his voice made a peculiar, rather amusing sound, like a bluebottle trapped inside a metal watering can that takes a brief rest before buzzing even louder until it finally finds its way out of the spout. But Erneste couldn't find his way out of the hole.

The boys stood around him, convulsed with laughter, until one eventually got scared and tried to help the poor creature. He grasped the cursed chamber pot with both hands and heaved it up, which only made Erneste howl even louder, so the terrified boy let the pot sink again. In the meantime, Erneste's mother had raced to the scene. She too seized the pot with both hands and lifted it up, together with her son. The boy thrashed around with his legs and remonstrated hellishly. The neighbours came running as well and tried everything they could, but were left wringing their hands. 'He'll starve to death,' Madame Besnard said, starting to cry.

Fearing the worst, the unfortunate mother took her son with his iron mask to Schlump and asked him whether the poor boy would have to spend his whole life in a chamber pot. What would happen when the pot got too small? another woman asked. Schlump said they had to see a doctor; he would give them all a pass so they could get there. They thanked him for his smart suggestion and begged him to prepare the passes at once. But Schlump announced that he wanted to go with them.

By this time a large crowd had gathered outside head-quarters, which parted respectfully when Schlump appeared with the sorely tested mother and the boy wearing the chamber pot. Then they all filed along behind Schlump to Mons-en-P. When they came to Deux Villes, all the people came running out and the poor mother, in floods of tears, had to tell the story again, while the boy started buzzing and droning once more in his prison. Then they continued on their way, with the people of Deux Villes joining the procession.

Arriving in Mons-en-P, they called out the doctor, and there was silence as he examined his patient. He made a serious face, put his head on one side, screwed up his eyes, and pondered for a while. Finally he declared that he could be of no help in this case and that they needed to see the tinsmith. The crowd realised how right the experienced doctor was and expressed its agreement with him. The mother was filled with hope and the procession moved on. By now a huge mass of people swarmed around Schlump and his entourage, and the murmurs and excitement of the throng were so great that you could hardly hear the blue-bottle buzzing in its chamber pot. Finally they arrived at the tinsmith's and Schlump went in with the mother and boy while the rest waited outside.

The captain commanding the battalion of recruits, who was staying opposite the tinsmith, was an excitable fellow. When he saw the effervescent crowd, all speaking animatedly and waving their arms in the air, he thought an attack on the army was imminent, and that this throng was on its way to procure arms from the tinsmith in broad daylight. Rushing to the telephone, he informed the guard and issued the alarm to the entire garrison. Five minutes later the troops arrived to the rolling of drums, on the double and with bayonets fixed. They encircled the inhabitants of Mons-en-P., Deux Villes and Loffrande, and a lieutenant came forward brandishing a sword and demanding their surrender. Terrified, the poor crowd fetched Schlump, who stepped up to the lieutenant, stood to attention and explained the situation in a few terse words. The lieutenant smiled, returned his sword to its scabbard, ordered the soldiers to lay down their arms, and handed over command to a sergeant. Then he went in with Schlump to see the tinsmith, who was grinding and crunching away at the metal chamber pot with his pliers. The boy stood perfectly still; his mother told him to close his eyes. A few seconds later she was holding her son in her arms, and as she wept she wiped away the two trails of snot that ran down to his chin. The lieutenant sent his troops home and went to report to the captain, who in the meantime had put on his helmet. Schlump, however, strode back to Loffrande in triumph, his subjects in tow.

Madame Gaspard from Drumez stood before Schlump, resting her bony hand on the desk. She was wearing clogs and looked like a withered old Christmas tree. She was as tall as a hop pole and from her clogs rose a pair of thin sticks wrapped in thick woollen stockings. Her long black skirt hung in dense folds around her waist, and a woollen jacket was bound tightly over her meagre breasts, covering half of her scrawny neck. Like a man she had a pointed Adam's apple, which gaped out between the two steep sinews that held her sharp chin in place. Her face had the appearance of an old Camembert; two grey eyes cast an ice-cold stare from between colourless lashes, and there was no hint of any eyebrow in her precipitous rectangular fore-head. She was as thin as a hop pole too; only her hips stood out at right angles, like a pair of branches from which no more green shoots would ever grow. 'I've come to complain about Madame Fontaine,' she said, casting him a fierce look.

'And?' Schlump asked.

Now this arid creature became animated and started talking verbosely.

'Well, that woman said that I'd said to Madame Aulnoy that Madame Patard had said that she'd shared a bed with Carolouis. Of course she's shared a bed with Carolouis, she still is, I know she is, I know for a fact or my name's not Madame Gaspard, because those sorts of people have got no sense of honour, and they've got no shame sleeping with a Prussian, not to mention one with bandy legs. But these are wicked people, you know, and impertinent to boot. They're saying that's what I said to Madame Aulnoy, but Madame Aulnoy will vouch that I never said a word to her about that woman. Madame Fontaine is lying, I tell you; she ought to be locked up, that one. She's a shameless hussy, she lets her cows graze on my meadow day in, day out, and she's also nicked clover, and then her brother, well…'

'Just wait a moment,' Schlump shouted in a pause for breath. 'I see Carolouis passing by outside; he can go and get Madame Fontaine.' Schlump was relieved to have shut the woman up.

'Oh yes, get Madame Fontaine here. Tell him to fetch her.'

Schlump opened the window, called Carolouis in, and told him to find Madame Fontaine because Madame Gaspard had come to lodge a complaint about her.

Madame Fontaine arrived five minutes later. Around her shoulders was a filthy woollen scarf, and she was wearing a pair of felt shoes, or something similar. She immediately thrust her hands on her hips, which, next to Madame Gaspard's, looked broad and healthy. Her face was as black as a stove door, and around her mouth long blackish-grey hairs knitted together to form a patchy moustache, giving this part of her face the appearance of an English park. But her eyes, set either side of a hooked nose, were full of life and as black as coal. They twinkled and shone from between long dark lashes, above which a pair of bushy matted grey eyebrows hung down. The black hair on her head sat in greasy strands; it looked as if she'd never washed it in her life. Staring straight past Madame Gaspard and opening her mouth, she asked, '*Eh bien, quoi?*'

'Madame Gaspard says you said that Carolouis... hold on... what did you say, Madame Gaspard?' Schlump asked. But when the raven-haired woman heard the name Carolouis, she went as rigid as if she'd been stabbed.

'What?' she screamed. 'What? Has she been gossiping about Carolouis again? And what about the three men *she's* had?'

'*You've* had three men,' the arid creature ranted, 'and at the same time, too, not one after the other like me, and—'

'Three men, *and* she slept with the hunchback. If you ask me, she's a brazen hussy, a haughty cow, a filthy—'

'Filthy? Who's the filthy one around here? Who's ridden with lice like a Prussian? Who's whoring herself up and down the village? Who nicks and steals at night? Who set Célestine up with the gendarme for a few miserable sous? And now the poor girl's got a child by him. Who—'

Madame Gaspard raised her claws and was about to grab the other woman's hair, but Madame Fontaine was prepared for a struggle. She bared her own claws, then the two women set upon each other, opening wide mouths full of gaps where teeth should have been. At the sight of this performance Schlump started to laugh so loudly and uncontrollably that the quarrelling women stared at him in bewilderment. They turned around and were about to exit the office when their bottoms collided, sending the door flying and smashing a hole in the wall with the handle.

A horrified Madame Doby came out of the kitchen and looked wide-eyed at Schlump, who was wiping the tears from his eyes and pointing at the hole in the wall.

Summer was long past, and autumn too. It was that time of year when you couldn't tell if winter had arrived yet. At times a humid wind rustled the treetops, the bushes dripped with the perpetual fog, door handles were wet, and thick drops of water fell incessantly from gutters on to the street.

They had started threshing. The threshing machine gave out a high-pitched whine that resonated throughout the entire village. And if it was given too much to eat, its monotonous melody would climb by a minor third, before soon falling back to its old tune. In the distance the cannons beat out a fast rhythm as an accompaniment. The girls loaded the sheaves into the thresher, and from time to time one of the young lads would skip into the barn and pinch their legs, producing squeals of delight. The cart, heavily laden with yellow wheat, rocked and rattled past Schlump's headquarters, making way for the other cart that was taking away the straw to be added to an enormous stack.

The short major from the agricultural section, to whom Schlump sent his weekly reports, had paid a visit a few days previously. He asked Schlump about supplies, about hay, how much seed there was, and how much butter he was

43

delivering. Schlump made a succinct report, gave him the figures, and stated that butter was churned every Thursday so that the peasants could deliver punctually. An energetic mayoress looked after this and settled the accounts every week. The major appeared to be satisfied. He clicked his tongue, tightened the reins, and rode off.

Louis Gez came into the office after the major. He was exactly one metre fifty tall and just as wide, even though he had sloping shoulders. He unashamedly wore a very baggy pair of corduroy slacks, which were tied above his shoes, a red handkerchief around his neck, and a cap on the back of his head.

'You ought to grow a moustache,' he said to Schlump. 'The girls love them. There's a real pretty one I've singled out for you – a hard-working, sturdy girl, let me tell you – but I need you to do me a favour…'

Schlump knew who he was referring to: Helen over in Marchelles, but she was well known far and wide; she'd already lent her favours to the entire artillery regiment stationed there.

'What's on your mind?' he asked.

'I'm right out of chewing tobacco, Monsieur Jean, and you know jolly well that a man without tobacco is only half a man.'

'Indeed,' Schlump said. 'Tomorrow I'll go to the mess and fetch you some, and some snuff for your neighbour, Madame Héaulmière. But tell me, Louis, is it true, you know, the story in Arras?'

'True? Why of course it's true. You know, times were very different then, you could still get chewing tobacco and cognac. My goodness, cognac! Do you have any of that in the mess too?' he interrupted himself.

'You'll get a half-bottle, Louis. That's a promise.'

'*Merci*, Monsieur Jean, *merci*. Oh yes, you could still get chewing tobacco and cognac in those days. The fair was on in Arras, and they'd organised a prize bull exhibition. Well, the richer peasants were strutting around the streets with their fat sticks, making all manner of lewd comments to the girls, twirling their moustaches and jingling the large coins in their pockets. They looked just like their bulls. And horns had been put on their heads, too, only you couldn't see them,' he said, giving Schlump an exaggerated wink. 'I was supposed to be operating the big machine at the fair, which was beside the cinematographic theatre and drove the dynamo. But it worked by itself, so I spent the whole day with the beautiful Céline in the bar in the market square. Quite a woman, that Céline, let me tell you. Oh yes, and as I'm drinking my cognac, all of a sudden out in the street they start running and screaming, and the peasants come running too, scarlet-faced, waving their sticks, and they scramble into the bar. The women are screeching, and one literally leaps through the window, cutting her chubby cheeks. In no time at all the bar is jammed and the market square is dead. I go to the door to take a look, and in the middle of the square I see a huge bull. Quite a fellow, you know, with powerful horns, and what a neck! He's bracing his front hooves against the ground, nodding his head up and down, then jerking it in the air like horses when the oats prickle them. And – I can still picture it today – in front of it, not ten

45

paces away from the beast, there's a child playing by the fountain, a little girl. She's beaming with joy and singing, blissfully unaware of what's going on. The women have yanked open the upstairs windows, and now they're screaming and wringing their hands helplessly. All of a sudden a door opens on the far side of the square and out rushes a woman, a pale, delicate thing – why, she couldn't have weighed more than forty kilos. She runs straight past the bull, grabs the girl and dashes back, while the bull gapes idiotically behind her. I tell you, the women applauded from their windows and cried "Bravo!" like those crazy ladies do at the Paris opera.

'I felt ashamed, I was furious, because the women in this part of the world are manly enough as it is. But I wanted to show them. I creep slowly up to the beast, which has started pawing and shaking its head again, and then I'm right in front of him, and he's staring at me! As quick as a flash I grab it by the horns, and before you know it, the thing's lying there on its back!

'Well, the women came running and applauded once more and, I have to say, Monsieur Jean, I had a good time after that... Nice work...'

As he laughed, he spluttered, rocking back and forth on his short legs.

Schlump again promised him the tobacco and cognac, but Louis said that wasn't the reason he'd come. 'I'm sure you know how poor we are, and little Célestine, who has the child by the gendarme, is living with me. We need wood, so please give me a permit to collect some in the forest in Marchelles.'

Schlump gave him the permit, for he knew that Madame Drouart lived there. And Louis Gez loved her.

His comrades, the recruits he'd come with from home, had long since been sent to the Front. Others had arrived who were now being trained in Carvin. Only a few clerks had stayed put.

The wind blew colder and Christmas was round the corner. Every day an orderly would bring Schlump his instructions and take back his reports. One day he announced he'd probably be getting billeted there soon with the service corps, to take over from Schlump. An hour later the telephone rang; it was Corporal Nebe from headquarters in Mons-en-P. He was the NCO to whom Schlump had to deliver butter and eggs, and who was then supposed to forward the goods to the military hospitals. Schlump couldn't bear the man because no matter how much he delivered, it was never enough, and because he was a deceitful, rotten soul. Corporal Nebe told him that a service corps unit would be arriving in two days' time to replace him. Schlump would soon learn when he was leaving. He hung up angrily, for he'd detected an unmistakable *Schadenfreude* in Nebe's voice.

That afternoon Schlump stormed out to Mons-en-P. to get more detailed information. The days were short, and when he arrived at headquarters it was already pitch black outside. He went in and announced himself. The corporal let him stand there for a while. Then he stood before Schlump, legs apart, hands in his pockets, and started to laugh. 'Well, well, whippersnapper,' he sneered, 'your mother's

47

going to be in floods of tears when she hears her little boy is off to the Front!'

Schlump had just turned seventeen and still harboured something of a sense of honour. He felt as if what was most sacred to him had just been defiled. It was a similar emotion to the one he'd felt when hurling the plate in the cavalryman's face. Seeing nothing but black and red patterns dancing before his eyes, he was seized by an indescribable rage. Schlump punched the corporal square in the face, sending him reeling, and was never quite sure what happened after that. He turned around and ran off, leaving a hell of a racket behind him. Chairs were overturned, and he heard a rattling and clanking like rifles clashing together. He thought the guard had been set on him. But he'd already vanished into the darkness.

Schlump ran and ran, down to Deux Villes, without knowing where he was heading, until he came to an isolated little house whose friendly owners he knew. He entered and said good evening as softly as he could, then sat down by the stove. The occupants weren't surprised, because he'd often popped by for a little chat.

'*Chauffez-vous, monsieur*,' the woman said, pushing a chair across. She gave him a cup of coffee with some sugar. She was sorry she couldn't offer him any cognac, and began to complain about the miserable war. Schlump listened with one ear and essayed some absent-minded answers, but with the other ear he was listening to the night outside. Surely the guard sent to look for him would turn up at any moment. Each time he heard a noise outside, he froze and his heart started pounding. And when he heard footsteps outside, he leapt up from his chair in horror. Composing himself, he sat back down and started talking nonsense. The surprised woman asked him what was wrong. He tried to smile and said, 'Nothing.' All of a sudden he felt unsafe where he was, and bid a hasty goodbye. The woman stood there, shaking her head behind him, for he'd interrupted her mid-sentence and scarpered.

Full of fear, Schlump listened out to hear if anyone was coming, then darted across the field to hide behind a bush. Holding the branches together, he squatted on the ground, trying to collect his thoughts.

Now you're a deserter, he told himself. When they get hold of you they'll haul you up before a court martial and you'll be found guilty of violent insubordination in the face of the enemy. And then you'll be shot. And what about your mother? And father? Think of the distress you're causing them! He pictured them distraught at home, giving a start every time the doorbell rang, for they'd be ashamed of seeing anyone; they'd be afraid. He started to concoct madcap plans to spare them the distress. He was going to confess everything and tell the army that they had to show sympathy and take into consideration the reason for his crime. But then he pictured those smug fellows sitting there, and him standing helplessly, unable to utter a word. No, that wasn't going to work.

But it was still night-time, and if he left now he could get far. He could flee to Holland. That would be a march of several days, and he'd have nothing to eat, but this was the least of his worries. He had no pass, and the gendarmes would apprehend him at once, for the authorities everywhere would have been notified of his flight. Well, he could creep back into his office and make himself a pass, using a different name and stamping it a few times. But surely his head-quarters would already be occupied, as that was the first place they would have gone looking for him.

He'd run out of ideas. He was squatting on the ground and time was passing. His teeth chattered as he started to freeze.

He fell asleep, woke with a start, and fell asleep again. He dreamed, half asleep and half awake.

The first cracks of light appeared in the east. Schlump made his way to Seclin. He looked around carefully, watch-fully. But there was nothing to see. Everything was quiet. A dog barked in the distance. He had a friend in Seclin, a telephonist who'd been commandeered from the recruits at the same time as him. Schlump wanted to ask whether his flight had been reported.

He called in at his friend's lodging – the man lived with an elderly couple – and found out that he had night duty until eight the following morning. That was useful. With the utmost caution he sneaked into the telephone office and woke his friend, who was sleeping on a camp bed. The friend knew nothing; no notification had been sent through. Schlump breathed a sigh of relief and became perfectly calm. The corporal must have a bad conscience, he thought. He never passed on the deliveries of butter to the military hospitals in full. I know he sent some home and gave some to the sergeants, who he's in cahoots with. I also know there are a few women in Mons-en-P. he slips all manner of things to. Schlump used to have to supply him with pigeons for the women. 'He's got a bad conscience and so he's not reporting me. But then it struck him that there'd also been someone else present, a lieutenant from the Hussars he didn't know, and who had heard everything. Schlump was seized by fear once more. The lieutenant wouldn't be able to let an incident like that pass. He was an older man – they probably assigned him to the corporal in order to sign documents. Perhaps he was a decent sort.

Schlump decided to wait till eight o'clock and then call the corporal, who he knew would be on his own in the office at that time. He resolved not to tell him where he was telephoning from.

He rang just after eight.

'Now listen here,' the corporal said gruffly and angrily. 'You know damn well what you did and what's in store for you!'

Schlump didn't reply. The corporal continued: 'In view of your age I've decided against filing an official statement. Report at once to the lieutenant, who saw the whole thing. And then come and apologise to me!'

Schlump was ecstatic. He knew he'd won. He ran back, still circumspectly, as he didn't trust the corporal. He reported to the lieutenant, who proved to be a reasonable man. He invited Schlump to sit down, then interrogated him, asking about his parents, his age – everything. Then he chastised him for his behaviour, pointing out his offence and the potential consequences, and urged him to offer his apologies to the corporal.

Schlump thanked the lieutenant and went to the head-quarters. The corporal flew into a rage when he saw him.

He screamed and swore, calling Schlump a rascal, a villain, a tramp – he served up all the pet names that were popular in the German army at the time. Throughout the entire tirade Schlump stood rigidly to attention, his hands alongside the seams of his trousers. Then the corporal spat at him, 'Now get the hell out of here!'

Schlump went home like a condemned man who's been pardoned on the scaffold. He thought of his mother and breathed a massive sigh of relief.

The billeting officer for the service corps walked through the village with Schlump, making a detailed examination of all the lodgings, and noting everything down.

The following day the service corps detachment arrived on their wagons. They wore lederhosen and brand-new sheepskins, and their feet were clad in new boots. Schlump marvelled at how smart they looked, and asked one of them where they'd got their new things from. He laughed and said, 'There are plenty of new clothes around; we're not going to put on any old rags, we're not that stupid!'

They had jangling spurs and long swords dangled from their waists. They'd also slung a carbine over their wagon, as decoration. The soldiers stabled their horses, moved into their quarters, and had a good night's sleep. The following morning – they were off duty all day – one of them came to see Schlump in his office. Irate and agitated, the soldier berated him, 'What the devil do you think you're playing at giving me a billet like that? What on earth do you imagine we've been through? We need sleep and rest! I can't sleep on a straw mattress; I must have a proper bed!' Schlump shifted the blame on to the billeting officer, but promised to find him something better.

Behind him, the service corps lieutenant hobbled in with a stick for support and a stern face. He was a young man studying agriculture back in civilian life. He'd brought with him a sergeant, a corporal, and two clerks. The lieutenant took occupation of Schlump's headquarters by sitting on a chair in the middle of the office, resting his hands on the stick and enquiring loudly and pompously about everything: the tasks and duties of the headquarters, the number of people under its command, the senior authorities, and the attitude of the French. Then he groaned and limped out, gritting his teeth. From the door he ordered Schlump to give the sergeant, the corporal, and the two clerks thorough instruction to enable internal business to continue as normal when Schlump was relieved of his duty. The lieutenant intended to look after the external work himself together with the men from his unit.

Schlump was now catered for by the service corps. As the wagon drivers fed themselves in their quarters, their rations came in the form of ingredients. Schlump took advantage of this perk, obtaining so much meat, salami, coffee, sugar and other lovely things that he felt quite proud. Every day he would fetch his rations and then sit with the drivers for a while. To begin with they were terribly nervy. They told him of their experiences. They'd just come from Notre Dame de Lorette, where things had gone disastrously. The French had sent forth their blacks; those devils came skipping down with flashing eyes and knives in their mouths. They would have slit our throats if the artillery hadn't started firing. But at night you couldn't see their black faces. They slunk up like snakes, knives still between their teeth, and silently strangled our poor chaps to death. Schlump listened attentively and in awe. The enemy fire had been horrendous; the Guards managed to break away, but not a single one of the green Chasseurs returned. The dead lay in piles in roadside ditches; if you touched the corpses they fell apart. These men had been shot dead in the advance. And still the French hadn't made any headway.

The soldiers looked Schlump up and down, then straight through him as if he weren't there. They nodded their heads, took their pipes out of their mouths, and said, 'Oh yes.' Schlump gently asked them how many losses they'd suffered.

'They shot the lieutenant's horse in the leg. He fell from the horse and ripped his bottom on the barbed wire.'

Schlump laughed, but the soldiers cast him angry glances and spat. They said this was bad enough; the lieutenant could have died.

Schlump returned home deep in thought. He didn't believe them, even though they hadn't lied.

Schlump hadn't believed a thing the soldiers had said. But their stories made him think. He knew that the trenches lay in wait for him, and that he'd have to move on from Loffrande soon. He felt as if he were having to bid goodbye to home a second time.

It was Christmas. Outside it was raining and the wind was clattering the bare branches against one another. His mother had sent him a package, which he unwrapped delicately, carefully laying out the contents before him. On top she had put a small green fir twig; its aroma, together with the smell of the stollen, which he now unpacked, enveloped his soul lovingly and carried him back home. He peered through the keyhole, saw his mother beaming as she lit the candles on the Christmas tree, and his impatience grew. His father was working next door as he still had a suit to deliver that evening, and the sweaty vapour of the iron wafted over to him. They had just returned from Midnight Mass, trudging through the narrow lanes and between the gables whose brows huddled close together as if they were trying to whisper to each other. The snow fell gently and with a soft, delicate rustle.

Schlump looked up. It was getting dark outside and a fine rain was falling. His mother had sent him a cake, a pair of woollen stockings, and everything else a concerned mother could conceive of. She'd included a book, too, containing short poems about spring, love, autumn, and longing – exactly what he might have wished for. He spent ages at his Christmas table. Then he went over to see the French, who didn't have a clue about Christmas. Little Hélène was sitting at a table in the corner, reading an old dog-eared picture book. He sat down beside her, and she immediately asked him for a fairy tale, because he'd once told her one. He was alone with her in the room, the only other presence being the ancient clock that snored out the time.

But Schlump was thinking of his mother. In the evenings he used to sit in her lap while she told him fairy tales, which he firmly believed and knew so well, as if he'd actually lived through them himself. 'Now listen, I'm going to tell you the tale of poor Gil:

'Once upon a time there lived a poor tailor's apprentice by the name of Gil. He had a wicked master who would beat him with his measuring stick if the stitches were too far apart, and poke him with the scissors if he didn't put the needle close enough to the edge, and jab him with the needle when he stared dreamily out of the window. And as for the tailor's wife! She couldn't bear the boy, for on occasion he wanted to eat until his belly was full. When he ladled a spoonful of soup from the dish, she would throw him a dirty look. Once he helped himself to a piece of dry bread to eat with the soup, because it was too thin. And when he cut into the bread a touch too deeply with his knife, the old woman snarled at him, "Eat the whole lot of it then!" For that he had to sew long into the night, attaching buttons, and when the first cockerel crowed the following morning, the woman made him mop the floors, carry out the ashes and fetch up the coal.

'But the master tailor became ever crueller, and his wife ever more miserly, until the boy could no longer cope with his hunger and he ran away. As poor Gil's parents were both dead, he didn't know where to go. He wanted to make his way to the city; surely there he would find food. One last time he wandered through the narrow streets with their pointed roofs and said goodbye to the tall gables, whose brows huddled close together, as if they were discussing the unfortunate young lad's fate. Then he left, heading across the fields to the city.

'He could see it from far away, for a large black cloud of smoke hung above the countless tall chimneys. He first came to magnificent wide streets, on either side of which stood splendid gardens full of wonderful flowers. Behind these gardens, between the trees, lay fine houses with huge windows. Gil couldn't believe his eyes. Then he came to another area, where the houses were black and extremely long and tall, but with nothing in bloom. A mass of children with snotty noses played on the street corners, and lorries raced past, disappearing through the wide gates, behind which he could see more tall black houses. With a degree of apprehension, Gil walked through one of these gates.

'From the sooty windows of one of the rear houses he heard the din of machines pounding and rattling, and the drive belts smacking against the broad rims of the busy wheels. He asked for work and was given a job immediately. All day long he had to sit by a gigantic machine in front of a clock face with a single hand that continually flipped up and down. On the dial was a red line, and if the hand went beyond this he had to push the button of a bell, which let the stoker know that the machine was approaching dangerous levels. But the hand never flipped beyond the line, and Gil sat there the whole day staring gormlessly at the jittering hand. He'd been given a key and a number. Every morning he had to insert the key into a large iron box, above which sat a proper clock. Many numbers were on this box, one for each worker, where they had to insert their individual keys. This meant the clock knew whether anybody had arrived for work late. On pay day there was an envelope by each number containing the worker's wages. Gil felt as if he had turned into a number, or a component of the machine he had to sit in front of all day long.

'As his earnings were meagre, he looked for other work.

He became an assistant stoker. He was given another number, but this time he spent all day at a furnace. His job was to fetch coal and take away the glowing ashes. Sometimes the stoker would open the huge furnace door, and Gil had to help him with the unbelievably long rake to remove the burning slag from the grate. They had to take care not to burn themselves. Once the stoker tripped and fell, and the red-hot slag toppled on to his chest and legs. The man screamed blue murder. Gil dragged him out, but he was already very badly burned. An ambulance took him away. Now Gil became the stoker, but he thought about his predecessor, who had died in hospital, and looked for another job.

'He went to a mine, but conditions were even worse there. First he had to push the cars, taking great care not to bang his head in the low passageways, as well as to avoid being run down. Then he was promoted to the position of cutter and had to work tremendously hard. Bare-chested, for it was infernally hot down there, and on his knees, he had to cut out the coal. He thought he'd suffocate in the poor air. And if he hadn't cut a sufficient quantity of coal, the overseer would jump down his throat. In the morning the miners would return above ground and sit silently in a train that took them home. Gil slept in a miserable room with another man he didn't know, and when they were working in the mine at night, two other men slept in their beds.

'One night, when Gil was at work, he heard an ominous cracking and rustling beside him, then his lamp went out and all he heard was a single thunderclap. When he regained consciousness, he was lying in hospital next to several of his fellow miners. The spotless nurses attended to him, and spoke softly and kindly. He didn't know what had happened to him, but the sister said he'd lain unconscious in bed for three days. Whenever he breathed, Gil felt a terrible pain in his chest, and he was so exhausted that he couldn't even lift his arm. But he was young and he got better by the day.

'Eventually they released him from hospital. He received a further month of financial assistance and didn't need to work. He took walks in the big parks and thought about his future. When the month was up and he had his last six-groschen piece in his pocket, he decided to pay a visit to a card reader and ask what lay in store for him. If things weren't going to get any better, well…but he didn't want to follow this thought to its logical conclusion. He gave the card reader his last six-groschen piece. With her hands, which looked like two giant spiders, she picked up a dirty pack of cards. Gil had to cut, then she shuffled, and wiggled her fingers back and forth, mumbling to herself. Finally she said, "Your fortune is on its way. You'll come across it when you step out of the house. Hold on tight so it doesn't escape."

'Gil left feeling disappointed and regretted having given the mysterious woman his last remaining money. As he turned the corner, deep in his thoughts, he bumped into someone so hard that he fell over on the spot. When he glanced up, stunned, there was a person on the ground opposite him: a pretty young girl with blue eyes. She was looking at him with such a friendly expression that Gil thought, This is my fortune, hold on to it tight. He swiftly helped her up, and because she was not at all angry, he asked whether he might accompany her some of the way.

'Gil did not let go of his fortune. She secured him a job as a packer in a large business. For she was a seamstress and had many grand customers amongst whom she was able to find something. On Sundays they took walks together. Gil was happy. He loved it when she wore a new dress; sometimes he'd take a pencil and design a different dress and tell her what colours it should be. The seamstress was astonished by his good taste. And because she was an industrious girl who had saved up her money, she persuaded him to attend a tailoring academy so that they could start a business together in the future.

'Which is exactly what happened. Gil became a master tailor for ladies. And when the grand ladies came he designed wonderful frocks for them, producing coloured drawings that delighted his customers. His wife cut out the patterns and oversaw the sewing, the apprentices and the girls.

'And the two of them lived happily ever after.'

Little Hélène slipped down from his knee. Monsieur Doby came in, and the cannons at the Front thundered more menacingly than ever.

The service corps annoyed Schlump. They did very little work; a few of them would go ploughing in the morning, and then they would pose arrogantly in doorways as if they'd just conquered the entire country.

Once the sergeant asked him what was going to happen to him when he moved on.

'Trenches,' Schlump replied.

'Really?' the sergeant said. 'I've two cousins with school qualifications who volunteered, but none of them is in the trenches with the infantry. One is with the heavy artillery, the other with the cavalry. Only fools end up in the trenches, or those who've been in trouble.'

Schlump said nothing. He knew as much already following his brief act of desertion.

But he didn't want to be regarded as a fool. Nor did he want anyone looking down their nose at him, and now he regretted not having signed up for the artillery. But they've got flat feet, he consoled himself; strapping young men who can march all day belong in the infantry.

So Schlump was annoyed. It was New Year's Eve and he wanted to enjoy himself. He fetched Carolouis and they went over to Fourbevilles, where the drivers of an artillery regiment had been doing very little for months. Their only task was the occasional transport of munitions to the Front, and for this they chose the darkest nights. Carolouis had his own worries. He talked about his Gret back home, with whom he had a child. But there were French prisoners in their village who'd helped out with the harvest, and he didn't trust his Gret. 'If that hussy gets a child from one of those Frenchies, I'll ditch her and find myself someone else. I mean, there'll be plenty of them after the war.' They were sitting in the artillery mess, drinking beer. The place was soon full of artillerymen and such thick clouds of tobacco smoke that they could hardly see each other. The soldiers became louder and merrier by the hour, and some were squabbling over card games. Schlump remained calm and was looking forward to the imminent punch-up. By ten o'clock the beer had run out, and now they started drinking cognac out of beer glasses. Before long all the tables and chairs had been overturned, and the legless staff sergeant was snoring on the floor. As they stormed out at midnight, violent cannon fire thundered down from the north. The drivers stumbled into their billets, fetched their carbines and fired shots into the air like madmen, before returning to the mess.

From that point on, Schlump's recollection of what they got up to was decidedly hazy. At any rate, it was already getting light when they set off for home. A little snow had fallen in the meantime, gracing the fields with a thin covering of white. Spying these white sheets, Carolouis was convinced that here was his bed. He stopped abruptly and took off all his clothes bar his shirt. Beside him Schlump looked on in amazement. Then he realised that Carolouis was going to bed, so he lay down next to him, although he hadn't undressed. Soon the two comrades were sleeping peacefully side by side, and Carolouis snored as he dreamed of his Gret, who he didn't trust.

Schlump suddenly woke up and listened. He could hear a strange ringing and gurgling in his ears. He stood up and felt sober immediately. Next to the path babbled a small stream. Carolouis was still lying on the ground; the two of them had slid head first into the water. Schlump pulled his friend out and tried to wake him, which proved an impossibility. So he covered him with his clothes, then ran back to the village to find a handcart to transport Carolouis back in. By now it was quite light, and people were going about their business. Finally Monsieur Doby gave him an old pram. As there was nothing else and Schlump would not leave his friend in the lurch, he had to make do with this. He found a pillow and left again.

Carolouis was still snoring. Schlump put the clothes at the bottom of the pram and, with tremendous difficulty, Carolouis on top, covering him with the pillow. A hairy leg dangled out here and there, to which Schlump had tied on boots as he was unable to find the stockings.

The two men arrived like this in Loffrande, met with cheerful greetings from the women who were on their way to work in the barns. It was Monsieur Doby, however, who laughed the loudest when he saw the peculiar transport arriving.

Schlump cut a solitary figure as he wandered through the snowy fields of France. Over the meadows the bluish snow formed no more than a thin shroud, and on the fields it had melted save for between the furrows, and the jagged dark-brown clods of earth peered out earnestly and silently. There had been a light frost. The broad ruts that the cart had channelled in the mud the day before ran deftly ahead of the wanderer, glinting faintly in the dim sun that peeked through the misty sky. Schlump slung his rifle across his back and pushed up his grey helmet. He was no longer used to marching or heavy baggage. He kept slipping in his boots, so dug in hard with the hobnails; the metal on his heels jangled. He wandered through dirty villages and once again was surprised by the ugly houses. The French people at their doors, their hands in broad trousers, darted him hostile looks, for he was a total stranger to them.

Two days before, the telephone had rung and he'd received the order to march to Carvin. The whole thing was like a dream. Then yesterday, the major from the agricultural section had come and given a short speech in praise of Schlump, even holding him up to the lieutenant as a fine example of a man. Schlump had felt quite proud, but it was of no use to him. He'd still had to pack his things this morning. Estelle had come over with her godmother and helped him roll up his coat and strap his blanket to his backpack. Thick tears ran down her cheeks, dripping on to the crockery.

Although Schlump could picture this very clearly in his mind, it all felt as if it had happened a hundred years ago. He was in a very strange mood; he couldn't be absolutely sure whether the past few months had actually been real. He was neither happy nor sad. Just surprised and a little dazed. He'd hauled his kitbag on to his back, attached his belt and ammo pouch, and put on his helmet. Estelle had taken a few steps backwards and stared at him in astonishment, as if she didn't know him. He'd gone over to the bar, where little Hélène was playing with her picture book. He shook their hands, Madame Doby had cried, Monsieur Doby had made a serious face, taken his pipe out of his mouth, given him a meaningful handshake and said, '*Courage!*' Estelle had disappeared.

Schlump arrived in Carvin around evening time and reported to the sergeant, who gave him a rude look of indifference and assigned him to the fifth platoon.

BOOK TWO

It was dark. The stars were twinkling and glittering, promising an icy night. Schlump had finally found his quarters. The fifth platoon were billeted in a cellar that was entered via a low door on the street. Schlump went down the stairs. His nose was assaulted by a nauseating stench of people, leather and wet rot, and the smoke from the stove stung his eyes. The soldiers were lying on straw playing cards, writing letters, or devouring the contents of packages sent by girlfriends or mothers. One was cleaning his things and another was delousing himself. Schlump searched for a free corner, dropped his kitbag, undid his belt and sat down. One soldier asked what he was doing there; the rest ignored him. Schlump looked around. The rear door led into a courtyard, but like all doors in France it didn't shut properly, and an icy wind blew in constantly. The small stove glowed from the wood fire inside it, as did the chimney pipe, for which a hole had been made in the wall. But the hole was far too big and you could see the stars shining in the sky outside.

His soldiering duties were to begin again the following morning. Schlump looked at his things. On the frozen soil his boots hadn't become muddy, and his belt was still gleaming, as Estelle had lovingly polished the leather. But his rifle was rusty and the metal plates on his heels rattled. He started eating; he'd brought bread, butter and tinned meat from Loffrande. Then he lay down and slept as deeply as only young people can.

They were woken by the guard early in the morning, a long time before sunrise; the stars were still twinkling in all their brilliance. Schlump offered to fetch the coffee, as he wanted to get on good terms with his new comrades. He was given eight mess tins. A soldier from the fourth platoon, which was housed next door, showed him the way. They crept through twenty hedges and clambered over just as many walls and fences; the narrow path had been created by the soldiers. It led past the rear of the plain workers' houses, through narrow yards, and over all manner of obstacles. The other platoons were there already because their billets were closer to the kitchen. With the mess tins full, they went back along the street at the front of the houses. This way was considerably longer, but more comfortable. The coffee was practically boiling still, and the scalding steam burned Schlump's fingers. Then an icy wind cut into his skin, making him feel as if the nails were being torn from his fingertips. The other soldier said, 'You need to wrap foot cloths around your hands.'

They went to practise drill, which Schlump no longer enjoyed. He found it somewhat below his dignity to still play the recruit. The others, his comrades, seemed so young and green, even though they were two years older than him. They were drilled long and hard, and had to run and march until they were roasting hot. Then they practised swarming, and lay down in the snow, cooling their knees on the frozen earth, followed by target practice. The afternoon was given over to rifle drill in an empty factory. For hours they practised loading and locking. Schlump behaved like a convict and sulked the whole time; he was sick to death of all of this stuff. His mind strayed back to Loffrande and the service corps, and he remembered what they thought of infantrymen. Then he marvelled at how thoroughly the factory had been stripped; even some of the floorboards had been ripped out. Finally it was time to return to their quarters.

The soldiers were given neither wood nor coal, so they had no other choice but to steal if they didn't want to freeze, even though a battalion order had strictly forbidden this. Schlump accompanied two other soldiers on a sortie to pilfer wood. One carried a pickaxe, the others spades. They slipped into the factory where they'd exercised that afternoon, creeping through the cellar door as the main door was locked. It was tricky, because the ladder only had three wobbly rungs. Above them the second and seventh platoons were already busy hacking away at the floorboards. Schlump got down to work. You need to make a mental note of the holes, he thought. You could break your neck otherwise.

A pair of unknown faces appeared from the cellar hole. These were soldiers from another regiment. 'Oi!' shouted one of the recruits, raising his spade. 'Go pinching on your own patch, you bastards!'

'Shut your mouth!' the other soldiers retorted, but soon scarpered.

They had enough wood and threw it down into the cellar. There they bagged as much as they could carry and hurried back to their quarters, each one taking a different route. When they were back, one soldier set about splitting the boards, while another fed the stove till the fire was roaring.

And so it went on every day.

After a fortnight, the company was told they were moving to L. to dig trenches. Schlump was looking forward to this; after all, it was better than mere exercises and rifle drill. And then they were actually on the march. It was a beautiful day. The sun shone, sparking thousands of tiny diamonds on the frozen earth. The air was clear and icy. They passed rusty lengths of barbed wire and a large military cemetery, the resting place of hundreds who had marched forth in 1914. Past houses that had been shot to pieces, up the hill towards L.

They were given a stable as their billet. The horses were housed below, well protected from the wind and the cold. Above, where hay used to be dried, the recruits were to make themselves at home. Here the wind blew in, for the walls were crumbling, comfortably allowing the air to pass through. The roof had also vanished save for the beams, which towered above them, bare and barren; from a distance the stable looked like a devoured herring. The few sheltered spots were soon occupied and soldiers fought for a scrap of space beneath a beam. Schlump had ended up amongst the Polacks from the first train and couldn't understand a word of their gobbledegook, for their mouths chattered and rattled away like machine guns. They made themselves as comfortable as they could for a brief rest after the march. Then it was time to fetch the coffee. Before he went, Schlump hid the butter he still had left over from Loffrande, because the Polacks thieved like magpies.

At eight o'clock that evening they assembled for duty again, with rifles, large spades and cartridges, but no coats or kitbags. They marched to the village, which comprised a few miserable little houses, though at least they had roofs. Hussars leaned in doorways just as pompously as the service corps back in Loffrande. Schlump gaped at them in surprise, for he couldn't fathom why they were at war. To his mind they were only needed for parade, when the Kaiser was there.

The corporals and lance corporals marched in front, and the company was led by a sergeant major. They were allowed to sing for the first quarter of an hour. One of the lance corporals, who knew a whole raft of songs, sang the verses, and the company responded with the chorus.

They had just got to the final verse:

> Now had passed one whole year
> Since that beautiful moonlit eve,
> Once again I sat down here,
> And my heart began to grieve.
> In the rays of the silver moon that night
> I saw a tombstone shining bright.
> It read: Here lies a mother and her son,
> O wanderer, pray for those who've gone.

They were passing a farmhouse encircled by bushes. The

company fell silent and all that could be heard was the uniform step, the spades knocking against the rifles, and the canteens clanking against the small picks.

Something whizzed through the air high above the farmhouse – a tiny, fiery red tongue – and exploded with a short, sharp plink.

'Shrapnel,' the lance corporal said. The recruits were astonished. They'd never seen or heard anything like it before.

Then the company continued on their way in silence. Schlump's ankle was sore. He'd got a new pair of boots from the quartermaster. But as there were so few left, he'd had to take what was there. And these new ones rubbed his ankle so badly that he'd started bleeding. Every step was torture.

At last they were called to a halt. The cannons sounded different from the ones in Loffrande. Here they seemed to fire less frequently, but the sound was much more violent, much crueller. It was still two or three hours' march to the Front, one of the soldiers said. They were on a bare patch of land and could see nothing apart from the night, in which a little snow shimmered. They were to dig. The sappers had already marked the course of the new trench, and the recruits got down to work. Each one of them was given a section of a metre, in which they had to dig two metres down and two metres across. The earth was frozen solid, and beneath the thin topsoil was hard limestone. It was a hell of a job.

They shovelled all night long. Schlump sweated like a peasant in high summer. But he couldn't keep up with the

Polacks. They were miners from Westphalia and Upper Silesia, and far more skilled at hacking and shovelling than he was. They swore like troopers and were on the verge of giving him a good thrashing, because the large sods of earth he dug up rolled over to their sections. Schlump worked like a man in desperation. Once a shell exploded nearby, and the fragments hissed through the air like a thousand cats, some wailing and howling like cursed souls. The recruits all threw themselves on the ground, but Schlump went on working; he wanted to make use of every moment to catch up with the others.

Finished, the others rested their hands on their spades, and their chins on their hands. Schlump was still working. But it was getting ever slower. He couldn't do any more. Gradually his limbs grew stiff from overexertion and the cold. The corporal came over and swore at him. But nothing helped. They could have struck him dead; he couldn't go on any longer.

It was beginning to get light in the east. The sergeant major barked, 'Shoulder arms! Fall in!' and they marched back home.

More torture for Schlump. His ankle had swollen, and with every step he felt as if his skin would be flayed. He moaned and gritted his teeth. The road went on for ever.

But everything in life must come to an end, and finally they arrived back at their village, utterly exhausted. They wrapped the covers around themselves, laid their coats over their shoulders and waists, and fell asleep. Early in the morning, before the sun came up, it was icily cold. They stood old petrol cans beside them, in which they made small fires. But the warmth barely radiated a quarter of a metre.

Schlump woke at eight the following morning. He tried to get up, but couldn't. His limbs seemed paralysed or broken; he couldn't tell. He finally sat up, but this was excruciatingly painful. He was rigid from the cold. But when he glanced next to him he was even more amazed. He was able to look through a large hole into the stable below. The rim of the hole was charred and the petrol drum lay below. Schlump couldn't believe his eyes. Had he moved even a fraction he'd have been lying down there too. And the straw he'd been sleeping on was also singed. It was a wonder he hadn't gone up in flames.

The Polacks were already up and warming themselves on the fire in the other drum. Schlump got up and sat down next to them in a state of shock, for he didn't know whether he'd almost burned or frozen.

Then it was time for roll call.

Roll call was over. Schlump was sitting beside the drum, cutting out a piece of his underwear, a rag from each leg. Unscrewing the bolt of his rifle, he used it to stuff the rags into his boots below the ankle, for they still hurt with a vengeance with each step. Then he smoked a cigarette and warmed his fingers. Beside him sat a soldier from the music corps, a handsome chap, slim and muscular, with a chiselled face. But he seemed beset with worries. He was staring vacantly into space, and he dropped into the fire the cigarette that Schlump had given him, even though he'd only just lit it.

Schlump asked him how he'd come to be there. 'We've got to dig trenches too now,' he said. He was no longer a recruit as he had the Iron Cross. He must have already been in the army as he also wore the marksman's braid, which was awarded in peacetime. Schlump asked him how long he'd been a soldier. 'I was in my second year of service when the war broke out.' After a while he continued, 'Until nine months ago I was at the Front. Then I was transferred to the music corps. I played the trumpet, although my main instrument is the cello. But I signed up to go back to the Front.'

'Why?' Schlump asked. 'Surely you lot don't need any more training, do you?' Schlump was fascinated by the trumpeter. The way he spoke was so refined, even though he'd been a soldier for four years now, and then there was the way he looked so sad and chose to sit amongst the recruits, the Polacks even. Something wasn't right.

'Why are you looking at me like that, comrade?' the trumpeter said. 'I'm in no mood for laughing. I feel as if I'm about to go mad. Listen to me, comrade, just listen. You seem to be a reasonable fellow, the kind of chap I could pour my heart out to. Do you have time?'

'Until they call us,' Schlump said.

'Well listen then.' And he started to talk. Schlump had the impression that the man next to him was trying to give a confession, for he spoke long-windedly, sometimes confused, and his eyes were as wide as saucers, as if he were reading everything from the past.

'I was telling you that I was already in the army when war broke out. We went to the Front, I was there before

Paris; wherever something was happening, I was there. I was the first in my regiment to be awarded the Iron Cross, and that meant something back then. I was the first one given leave; that was Whitsun 1915. And then my bad luck began. Let me tell you the whole story, comrade. I went home. You can imagine how proud I was to be the first one back from the war. I was invited by everybody, and wherever I went they fed me until I was bursting.

'Well, one day I was invited to a birthday party. Not too far away, about half an hour's tram ride. I arrived, greeted everyone, and there, sitting at the table, was a girl. Comrade, this was a girl the like of which you'll never have set eyes on in your life. You're laughing, but don't imagine that I'm in love – all that is past now. But just so you know how beautiful she was, let me tell you one thing. I ask the other people who she is and why she's dressed in black. "What?" they say. "Don't you know the fair Lieselott? Why, she is renowned for her beauty." So why is she in mourning? "Her brother was killed. He volunteered, and people even say that he was seeking death because he'd fallen in love with his own sister. But she's an upright girl, too upright; she won't look at another man, although many have tried with her and failed. So just watch out!" That's what people said, so you can believe me when I say she was beautiful.

'I watched her dancing. Oh, how she could dance! It didn't happen often, for she didn't want to on account of her brother's death. But when she danced, comrade, it was like listening to an unearthly music. Her body played as it danced; I fancied I could hear a wonderful, joyful *allegro*, followed by a soft, divine *andante*. She had a very slim waist and a powerful body. And her mouth! So elegantly curved and blossoming red. Curved as Mozart's lips might be as he conducted a graceful minuet. And her nostrils would flutter slightly, just like a butterfly about to take off from an apple blossom. I could see nothing but her; everything else blurred into a fog. I don't know what I said or did that evening. I just saw her, even when I wasn't looking. It felt as if everything had become transparent, as if I could see Lieselott through all those standing in front of her, as if I could see through myself when I turned my back to her. Comrade, I was bewitched.

'She allowed me to take her home. Just imagine, comrade, I told her exactly what I thought of her. And she wasn't angry, not at all. Do you know what, comrade? I kissed her.'

Suddenly he grabbed Schlump by the arms and shook him. 'Comrade, can you understand what that is like, have you ever loved a woman like that?' Then he spoke softly again. 'No, that can't happen more than once in the world. You cannot understand.' The trumpeter followed this comment with a long pause.

'To cut the story short,' he continued, 'she was kind to me too. I only had eight days' leave and these soon came to an end. I spoke to her father. It all felt like a dream, and on the day before I left we had a war wedding.

'Her father had rented a small attic apartment. I can't remember who was at the ceremony; I think it was just our parents. I could only see her.

'Then they were all gone.

'The following day I had to return to the Front.'

The trumpeter didn't say any more. He poked around in the ashes, tossed in a piece of wood and stared at the flames.

Then the corporal arrived with the order to fall in. Schlump took his rifle and went outside. They practised falling to the ground and standing up, and for this exercise the corporal had chosen the dirtiest place.

That evening the trumpeter returned. Schlump sat next to him. 'I left early that morning, comrade.' The trumpeter continued the story. 'You can imagine how I was feeling. I'd never feared death before; I'd always been reckless in the face of danger and gone on the craziest escapades. But now! I wanted to live, I didn't want to lose my happiness; I shivered when I thought of it. I went back to the Front. And just imagine, my captain was assigned to take over the battalion of recruits and he wanted to bring me with him as a musician! How willingly I followed him. I didn't have to go to the trenches, I was certain to see my wife again!

'We wrote each other letters. Every day. I couldn't bear the separation. I thought hard about how I could get home again. I cooked up the most idiotic plans. But I had to wait.

'I noticed that she was writing more seldom. The way in which she wrote her letters changed too. It sounded as if she was preoccupied. I sensed this acutely, I wasn't mistaken. I racked my febrile mind as to what it could be. Finally I thought, we're going to have a baby, and wrote to her even more tenderly than before.

'And then at Christmas I struck lucky. I was given leave!

The captain was sending his clobber back home and a stack of presents to his wife. I was allowed to go too, as the orderly couldn't manage it all on his own. Besides, the orderly didn't know the city where the captain lived, whereas I hailed from the same place. And so we left. Arriving back home, I ran up the steps. Rang the bell. She opened the door, gave an ear-piercing scream, and was about to collapse. I caught hold of my wife, took her indoors and gave her a kiss.

'When she came round, she pushed me away, dashed into the bedroom and bolted the door behind her. I could hear her sobbing loudly. I was speechless with shock.

'I knocked and she unbolted the door. I went in and tried to calm her down. She pushed me away again. I asked her what this was all about. Finally she began to speak, in fits and starts. Gradually her eyes dried altogether and she stared straight in front of her as she talked. Talked harshly, soberly and defiantly, as if she were in court. And comrade, just listen to what she had to say.

'She'd been invited back by the people whose house we'd met at. Once again there was a soldier there, just as before, only this time he was a lieutenant in the flying corps. And apparently he looked so much like me, so similar, that she'd been taken aback. And he behaved just like I had: he never let her out of his sight, following her wherever she went. Everything was just as it had been on our evening. And he spoke the same words to her, and took her home too, and – well, comrade, you can imagine the rest.

'I staggered out of the room and sat down at the table; I sat there the whole night. I don't know what went through my mind. In the morning I even had a short doze. When I woke up she was standing at the door, dressed exactly as she'd been the night before; she probably hadn't slept either. She stood there, her hands clutching the frame. She fixed her gaze on me with her large, deeply sad eyes, and looked utterly submissive, as if begging me to strike her dead.

'She served me, she obeyed me like a dog. I could have trampled her to death, she wouldn't have complained.'

All of a sudden the trumpeter stood up, rolled his eyes terrifyingly, grabbed both of Schlump's shoulders with his hands, and yelled so loudly that the Polacks rushed over to see what was going on. 'And three days later, comrade, three days later she drowned herself!'

The trumpeter laughed, a frightful booming laugh. Then he sat back down and spoke very softly. 'I went straight to the sergeant and told him I wanted to go to the Front, and that the next day I'd be right in the thick of it, and,' now he was speaking very quietly, 'and I promised him that I wouldn't be coming back.'

That night they went out again to dig trenches; the musicians joined them. Once more the lance corporal sang the verses and the company the chorus:

> Three lilies, three lilies,
> I planted on his tomb.
> Then came a proud horseman
> And snapped them bloom by bloom.

The French had long since realised that trenches were being dug throughout the night. They shelled with their heavy coal boxes. And this time there were casualties: two wounded and one dead. The dead man was the trumpeter.

For eight nights the recruits dug trenches, then marched off again. Not back to Carvin, but to Mons-en-P. Drill and exercises continued. They practised assault, they learned how to negotiate obstacles, they attacked and took trenches with hand grenades, they ran across boggy meadows and wallowed in the mud. They often returned home like pigs, caked from head to foot in muck. Sometimes they went to Loffrande, and Schlump gazed longingly at the houses whose occupants he knew so well. He felt like a deposed king, ashamed to march through the village as a recruit where he had once been in command, and was glad when they failed to recognise him amongst the many faces. The soldiers had practically no free time, for everything had to be kept clean, and there was muster every day, today with mess tin, canteen and kitbag, tomorrow with spade, rifle and cartridge belt, the following day with shoes, boots and coat.

Once, in one of the rare free quarters of an hour, he was standing outside his old headquarters as a group of Loffrande girls arrived to have their passes stamped. Not recognising Schlump, they walked straight past him. When they came back out, he approached them: Marie, Jeanne and Estelle. Estelle let out a cry, blushed and jumped for joy. Then she turned very quiet and sad once more. The other two laughed and went on their way. But he could only exchange a few words with Estelle. As she bid him a sorrowful goodbye, there were tears in her eyes.

Finally they were going to the Front. In the morning,

they paraded in the market square; the sergeant major filed up and down the ranks, first on his own, then with the captain. The musicians moved to the front, the captain mounted his horse, then they marched in an arc around the market square and off to the west. The sergeant major stood in the middle of the square, leaning on a stake to which pigs or calves would be tied in peacetime, and watched thoughtfully the long procession of recruits heading for the Front. This was not the first, nor would it be the last. How many had he seen go before them, and how many of those were still alive now? Perhaps he was wondering where all this young blood was coming from, which never seemed to run out and marched so cheerfully to the Front. Perhaps he was wondering why he had been spared.

As Schlump marched off, he noticed the strange expression on the sergeant major's face, and he had a peculiar, unpleasant feeling.

The captain accompanied the soldiers for a while, then he turned around and the band followed him. The recruits marched onwards, each company led by a staff sergeant. Then the companies separated, each one going to a different regiment.

It was a long march, at the end of which they had to wait outside the regimental office. It was a long wait. At last a clerk came out of the large building and assigned each platoon to a different battalion. Then they waited outside the battalion office, another long wait. Eventually another clerk came out and assigned them to the companies. With twenty others Schlump was assigned to the seventh company, which was quartered in a former bread factory, an hour from Carvin. It was another long wait outside the company office. After an eternity the sergeant major appeared and inspected the new recruits. He stopped in front of Schlump, who'd attracted his attention on account of his threadbare uniform. Stabbing his finger into Schlump's chest, the sergeant major questioned him about it. Schlump replied that he'd been drafted a long time ago and so his clothes were no longer new. 'I see,' the sergeant major said. 'Drafted. And you couldn't get yourself a decent uniform? You must be a right old fool, my friend!' He turned around and left the recruits standing there. After an age the company clerk came out and told them, 'The company is about to be relieved. You'll be leaving tonight for the third line, where you'll wait in reserve.'

They took up position around ten o'clock that evening, ready for their lengthy march on the main road that led to Aubines. It was a starry night, and freezing. Their combat packs – a sandbag with bread, iron rations, and mess tin – and the steel helmet were new to the soldiers, for as recruits they'd still been wearing the old leather helmets. They also had blisters from the ten-hour march they'd done earlier that day. The soldiers were led by a quartermaster from Upper Silesia, an uncouth, boorish man, but a decent soul. He told them about where they were being positioned. 'They'll be happy to see some reinforcements,' he said. 'The company's too weak. The group of eight has to man three or four posts; that's too much.'

They arrived at Aubines around midnight. It was a dark village that stood on the far side of a hill above which the moon was yet to rise. They passed by a guard who didn't move a muscle. Light slanted through tiny cracks in cellar windows. 'That's the heavy artillery in there,' the quartermaster said, mentioning the calibre. They crossed a railway embankment to an overgrown dirt track. The recruits were no longer saying much, and because it was so quiet they held on tight to their spades to stop them clanking against the rifles. With the other hand they tugged on the rifle straps to prevent the guns from slipping from their shoulders. Now the moon was brightly illuminating the men. They all marched in a semi-doze, with their heads bowed. Schlump thought about many of the things he'd experienced since the day he'd moved into the barracks. Then he remembered the barracks he was about to become acquainted with. Invigorated by his curiosity, he looked keenly into the night before him.

By one o'clock they had arrived at Saint-Laurent. 'Here's the field artillery.'

Bang! Bang! Bang! Behind them the guns fired. It sounded as if something was bursting with excessive pressure. Then the shells wailed into the distance, hissing as they got ever further away. After a while the echo came from the other side, the impact a muffled bang.

The quartermaster cursed. 'Stupid bastards, why the hell are they giving us trouble now, just when we're trying to get past? It won't be long before the Frenchies start firing.'

They moved through the heavily shelled town. Barely a single house had its roof left. On some you could still read the shop signs and advertisements for a brand of cognac. In many cases, however, the facade had been torn away, leaving the house's intestines hanging out and allowing passers-by to peer into the rooms. On one wall was a picture with a dedication: *Hommage à mes parents*. A child's tentative hand had written this in large writing: To my parents. And the child's parents had been so delighted they'd proudly framed its work. What a surprise they'll get, Schlump thought, when they see their house again.

The soldiers had to cross an open square, in the middle of which was a severely damaged iron pavilion where the band used to play when the fair was on. 'A cursed spot, here,' the quartermaster said. 'This is where the Frenchies always fire their artillery.'

Having stumbled over the debris of the wrecked houses into the middle of the square, they suddenly saw a red light beyond the hill on the other side. There was another bang. A few seconds later a shell hissed towards them and buried itself with a whine in the frozen ground, about thirty paces away: *peeoow* – like a locomotive exploding. Schlump jumped at the evil wailing of the shrapnel as it spat through the air. That was the French response. 'Bloody lucky we weren't over there,' one of the soldiers said. They passed the fresh shell hole with trepidation. If one comes now, Schlump thought, there's nothing you can do, you're helpless.

They crossed another field sown with duds and shrapnel, and came to a wood. 'This is the third line. Over there, beyond the last row of trenches, are eight thousand British and further on thirty thousand Germans in a mass grave, from the big offensive last autumn when the British were already in Aubines.' Schlump didn't believe the numbers the quartermaster was quoting. But a lot of what he says must be true, he thought, and now the poor fellows are rotting away. And next year others will be thinking the same thing when we're under the ground.

Arriving at the place where the trenches began, they climbed down. The passageways were narrow, supported at the sides by woven branches. In places the rain and mud had brought the walls so close together that the soldiers' kitbags got stuck. Elsewhere, they hit their heads on the planks or trench railway tracks above them, or their rifles would become caught. In some places the trench had been shelled, leaving a yawning hole in front of them. Progress was arduous, and they started to sweat for they were not used to this.

'This is the lieutenant's dugout,' the quartermaster said. 'Wait here.' He climbed down. Alongside the steps that led down was a neat banister, and a roof decorated with logs had been built over the entrance, making the place seem almost cosy. The quartermaster didn't return. After a while the lieutenant's orderly came out and took them with him. Schlump was disappointed. He'd thought the lieutenant would come in person, shake their hands, and give them a warm welcome as new comrades. But this! It was as if the quartermaster had announced the arrival of a few sacks of peas.

On and on they stumbled, squeezing themselves through the narrow trenches, which snaked this way and that, sometimes branching off forward. It was a quiet night, the stillness punctuated only by the occasional hammering of a machine gun. They passed other dugouts that were no more than holes at the base of the trench wall, and if smoke hadn't been rising from the chimneys that stuck out of the holes, they would have fallen in. The orderly instructed two men into each bunker.

They passed a guard, a veteran of the army. He turned round and asked, 'Replacements?'

'Yes.'

'Thank God for that!'

At five o'clock in the morning Schlump went on guard. Exhausted from the previous day's march, he staggered along the trench, at a loss as to why it curved every few metres, as if forever having to give way to someone. He patiently negotiated the twists and bends in search of his post. All of a sudden he stopped in his tracks, puzzled. There, on the fire step, in the dim light of dawn, stood Lemke. Lemke came from Brandenburg and had arrived in the trenches with Schlump the day before. He had red hair and his face was a sea of freckles. All alone he stood there facing the enemy, his rifle at his side. From the other side a machine gun rattled at regular intervals: *tak-tak-tak-tak – tak-tak-tak-tak – tak-tak-tak-tak*. And with the same regularity as the machine gun, a serious-looking Lemke bowed towards the French, as if trying to introduce himself to the enemy. Schlump stood there agog and cheered up. It was such a funny sight that, try as he might to restrain himself, he burst out laughing.

'What the devil are you doing clowning about like that?'

'Those buggers over there are shooting so close to the ground that the mud sprays into your face!'

'But why do you bow every time they shoot?'

'You'll see. If you don't duck, you'll get one right on the bonce. Then you're a goner.'

Lemke jumped down. Schlump climbed up and looked out eagerly at the enemy. On the other side it glowed red again behind the mound, and large shells hurtled over his head towards the artillery. Then came the machine-gun fire: *tak-tak-tak-tak – tak-tak-tak-tak – tak-tak-tak-tak*. The bullets whistled around his ears like swallows after a storm. Schlump thought, If you can hear them whistling, they must have gone past you. Which means there's no need to worry about them any more. It went on: *tak-tak-tak-tak – tak-tak-tak-tak – tak-tak-tak-tak*. Suddenly there was laughter behind him.

Startled, Schlump turned around. The redhead was smirking. 'Crikey! You bow more elegantly than I do!' Schlump hadn't noticed he'd been doing it. They both laughed and Lemke walked off.

On sentry duty, time went slowly. It began to get light. Schlump stood motionless at his post, looking neither right nor left. Only one hour had passed, and he would have to stand there for two. They'd told him that the second hour lasted ten times as long as the first.

All of a sudden he felt the call of nature. He had an urgent need for that place where even the Kaiser had to go. But he was not allowed to leave his post. He tried his best to hold it in. Nothing helped. He was getting more desperate. He started to sweat and shift uncomfortably from one foot to the other. That didn't help. And time wasn't passing at all; his replacement was a long way off. Now he was even more desperate. He came out in a cold sweat. His knees were trembling. A soldier must never leave his post! Especially not in the face of the enemy!

What if he did it in his trousers? No, that wasn't on either! They'd think he'd done it because he was scared! For the rest of his life he'd be known as the man who'd crapped his pants: Scaredy Cat! Good God – he didn't have any paper either! He remembered the slim volume of poetry his mother had given him for Christmas, which he treasured and always kept in his breast pocket.

He jumped down. Beside him was the regimental boundary. There was a sign: *Infantry Regiment X – Infantry Regiment Y*. And at the foot of this marker he laid a different, far less glorious one. Visibly relieved, he climbed back up to his post and looked out with a keen eye to check that the enemy had not set off at a march towards them in the meantime.

It hadn't. Schlump let out a heavy sigh of relief.

At last his replacement came; Schlump could take a rest in the bunker. He fell asleep at once. He had two hours, then he was supposed to fetch the food. But he woke again after only one. His squad leader, Lance Corporal Golle from Saxony, was cursing wildly. Schlump listened intently. He had a bad feeling about this, and finally he worked out what was up. While on an inspection of the trench, the lieutenant had stepped in the new marker. He was apparently beside himself at this outrage because the general had planned a visit for the following day. The lance corporal was swearing his head off: 'If I find that bastard…! It's got to be someone who reads poetry. I looked at what he wiped his arse on. I thought it was a letter. But it's just poems

89

about spring and that. Well I'll get him, you mark my words. I bet it's one of the new boys, a one-year volunteer.'

Schlump broke out into a cold sweat again, feeling afraid and ashamed. He remained as quiet as a mouse, and when it was time, he gathered up the mess tins and dashed off to fetch the food.

When he returned, he had to go back on sentry duty. He took a spade and cleared away his shame with profound embarrassment. Then he leapt on to the fire step, unable to comprehend how others dealt with such an emergency.

But the incident was soon forgotten.

The general really was going to come. The soldiers who weren't standing guard had to dig trenches. In the evening they either shovelled out mud from the trenches that the rain had washed in, or worked out in the open. They had to clear the earth excavated from the trench to a distance of one metre, working as quietly as possible. But the French had got wind of what they were up to and opened fire with their machine guns. The bullets whistled and sang around their ears, and they kept themselves poised to scramble back into the trenches in an instant.

Suddenly one of the men cried out and fell into the trench like a sack of potatoes. As he toppled back, he had enough strength to say, 'I'm dead!' The others leapt down and stood around him. He opened his eyes and looked around quite cheerfully. It was Lemke, the one with the freckles. He felt to check he was still in one piece and found he was able to move all his limbs; just his left leg was stiff. He started moaning at once; the wound was hurting. Blood was seeping from his calf, but it looked like a harmless flesh wound. The old soldiers, who'd been playing at war for a year or more, cursed and envied him. It was outrageous that a recruit as green as he was should immediately get a bullet with 'home' written on it, without having so much as seen a Frenchie. They really wanted to give him a thrashing, but when he asked for a cigarette, they gave him that instead. Then two of them took him to the hospital bunker. The others climbed back up and carried on shovelling. The machine guns on the other side had stopped rattling.

The following day not a single aeroplane was seen in the sky. The weather was gloomy and the French didn't fancy shooting. The general definitely was coming. The more experienced soldiers were amazed: that would be a first. The lieutenant had gathered together all the platoon commanders and issued instructions. Schlump's lance corporal came back to the dugout looking serious and said. 'Right, the general *is* coming. If he addresses anyone standing guard, that man mustn't turn round, but answer the general while continuing to look straight ahead. Clean your rifles and boots, and smarten yourselves up so that no one in my platoon stands out.' They all laughed and cracked bad jokes about this general who was brave enough to visit the third line.

Schlump was lucky. He was standing guard when the general arrived. He heard a few voices. The general asked questions and the lieutenant answered eagerly and nervously. Several other officers were there too. Schlump, meanwhile, kept a sharp lookout for the enemy. Stopping behind him, the general asked him what his name was and what the password was. Schlump kept his eyes focused in the direction of the enemy, his back turned, and gave a terse but firm answer, without once averting his gaze. The general appeared to be satisfied. He resumed his conversation with the officers and moved on.

Schlump stayed where he was, deep in thought. He couldn't really tell what to make of the encounter. That general is a fool, he thought, if he thinks he can try to distract the soldiers for his own amusement. I hope the other generals have more brains, otherwise we're not going to win this war.

But he was doing the general an injustice. He wasn't being light-hearted. On the contrary, he felt deadly serious in the third line facing the enemy.

Schlump had lice. He'd picked them up a while ago, when he'd been digging trenches and he'd slept with the Polacks. But those were only the large white ones with the Iron Cross marked on their back. Now he had the small red ones as well, which hid in the seams of his shirt. Those were the worst. And when he was standing guard, he'd grab the front of his coat and rub his chest raw. But they saved their worst torment for the dugout, when you were trying to get to sleep, for they livened up when it was warm.

He sat beside the candle and deloused himself, holding the critters in the flame when he'd caught them. Or he let them march along the narrow board where the soldiers put their bread when they were eating, then ran his thumb over them *glissando*.

Up at the front line they were anticipating an attack. Every day the seventh company sent a group from the third line to the second, into the dugout beside the lieutenant of the first company, in case of an emergency. If the French mounted an attack they were to go straight away to the front line and close the entrances to the communications trenches that led to the rear. These were two wonderful days. They didn't have to stand guard and could while the time away. One soldier had brought along a pack of cards with him; they played the entire two days without stopping, only pausing to eat. The men were in excellent spirits, taking tricks and trumping with loud whoops of delight. They'd put a cover over the entrance to prevent their noise from reverberating beyond the dugout. The soldier who fetched the food brought back a couple of bottles of schnapps, too, which significantly increased the level of merriment. They failed to notice that the French were starting to fire their trench mortar shells with gusto, those huge things that buried themselves into the earth before exploding with a horrific racket, ripping out enormous holes you could comfortably build a house in. And when a thing like that struck, the dugout rang like a bell and it felt as if the earth was shaking momentarily.

The two days passed without the French launching an assault, however, and the soldiers were replaced by the next group. They walked back in single file. It really was quite an art to make your way through the thick mud, which would relieve you of your boots if you weren't careful enough in bracing your feet against the trench walls.

Back in the third line things looked bad. The Frenchies

had hit many parts of the trench with their mortars, and the soldiers had to climb through enormous holes. One dugout had been destroyed altogether, and no more had been seen of the poor blighters who'd been sleeping in there at the time. They went back to their own dugout. The artillery fire subsided somewhat, although every few hours a huge mortar shell flew over. One of them landed in the middle of the trench, right outside their dugout. But rather than exploding, the propeller broke off, ripping the cover with it, allowing them to scrape out the yellow filling with their fingers.

Schlump had become smarter. He now knew where to find the latrine: behind the third trench. One fine afternoon he paid a visit, relieved himself, and also took off his coat and shirt to delouse himself. You could afford to do that here in the third line. The sun shone, he was sitting comfortably on the beam, protected from the wind and out of sight of the enemy, an aeroplane revved high in the sky, a lark had even ascended and was singing its peaceful love song, free from any concern about shrapnel or shells. In the midst of this idyll Schlump was going about his business. And just as he was making good progress, having launched an assault on the terrified lice, regiments of which were perishing beneath his thumb, he suddenly heard the soft *sh-sh* — the firing of a trench mortar shell.

He looked up and saw the dark bird fly up almost vertically into the sky, slowly and majestically. And it was heading straight for Schlump and the latrine. He stared at the dark creature as if hypnotised, like a chicken spellbound by a snake. Finally it reached its highest point, the tip tilted, and

94

the shell started to plummet. It was still coming his way. Schlump couldn't move. He gazed up, and the next few moments seemed like hours. It was falling! Falling! Right on top of him. He jolted, grabbed both sides of his trousers, and ran as fast as he could along the trench, which curved left. The spell was broken!

Thud! The dull impact! Now it was going to explode. Schlump threw himself on the ground; here the communication trench was very shallow, giving only a hand's width of cover. Now it was going to explode. But it lasted an eternity; he could have got much further away. And still it didn't. Then, finally, came the dull boom, followed by a rumbling and drumming, as if a thousand horses were galloping towards him. And in the midst of all this, a strange splashing sound.

Schlump remembered nothing after that. When he regained consciousness, he was in the hospital bunker, where they were binding his wounds. The pain had brought him to. They had to stitch the skin where he'd suffered a graze wound to his head, while there had been minor damage to the skull, too, the surgeon said, holding his nose ...

Schlump closed his eyes again. He felt as if the thousand horses were still galloping over him. If he could have seen himself, he would have been horrified.

Schlump was fortunate. The summer offensive was under way, the field hospitals were being emptied, and he was returning home in the hospital train. When he turned on to his side, he could see the picture-perfect villages rushing past, nestling cleanly and cosily in the countryside. So different from the joyless bare houses in France. He couldn't get enough of the red roofs and green fields. The train ran along the Rhine, over proud bridges, slowly, but without stopping. They were unloaded in Bacharach and taken to a large, quiet house where they were cared for by silent nuns and examined by an elderly doctor. Schlump might have caught his attention because he was so young; the doctor always liked to joke with him.

Schlump was healthy and had young blood, which healed quickly. He had to stay in bed for a few months nonetheless. It was painful when they bandaged his head. And when once he grimaced, the doctor said, 'So, young man, why did you poke your head out just when the French guns were blazing away?' Schlump had a quick riposte: 'You're absolutely right, Herr Doctor, but what do you think they'd shoot at you if you poked your backside out?' Rather than take offence at this cheeky answer, the doctor laughed, for Schlump had already told him how he'd come by his wound.

Outside the sun was shining, the cherries were ripe, but the wounded had to stay in bed, growing ever more bored. Beside him lay a good old veteran. His name was written on the board by his bed: Paul Gottlob. He was a poor weaver from Treuen in the Vogtland. Schlump had told the man of his heroic deeds in Loffrande, and the weaver always wanted to hear more, for he'd been in the field hospital for an age. Gottlob had been shot in the stomach and his recovery was a slow one. 'Come on, boy,' he'd say in his thick accent, 'tell me another story. It makes the time pass quicker here.' So Schlump launched into one: 'Now, comrade, I'm sure you know that the peasants in France can't read or write. And their geography's even worse. One evening, Monsieur Rohaut comes into the bar. You know, the father of gorgeous Jeanne. We sit together for a while. Then he asks, "Is it true that there are still lots of bears and wolves in Germany?"

'Of course, I say, there's a plague of them in our country. We'd have ten times as many soldiers if the wolves didn't gobble up so many of our little children. But for many people it's also a chance to earn a crust, especially trapping bears. And trapping bears is a real art form back home in Germany. This is how we go about it. You need two men: one carries a noose like a lasso that you throw; the other puts on a pair of trousers like small boys wear, with flies that do up. Now as everyone knows, bears go crazy for honey, and this is what the trappers are banking on. To capture the bears alive – because if you shoot them, the bullets damage the fur, which then plummets in value – the second man undoes his trousers and the other one covers his backside in honey. This is normally done using a huge paintbrush. Then he goes on all fours and starts grunting amorously. This attracts the bears, as does the honey. They immediately start licking, and now it's easy for the second man to catch the bear with his lasso. He just has to be careful when he throws the noose that it doesn't stick in the honey.

'Now in our village we had two men who were experts in trapping bears. One was called Mouser, the other Louser. One winter's evening, it was about two years ago, they went into the forest to catch bears. It's better to go at night, because the bears can't see as clearly. So Louser takes down his trousers and lets Mouser paint him with honey. Then he goes on all fours and starts grunting amorously, an art in which he was peerless. But not a single bear showed its face. As it was miserably cold, his backside began to freeze. The men were about to pack up when all of a sudden an old beast came toddling along, droning loudly. Like all old bears, he had a real sweet tooth, and started licking the thick honey right away.

'Mouser ought to have thrown the lasso at this point, but he had an idea. Where there's a bear, he told himself, there must be two bears. So he covered the bear's behind with honey too. He'd brought along a whole pail of honey, because you have to keep applying new coats. And hey presto! A second bear comes creeping up, and Mouser paints his behind as well. As if the devil himself has a hand in all this, a third and a fourth huge bear appear. Meanwhile, Louser had started heading back to the village on all fours. The bears followed him every step of the way, and Mouser smeared the behind of the last bear with honey. By the time the procession arrived in the village, Mouser was painting the bottom of the twenty-second bear, and all the honey was used up.

'Louser skipped towards the fire station; Mouser, dripping with sweat, ran in front and opened the doors, and Louser entered with his sizeable entourage, marching round the walls until he came back to the doors. The last bear plodded in and, in a single bound, Louser darted out. Mouser closed the doors and congratulated his comrade with a shake of the hands. They'd caught twenty-two bears, and had become rich.'

Paul Gottlob split his sides laughing. He couldn't believe the French were stupid enough to believe such nonsense.

Schlump's head was full of the most outlandish ideas, and he was able to entertain the entire hospital with them. It was only after two months that he was permitted to get out of bed. He had a very cautious doctor, who liked Schlump because of his bright and cheerful eyes, and so he made him his clerk. This suited Schlump down to the ground because he was longing for some freedom; he wanted to show his gratitude to the girls he'd met some time before at the garden wall – each day he was allowed to stroll for two hours outside – and who'd given him chocolate and other goodies. Now he was able to go outside and return their favours.

As the autumn of 1916 slowly drew in – the rowan trees were starting to change colour – he had to take the soldiers who'd had their legs shot to pieces to see a doctor at the other end of town. This man had all manner of torture instruments, which he used to rack and twist the soldiers' injured limbs to make them flexible again. Schlump would deliver the heroes to the doctor at two o'clock in the afternoon and pick them up again at five. In between he was free. In this beautiful old town he'd discovered a wonderful, charming inn, covered up to the eaves in a vine. A romantic arch inscribed with an old, faded date that nobody could read led into this little paradise. Schlump went into the low bar, beneath the panelled ceiling, where at the counter stood the friendly landlady with her strong arms, red cheeks and gold teeth. Two lovely young creatures,

Elly, her niece, and Nelly, her daughter, served the customers. But there were seldom customers in the afternoons. Only in the evenings did the red noses assemble to win the war with their grand words.

Elly was exactly Schlump's age and had a sergeant for a sweetheart. Nelly was barely sixteen, and shone white and rosy like apple blossom. Her father was with the artillery at the fortress in Metz and wore a huge sabre whenever he was on leave. But he was rarely on leave, and the landlady, who loved him very dearly, had to make do with a fat paymaster who paid court to her every evening. On occasion she'd go away with him, which was good news for the impoverished Schlump because it meant he didn't have to pay for his beer. On those days the inn was a heavenly place to be. Schlump sat on the old-fashioned curved sofa, a lovely young girl either side of him, and was able to kiss them to his heart's content. Sweet little Nelly would sometimes unsheathe her claws if he got too close, for she was still a virgin. But Elly had a sergeant for a sweetheart and she knew that you had to keep still when a soldier kissed you. These were delightful afternoons. The sun spun golden threads through the bar and shot glowing white sparks in between. The vine in front of the window wove a lovely pattern into the light. The only sounds to be heard were Schlump's kisses and the girls' giggles. Sometimes Schlump wasn't so lucky: the girls would assault him with waves of tickles until he could bear it no longer.

One day Elly was in a bad mood when Schlump arrived, while sweet little Nelly was nowhere to be seen. Schlump crept out of the bar, but rather than go back out into the street he headed up the narrow staircase to seek out his little creature. The doors were not locked, and he went along dark, narrow corridors from one room to another. In the living room he discovered a small concealed door. Approaching it with caution, he opened it as carefully as he could, and stuck his head in the tight opening. What a sight met his eyes! Two steps led down into a small, bright white room, into which the sun smiled just as it did in the bar below. Behind the curtains by the window he saw red and blue flowers in full bloom, and on the table in front of the window gleamed large white roses. But behind the curtain by the wall was a sweet little bed, painted white. And beside the bed waited a pair of charming slippers, one leaning wearily against the other. Schlump could hear his heart pounding and didn't dare move a muscle. For he saw a slender little foot peeking out from behind the curtain!

He stayed where he was for ages. Then, plucking up courage, he closed the door behind him and went down the stairs with the utmost circumspection. With each step he'd wait in trepidation, as the floorboards creaked terribly. Eventually he was standing by the curtain, which he lifted gently. There was sweet little Nelly, sleeping on the bed, her cheeks as rosy as wild poppies. She lay there without a cover, dressed in only a pair of see-through knickers. Her stockings had slipped to reveal two charming dimples on her knees. One hand was by her nose, the other where the great artists tend to paint it when they don't want to reveal everything. Throwing caution to the wind, Schlump kissed her on the lips. With a jolt she opened her eyes, turned as red as a peony, fended him off and was on the point of turning very angry. But with the other hand she held him tight and pulled him down to her small breasts.

On this occasion Schlump arrived back late at the military hospital. He would have happily taken any punishment they might wish to throw at him, but they did nothing.

Every day from now on he went straight up into the tiny bedroom, where Nelly would be waiting impatiently for him. She now kept her claws retracted, showing him her velvety paws instead. Elly made sure that nobody disturbed them, for she had understanding for such matters. Nelly's mother happened to be away for a particularly long period of time, and the honeymoon lasted until autumn had sacrificed her last leaves. Then the mother returned and the sabre-bearer came back too, on four weeks' leave. By now, however, Schlump had fully recovered, and when a rather severe army panel made a round of the hospital – wicked military doctors who threw out all shirkers – Schlump's days were numbered.

Half a year later, sweet little Nelly wrote to him in the field that she was expecting a little Schlump. But he should not fret about it. Her mother wasn't angry; she herself was expecting a little paymaster. And her father, too, had commissioned a little sabre-bearer in Metz, while Elly would be giving birth to a little sergeant. What a christening there would be! She, Nelly, had found a sweetheart who wanted to marry her, a man who no longer had to play at being a soldier as his right arm had been shot off. So the wedding would probably be soon. This long letter had come in a big package of goodies containing salami, bacon and ham, all from a pig that had been slaughtered in secret, for by this time people in Germany were already starving.

Schlump was discharged from hospital and transferred to the reserve battalion in his regiment. He travelled home and even obtained a fortnight's leave. He would be seeing his mother again!

When he caught sight of the house where they lived and where he'd grown up, he quickened his pace, then started to run, finally charging up the steps. He rang with such fervour that he broke the bell. Although his mother knew that her son was coming back, the shock when she saw him at the door was so great that she screamed out loud and fainted in Schlump's arms. But her joy revived her at once. Although she was beside herself with happiness, the thought that her child might be hungry kept her mind straight. She placed everything in front of him that she'd put by from her own meals. She didn't tell him she'd starved for his sake; when he came back to his mother he should find bread on the table, and be able to eat heartily. Fear that the bread might run out threatened to ruin a portion of her happiness. They were rationed down to the last gram, and Schlump's father needed to eat as he worked hard in a factory. He'd given up tailoring because there was no longer a man in the land who wanted a suit. The mother felt sorry for the boy because he'd have no stollen for Christmas. She only had a tiny amount of flour left, which she wanted to use to make a cake for him.

But Schlump came to the rescue. He'd brought home a huge sack, which he proceeded to unpack. It contained two enormous stollens that Nelly had given him. There was no danger of starving at their inn, for they were amongst the lucky people in Germany to have a field where they could grow their own grain. Schlump's mother was proud of her son when she heard that the stollens were from a girl; all mothers feel pride and delight when girls spoil their boys.

That evening Schlump's father came home from work, shook his hand earnestly, and enquired about the war. The question troubling him was whether Germany would win. Schlump couldn't give him an answer to that. He told them about Loffrande and the French people he'd met, and his parents listened blissfully to their son until late in the night. They became young, cheerful and lively again.

Schlump's mother was a very happy woman. Her son stayed for a fortnight. He seldom went out, for he knew that she regretted every hour he wasn't with her. She'd suffered greatly in his absence. It was like a knife in her heart whenever she saw his school friends in the street, still going around in civilian clothes because they hadn't volunteered. But she didn't reveal any of this to her son, because the last thing in the world she wanted to do was hurt his feelings.

Schlump was annoyed by many things at home. He despised the milk women, who put on airs and graces and demanded a fortune for the dribble of milk they handed out to the poor. Then the clerks at the town hall, who distributed bread coupons and behaved as if they were the Lord God themselves, snarling at the timid women. One afternoon Schlump went into the countryside with his mother to beg the peasants for some butter in exchange for money. But they were chased from the door at every farm they tried. Eventually they got hold of a pound of curd cheese and went home in fear of the gendarme who would confiscate their hard-won booty and eat it himself if he searched them. As they passed a barn, they saw a couple of plump maids enjoying breakfast with French prisoners. They waved to Schlump and his mother, each of them with salami in one hand and a thick slice of bread in the other. Schlump wanted to fire a volley of bullets in their direction, but all he had was his bayonet hanging on his belt, and you couldn't shoot with that.

His leave came to an end three days before Christmas. When he reported to his battalion, the sergeant sent him to the supply sergeant, where he was given new clothes. On Christmas Eve a transport was leaving for the Front. Two men had fallen ill so Schlump had to step in straight away. His mother was horrified when she saw him in his new uniform, because she knew exactly what that meant. He said goodbye to her; she was brave and didn't cry. He joked and laughed to comfort her. On the street he turned round and gave her another wave. She was holding a handkerchief and wiping her eyes.

On the bridge by the barracks he met a worker, a woman who was still young but had an old face. Noticing Schlump's new cap and uniform, she stared at him wide-eyed. She stopped to let him pass, then mumbled quietly to herself, 'Another poor animal off to slaughter. And such a young one, too.' Schlump heard her and couldn't help laughing.

Taking some time off work, his father accompanied him and his comrades to the station. The band played as it had that first time he went to France. The train pulled slowly out of the station. The soldiers lit candles, put up some fir twigs and celebrated Christmas. They smoked cigarettes and sang carols. Then most went to sleep, though some played cards.

Schlump had been in the trenches for several days, and this time he was in the front line. On the journey there he'd met an old friend, Willy, the tracer in the factory where he had once worked. Having joined up at the start of the war, Willy had been part of the advance on Paris before being transferred to Russia. His body had been subjected to the most unbelievable exertions – endless marches, hunger, thirst, and all-out assaults. He'd seen trenches full to the brim with dead Russians, while his entire regiment had got dysentery and many had died. Now he was on his way to France, where death was awaiting him.

For five days they stayed in the front trench, after which they would go back to the third line. They were not far from the place where Schlump had been injured. Twice the regiment had fought at the Somme, and twice it had haemorrhaged so badly that only the sergeants, their clerks, the kitchen boys and the supply unit behind the Front were left. Even some of those had copped it. The few who'd survived said that the war couldn't throw up anything worse than that. Schlump came across almost no familiar faces in the company.

In spite of the squad of reinforcements Schlump had arrived with, the regiment was still very weak, and the group had to guard three posts. The nights were painfully cold and during the day it snowed. And when the sun shone, the ground would thaw and everything would be wet. Schlump was in sap three. Now he was facing the British, who often fired with long-range ship guns. Those cursed straight shooters! Barely had you heard the shot than the shell was already there; you didn't have time to take cover.

Shioou! Christ, they're firing short today, Schlump thought. Have they forgotten where the second trench is? Up till now the straight shooters had always fired at the second trench, where the lieutenant was. Yesterday the lieutenant came forward with the sniper. From the sap here you could see the Tommies going to collect their food. They went quite a distance above cover, probably because they sank a metre in the mud in their trench too. Then they disappeared into a wreck of a house, behind which was a barrel. Yesterday the sniper got one. He was paid three marks for each Tommy he shot dead so long as there was a witness. The British had noticed this and had started firing early this morning at sap three with their straight shooters.

As Schlump lit a cigarette, his friend Willy came round the corner. 'Where are you going?' Schlump asked.

Shiouu!

Bullseye. Schlump collapsed into the parapet and vanished beneath his steel helmet. White smoke all around him, and more puffing from small cavities pitted into the chalk by the shrapnel. His rifle was smashed, and the gas mask over his shoulder full of holes. He was buried in dirt up to his waist, and there was a whooshing in his ears. With super-human strength he heaved up the mass of limestone and scrambled to his feet. There was Willy, bathed in blood. His face was green and his left hand quivering. His chest was ripped open, red lumps hung out, and in his neck was a hole the size of a fist.

Schlump leapt over the body and dashed away. Knowing that a second shot would follow quickly, he darted round the corner and fell into a tunnel that the sappers had dug. All his limbs were trembling, his teeth chattering; he was no longer in control of his body.

It went on like this for two days before his nerves calmed down. The others said his face had been as green as Willy's.

At eight o'clock in the evening it was his turn to go back on guard, sap three again. Three men from his group had dragged Willy's body away. The sap had caved in and there was blood everywhere. Only now did he notice that his coat was also splattered in blood, all over the breast: his friend's blood. He'd taken Willy's rifle because it was cleaner. The others had already squabbled over his bread and the rest of his things; that was how hungry they were. Comradeship was thin on the ground because these men barely knew each other and hadn't yet had the benefit of shared experience.

Front line, third line, rest, six days at a time – this was the gruelling and perilous rhythm in which Schlump was now fixed. It was thrilling and deadening at the same time. You didn't see an enemy; you were exposed to shelling and couldn't fight back. Just standing guard by the barbed wire, nothing but standing guard. And in between, fetching food, fetching coffee, digging, delousing.

Spring came. There were rumours of an offensive, the mood was bad, the soldiers were starving and openly expressing their disgruntlement. Rations were smaller and yet had to last just as long. They were usually gone by the first evening, which meant an enforced fast from one lunch to the next. And usually the soldier sent to fetch them dropped half on the way back or never returned at all, for the Tommies fired at each one of them with their cannon, hunting the men down like hares.

The twelve days were up and they were waiting to be relieved. Thank God, Schlump thought. Sleep, delousing, fresh underwear. But nothing came of it.

'The company's going to sector D.'

Which meant back to the front line, except this time to sector D, which was the best sector in the regiment: better dugouts and peaceful. The group had found a tolerable bunker. There was a draught, it was freezing, and water dripped from the walls, which was horrible when cold drops splashed your neck as you were trying to get to sleep. But the men were exhausted and had to put up with it, just as they did with the lice.

The group had chopped some wood for the platoon commander, in return for which they each received a slice of bread. Schlump was enjoying two hours' rest. He lay on the bunk with his metal mess tin beneath his head. The slats were hard and scraped your hips. In the wall beside him must be a rats' nest with several young, for they screamed like tiny children and made quite a racket. From time to time the mother would quite happily climb over Schlump's tummy to take a sniff of the bread. He let it scrabble around while he ate his slice of dry bread. He thought of home, of sweet little Nelly, and Estelle, and felt happy. Then he fell asleep.

'Guard duty!'

'Oh for God's sake,' Schlump cursed. 'I've just been dreaming of food and women. If only I could have a proper sleep, a proper sleep in a proper bed, as long as I liked, without freezing.'

'Guard duty!'

He staggered out, still half asleep. The rifle, the ammo belt, gas mask, hand grenades – he picked up all of these mechanically, his eyes closed. Outside it was bitterly cold; it was three o'clock in the morning. He wrenched his eyes open, violently, but could see nothing. He walked along the long trench, which was just a sunken thoroughfare. Tripping up, he swore.

Schlump relieved the soldier on duty, who left without a word. Now it was his turn to stand there again. His legs froze within seconds and the stamping began, the incessant stamping.

It was a godforsaken sap. Schlump was all alone; he couldn't see anything apart from barbed wire. The trench ran forward diagonally, turned on itself, then ran diagonally backwards. A Tommy could easily hop into the trench behind him and knock him silently to the floor with a crack to the skull. An unsettling thought. 'Watch out,' the soldiers from the other company said as they were being relieved. 'A Tommy came in from behind and slit the throats of two of our men.'

Then Schlump saw something black scuttling about. A

rat. His neighbour in the dugout, perhaps, the one with all those children. She came up to him, nudged his rifle, nibbled at his gas mask, sniffed the hand grenades, and gave him a long stare. She appeared to know him and wasn't in the least afraid. Standing on her hind legs, she started to clean her whiskers and wash her paws. Schlump looked at the rat affectionately. He was delighted with his new friend, and spoke to her softly. 'Stay a while. Why don't you sit down on the gas mask?'

'What are you thinking of?' she said. 'I've got seven children to feed who are crying with hunger. I've got to go home. Farewell!' She nodded to him a few times, then vanished. Schlump checked the time. Not even five minutes had passed of the two hours he had to stand guard here.

There was still ages to go until the two hours were up. Schlump was stamping heavily from one foot to the other.

There! There in front of the barbed wire! No, it was nothing. There it was again! It was eerie. The moon had not yet shown her face; it was pitch black. Schlump wanted to sleep – at his post! – and leaned against the trench wall where earlier he'd chatted to his friend. There it was again! Yes, no doubt about it. My God, bodies were creeping towards him.

He took his rifle and shot, shot blindly out of the trench. Sparks flew as the bullets clanged against the barbed wire.

Suddenly he stopped. It was deathly quiet, save for the odd shot to his left and right; some machine-gun fire, but that sounded far in the distance. The silence was creepy. His heart was pounding loudly, much more loudly than the report of his rifle. He heard footsteps behind him. He turned around. It was the corporal on duty.

'Anything wrong?'

'No, but shoot a flare, would you?'

The rocket raced into the sky with a whoosh and a hiss; on the opposite side the shadows sank slowly, the flare burned out. Nothing.

The corporal went on his way.

Loneliness again. Now the cold was torture; it bit into his knees, his feet. He was wearing threadbare socks, his boots stuck to his feet, and the lice were eating away at his scalp.

Four o'clock. The soldier responsible for maintaining contact between the dugout and the guard post hadn't shown up yet. He was probably sitting in the dugout, warming himself with the smoke coming from the pipe. Oh, to be sleeping in the dugout! Schlump pictured it in all its detail: the men snoring, the candle still burning, albeit weakly, the stove crackling. Paradise.

The second hour was an eternity. Would it go on like this for ever? Day and night, day and night! Good God!

It got increasingly colder and Schlump didn't dare move his feet any longer for fear of pain.

Five o'clock. No relief. 'Bastards! Always five minutes late.' Still no sign. Schlump began to curse loudly. Fury welled up inside him. He wanted to run over to the dugout and toss in a grenade. But what was that? To his left, a burst of fire erupted wildly, flares, colourful ones, and then a barrage! The Tommies were shelling with their artillery, too.

Whee-ee, whee-ee!

From the Tommies' trenches came the 'Christmas tree': red, green and yellow flares. Now all hell was let loose: grenades, heavy shells, light shells, shrapnel, straight shooters, small ones, big ones, small ones. The bombardment became more intense, wilder: trench mortars, aerial torpedoes. Schlump could clearly see them glowing in the sky, the mortar bombs, big ones and small ones, then the flares! Finally our artillery returned fire, but more sparingly. The shells whizzed right over Schlump's head and exploded on the other side, massive explosions. A thrilling spectacle! Schlump couldn't help laughing; he laughed out loud amidst this hellish turmoil. He was enjoying himself. To his left and right, hot pieces of shrapnel buffeted the wet mud: *pff, pff, pff*. Once the shells had exploded, the heavy fuses hurtled on their own through the air, humming like bumble bees. What a concert!

This lasted for an hour, until six o'clock, then it was over at a stroke. Silence. In the east the sky became a touch lighter. A star glistened cheerfully, shining innocently like the baby Jesus.

And then the relief came.

The British appeared to be on the verge of launching an offensive.

At seven o'clock Schlump was back on duty again, but this time he was posted in the trench and could move around freely. He didn't have to spend the whole time in one spot while his feet turned to ice. The trench was littered with shrapnel from the barrage. Schlump could scarcely believe that he'd come through it unscathed. Some of the hunks of metal he saw wouldn't have left much of him intact.

Now they started firing again: one, two smaller shells. And what was that? A really heavy straight shooter. To his left, directly behind the trench wall, a colossal sheaf of mud and stones flew up. And what an explosion! Schlump flung himself into a shell hole, which was rather comfortable as it happened and extended deep into the ground. In the subterranean world another war was being played out, maybe even worse than the one on the surface. You seldom saw these pale, nervous miners, these moles. They burrowed down below, always listening, and seeking to blow the Tommies into the air or crush them when they themselves tunnelled into the ground. Recently they'd blown a long section of trench into the air at Souchez. The valley smoked for days afterwards and stank of powder. An entire company of brave soldiers had been wiped out.

Schlump leaned against the entrance, to give himself at least a modicum of cover from the heavy shells. He smoked a cigarette. There they were landing again, right next to him, where the machine-gun nest had been built, bomb-proofed with cement. Beside it was a store for hundreds of hand grenades.

One, two! Those were the small shells; now the heavy one would be on its way. Yes, there it was. A terrible explosion, and Schlump was given a sharp jolt by the wall he was leaning against. A loud boom came from the dugout. Schlump teetered forward. The heavy shell had hit the machine-gun nest and the hand grenades had exploded.

Two soldiers shot high into the sky; Schlump had a clear view of them, their arms and legs spread-eagled. And around the two bodies innumerable tiny black dots reeled: fragments of stone and dirt. Everything landed on the Tommies' side. The trench was completely destroyed. There was no trace of the other two machine gunners. Schlump crawled out of the rubble and checked that his legs were still in one piece. The Tommies kept up their fire. Two small shells, then a heavy-duty one.

His relief arrived. 'You've got to get the food!'

Now? In this barrage? For Christ's sake! Schlump thought, pouring the last of the coffee into his mess tin, in an attempt to smear it clean with his filthy hands.

He set off, running as fast as he could, above cover; the trench was too full of mud and everything was thawing. Along the second and third line, behind the artillery position, back, back, back to the quarry. This was where the kitchen boys came with two barrels that they'd mounted on to a wagon. There was sauerkraut. First Schlump had them fill his mess tin and gobbled the whole lot up. You only got this privilege with the seventh company. They'd been put in charge of the kitchen and they were the best thieves in the whole company. Then Schlump had all the mess tins filled and went back.

It was like a punishment, having to struggle through all those old trenches with full mess tins. Trenches that had been fought over last year, where now the artillery stood. A dead infantryman lay beside the artillery; his body had been there for several days. He'd died going to fetch food. The shot had torn off the top of his skull. It lay beside him like a plate, and death had neatly placed his brain on top. Schlump clambered through the second position, which was now unoccupied, to the third line of the first position. He saw the holes they'd dug out with their fingernails in mortal fear after the assaults two years ago, in an attempt to afford themselves some cover from the frenzied fire. Schlump thought of the mass graves that the quartermaster had shown him last year, and the feeling he'd had then gripped him again like a cold fist.

At that moment a shell whistled past and plugged in an old grave ten paces from him. Bones soared into the air; the old leather helmet, which funnily enough had remained on its post all this time, spun around madly then slowly came back to rest.

Schlump had thrown himself on the ground, the hot sauerkraut all over his fingers and coat.

'They're going to be mad at me,' he muttered to himself.

The nights were still freezing cold. They were back in the third line and had just been given supper: a small chunk of bread, a little 'monkey fat', as they called it (some schmaltz substitute), and a teaspoon of jam. Starving, they ate the whole lot at once – they wouldn't be getting anything else for two days. Their next task was to haul timbers, eight per man. Those pieces of oak were unbelievably heavy, and Schlump almost collapsed. He decided to take two at a time so he'd only have to make four trips. An icy wind was blowing which cut into his fingers like a thousand knives. The cold crept under his fingernails and Schlump gritted his teeth so hard that tears came to his eyes. On the second trip he only took one piece of wood. The pain was so excruciating that he thought the cold would rip off his fingers.

He'd brought all eight pieces of wood into the trench, all eight. The others had finished too. The two men who were supposed to be on non-combat duty only – a couple of luckless fellows who'd been sent to the trenches four times, practically cripples – couldn't physically move the wood, so had to stand guard.

Schlump crept into the dugout. All of them were now starving, but the bread was finished. They cursed and lay down, but they were so hungry they couldn't get to sleep. 'They do as they please with us,' lamented someone who'd been at the Somme. 'If we avoid being blown to bits they let us die of hunger.'

Night passed. The following morning they collected unexploded shells because raw iron was needed back in Germany. The men were promised seven pfennigs for each piece. But they had to keep their wits about them, for there was no let-up from the Tommies' artillery. And nobody ever saw any money. When the offensive was launched, all that remained of the company was the sergeant and his clerks.

It was lunchtime, and the man charged with collecting the food set off. He came back a few hours later having spilled nothing. But their hunger returned in the afternoon. What a night it was going to be! And no food again till tomorrow evening! Schlump teamed up with another man to go and beg for bread from the artillery, who often had some left over. He and his companion made their way to the rear and although they weren't given anything in the artillery canteen, they came across the bread wagon as they continued towards the heavy artillery. They asked the two gunners sitting on the wagon if they could have some bread. 'What do you take us for?' the two cannon-cockers scoffed, and drove on. Schlump clenched his fists and said, 'Right. We're going to make mincemeat of those two. We'll give them a good hiding and then take as much bread as we need for the whole group ... But they've got rifles and we've got nothing,' he continued sadly. 'They'll just gun us down.' They cursed and returned to the dugout with empty hands.

There was one man in the group who Schlump found it impossible to get on with, who couldn't stand him, although Schlump hadn't the faintest idea why. He was a nauseating individual who made life difficult for Schlump in every conceivable way. 'You swine, I bet you ate all the bread you nicked on the way back,' he sneered. Schlump put up with a lot of abuse from him without saying anything in return. He knew that the slightest reaction was all the other man needed as an excuse to fly at him. But the entire platoon was exhausted and highly irritable. 'Hey, how about you get us some wood, too? We do all the hard work and he just sits by the stove warming his bones,' the man spat venomously. Maybe he'd taken against him because Schlump was a volunteer − a sabre-rattler, the others used to call him. Maybe he had a wife and children at home who wrote him sour letters. He was from Brandenburg, had a small head with straw-blonde hair and a huge nose that ended in a sharp point.

That night they had to dig again. They picked up their spades, but did nothing apart from grumble. Suddenly

Pointy-Nose lashed out at Schlump: 'Do something, you war-loving swine. Do something, or I'll smash your face in!' There must be something wrong with him in the head. But it was the tipping point for Schlump. There was only a certain amount he could take: 'Shut your big fat face, you prick!'

'What did you call me?' Pointy-Nose screamed, grabbing his bayonet and making for Schlump. The others stood in a circle around the two men and watched. Well, it was a bit of variety.

They fought that night, the two of them, in the face of the enemy. It was a struggle for life and death. Pointy-Nose was taller and stronger than Schlump, his eyes shone white and his face was crazily contorted, which they could just about make out in the faint illumination provided by the snow. 'Bravo, lad! Look at the young lad!' the others shouted, forgetting all else. Schlump was beside himself with fury, he was sweating... and now he had him, he was lying on the ground. Schlump was kneeling on his chest, both hands tight around the man's neck, his thumbs pressing on the throat. 'You're never getting up again, you bastard,' he panted. He wanted to strangle him, but the others pulled him away.

From then on Pointy-Nose gave him no more trouble. But Schlump was always on his guard; he thought the man capable of anything. It was dreadful – your own comrade!

Schlump wasn't in the least bit proud of his victory. He thought about the fight as he lay on the slats; it made him feel uneasy, as if he'd defiled himself somehow. In his mind he ran through the whole of the previous day. In the afternoon he'd tried to pilfer bread – in fact, steal it violently – and in the night he'd had a punch-up with his comrade. That was what it had sunk to, that was what happened when you came down in the world. And he remembered what the sergeant had told him back in Loffrande: 'Only the fools end up in the trenches, or those who've been in trouble.' Was the man right? There must be something in what he'd said, because plenty of people surely thought the same. Maybe they *all* think the same. It's just that we, the poor bastards at the Front, don't realise. Yes, that's right, that's how it is. We're treated with such contempt that even a blind man would notice. Those two gunners on the bread wagon yesterday, just remember how scornfully they laughed in your face. Two filthy infantrymen, begging for bread! And the sergeant who gave them a mere slice for chopping wood. He must have bread till it was coming out of his ears! 'Those poor bastards,' he must have thought. What's more, those were heavy logs they chopped for a slice of bread. And the lieutenant had forbidden them to get caught doing it! The Tommies, meanwhile, had been firing without any let-up, scattering their shrapnel everywhere! For one measly slice of bread!

And then that time when they'd been resting, when the first company had returned from the front trenches, those wretched fellows had looked ghastly: emaciated, ashen-faced, grubby chalk worked around the stubble, stooped, utterly worn out, filthy, terribly filthy, lice-ridden and bloody, and only twenty men left of the sixty who'd been positioned on the front line. These men were standing by their quarters when the fat sergeant major came out, who'd spent each one of the twelve nights playing cards and getting drunk. This sergeant major, the mother superior of the company, came and ranted at them as if they were common criminals. If that wasn't contempt, then what was? And sometimes, when you wandered past the lieutenant's dugout in the trench, a smell wafted out, a smell of frying and stewing! Did you ever see an officer eating from the same mess tin as you? No, never, just as you'd never eat out of the same dish as a dog! So it really *was* true what the service corps sergeant had said – no man with a hint of self-respect ends up in the trenches.

Schlump talked himself deeper and deeper into this bitterness; all of a sudden he saw everything with new eyes. He worked himself up and felt unhappy for the first time in his life. It was as if he'd awoken from a deep sleep; for the first time in his life he was thinking seriously about himself and the world. For a moment he lost his golden childish innocence. But it didn't last long.

Maybe those others who despise you are right. All this is just for the morons, the blockheads. Anyone with a brain in his head works his way out of it. Just like in life. A man with a bit of guts works his way above the masses, where you're a nobody, without a name even. 'Yes,' Schlump said out loud. 'Yes, you've got to get out of here!' But how? Join the artillery? They'd laugh in your face: 'Oh, young man, want a bit of life insurance, do you? You're no fool; I quite fancy that myself!' The sappers? But that's worse than up in the trenches. Those moles lie in wait for one another, and slaughter each other in the most horrific ways imaginable, without ever setting eyes on the enemy. What about the flying corps? Yes, that's it – the flying corps, that's the answer. There, a man is still worth something; there, courage and skill still count for something; there, every man is his own mini commander and has his opponent in his sights; there, respect and chivalry still exist. And when you're back from a hunt, you can be a human being! Yes, that's the right place. But how do you get in? The sergeant major would laugh at him. 'You want to fly? What, a clown like you? I recommend you learn how to march properly first, and how to handle your rifle, you fool!' But there was another way. He had to achieve something! Distinguish himself! And more than once; after all, he needed to get their attention. And then you'll be promoted, you'll be awarded the Iron Cross, and they'll have to take you seriously when you're a sergeant.

When I'm a sergeant, Schlump thought, I'll get a mess tin full of food, and won't ever have to fetch it myself. And I won't have to dig trenches or stand guard.

Schlump resolved to go out with every patrol and volunteer at every opportunity. He was pleased with himself. And if he should cop it while on duty, well, that could be no worse than the eternal misery of the trenches.

He went to sleep a happy man.

Their relief came, and now they were to have six days' rest. A chance to wash and delouse themselves, and put on fresh underwear. The march back to their quarters was long and arduous. They had to pass along a defile that was under constant shelling from the Tommies. At three o'clock in the morning, Monday morning, they arrived: exhausted, shattered, finished. Every muscle in their bodies was crying out for sleep. But they were woken again at six o'clock. Schlump was dreaming he'd been promoted to sergeant. When the soldier on duty came to wake them, he felt as if he'd only just gone to sleep. He cursed and shouted, 'Get the hell out of here!' The soldier heard him and Schlump was ordered out immediately to clean the large spades, while the others drank their hot coffee.

Then the day's activities began. One inspection after another: mess tin, helmet, overcoat, coat, rifle, canteen — everything had to be as good as new. In between these came drill: down on the ground, standing up, saluting. They had no idea how to get their things clean. There was no soap any more, or only poor-quality stuff. They scrubbed and cleaned, washed and wore themselves out, polished and patched up; the rest was out of the question. Schlump thought about his dream and had no desire to perform these mundane tasks. He was upbraided when they assembled for inspection: 'My God, what a mess we have here. Just look at this man!' And the sergeant major with the thick notebook on his chest pulled him by the buttonhole to the front of the parade and bellowed, 'Two hours' punishment drill, and report every half-hour in full uniform! And woe betide you if you're not clean! Go on, clear off!' Schlump realised that his dream hadn't come true.

They were permitted to sleep the following night. From the evening till the morning. But the night after that the alarm was sounded! At two o'clock they were wrenched from their sleep. Within five minutes they had to pack their kitbags and fall in outside. Then they marched off into the night. The artillery was moving into position so they had to dash past in the roadside ditch and were spattered with mud in the process. They marched for another half-hour. The path became drier. Up on the hill stood the regimental commander, who Schlump had never set eyes on before, staring at his watch. 'Seventh company ten minutes late!' Then they were allowed to return home – it was only alarm drill. They think they can do what they like with us, thought Schlump. He said nothing but he was furious.

They were allowed to sleep through the following night, but in the middle of the next night they had to fall in for duty. They were being sent to the second line in the first position to dig trenches. The company leader didn't go with them, only Lieutenant Grün and two sergeants. They marched in silence and half asleep. When they arrived, it started to rain. The lieutenant soon crept into a dugout, and the two sergeants vanished as well. The corporals stood there cursing: 'Come on, men, keep it up!' They were in a bad mood. The Tommies were attacking from the front and the side with machine-gun fire. Schlump toiled away to create himself some cover. The trench had been blown to bits and he thought of the trumpeter who had died. The rain stopped. It became icily cold. They froze miserably and stopped working. Then they lay down in the wet mud to afford themselves a little protection from the biting wind that was chilling them to the bone.

'Come on, let's get out of here,' came a voice. The corporals didn't say anything. They put their heads together and swore. No order came to march back. They waited for hours. It got increasingly cold. The wind turned humid; it blew sharp needles, half ice, half water. They were lying in the muck and freezing. The mud that they'd shovelled out earlier slowly started to drip down the trench walls, accumulating behind their backs.

At four o'clock the two shirkers-in-chief arrived. They'd been playing skat in a dugout. One was still laughing; he'd won. 'Well, boys,' he said, 'I can't dismiss you yet, the lieutenant's not here.'

At five o'clock, just as there was a glimmer of light in the east, the lieutenant came, still dozy. 'Easy march!' he ordered quietly. They were pleased. Nobody said a word, and they tottered sluggishly back to their quarters.

Saturday was a free day. The following evening they were to return to position. Schlump had been in the mess since lunchtime. He'd given his food to the kitchen boy as he couldn't stand the smell of swedes. But there was beer. After lunch the lance corporals came in and sat at his table, amongst them Paul Biersack from his home town, who'd just been promoted to the rank. Paul took six matches from his pocket, broke one of them and threw half of it away. Then he held up the matches so only the red heads were visible. Every man had to draw a match. The one who got the half had to pay for a round. Then the next man took the five and a half matches and let the others draw. This way nobody had to talk; they could just drink beer and ruminate, aware that the offensive was about to start and that some of them would never come back. They kept playing this wonderful game all day long and into the night, and through the night till the morning, and then to the following lunchtime, and after lunch till late in the afternoon. At the end, two of them were left: Schlump and Michael Quellmalz, the famous 'Michel' who went on every patrol. Paul had been the first to quit; the final two wrapped the game up at five o'clock. Schlump wrote a letter to his father, wishing him a happy birthday, and at seven o'clock they set off for the trenches.

A month later, when Schlump was in the military hospital, he remembered their lovely game. All the players had fallen, one after the other: first Paul and finally Michael Quellmalz, the famous Michel.

They'd been back in the trenches for God knows how long, but the opportunity for Schlump to commit an act of heroism still hadn't arisen. He was forever having to stand guard and dig, and had no rest, no sleep. Previously he'd sometimes been able to snatch a couple of hours' sleep at night, but even that was over now. Perhaps ten times in those two hours he'd get up, grab his rifle, hand grenades, and bullets, and clamber out into the trench. Once outside he'd be woken by the cold air, unable to fathom why he'd come out. Shaking his head and practically asleep again already, he'd crawl back down to get himself a few more minutes.

'On duty!'

He woke with a jolt. 'What is it? Where am I? Hey, what's happening?'

'On duty, for Christ's sake!'

He grabbed the rifle again, and the hand grenades, the gas mask, everything, but he didn't know whether he was asleep or awake or what was going on. Only when he was outside, when he froze bitterly once more and the lice commenced their torture inside his boots, could he be sure that he was awake, that he wasn't dreaming.

They'd been in position for twenty days now. The chalk ate into their backs; a few bits always crumbled and found their way into their clothes whenever they crawled into the dugout. His hands were cut open. Constant filth for twenty days, nothing but filth. There were no nice words uttered any more, just curses.

How fortunate are those who've had a leg shot off, or an arm. They're at home now, they can stay in bed and sleep, sleep, sleep.

Schlump was deeply disappointed by this war. And the opportunity to commit an act of heroism was still refusing to present itself.

But then, all of a sudden, the chance *did* come. One day, the soldier sent to fetch the food told them that the second position had been occupied by very unfamiliar-looking troops from the flying corps. They were building new dugouts. They'd come straight from Italy and were wearing Austrian uniforms. Apparently the wops got quite a shock when the heat was turned up on them.

The second position was some way behind them, up on a hill. 'We're not going to be relieved,' the food carrier said. 'We're to hold on to the last man and final bullet. We ought to be pleased if we get our rations. We're to make things difficult for the Tommies; if they storm our trenches, all they should find is a few dead soldiers.'

There was more news. A few days earlier, the British had made an assault on section B. The guards hadn't seen them coming as the Tommies had blackened their faces and crawled over like cats. But as luck would have it, at that very moment our artillery was launching its own attack. They fired too short, and the whole lot fell on to the barbed-wire entanglements between the lines. The result was horrific. Screams pierced the air and the Tommies raced forward wildly. Get out of that barbed wire! But they got stuck and fell over. Our guards were on their toes. They sent out the alarm through the entire trench, and now our machine guns got going like fury, while the others tossed hand grenades. The Tommies must have thought the gates to hell had been opened. Not a single bastard got into our trench. Our lads launched a counterattack and stormed over to the other side, where they were met with such intense machine-gun fire that they had to seek cover immediately. They crawled back slowly. The enemy artillery got going too, and picked off the ones at the back. One of them, a really young fellow, became stuck in the barbed wire and couldn't go forwards or backwards. He got shot in the stomach and his guts started pouring out. Grabbing them with his hand, he pressed them to his body and howled in pain like an animal. The Tommies were firing like crazy and the poor young man had to stay where he was. No one could come and get him. With his glassy eyes he stared at the trench, occasionally screaming 'Mother! Mother!'

Schlump listened to all this – by now it was afternoon – and thought about his decision. He went to section B and saw the poor lad stuck in the tangle of barbed wire, holding on to his innards. The Tommies had the section under constant artillery fire, and were spraying the whole area with their machine guns from the side. Schlump climbed on to the fire step. Scarcely had he poked his head out than he heard the short, sharp *tak-tak-tak* coming from the other side.

He climbed out of the trench slowly, as if nothing were the matter, and stood fully upright. The bullets whistled around his ears: *feeow, feeow, feeow…* He ran over to the poor young boy. He saw him coming, and it looked to Schlump as if he were moving his hand and head slightly to show his gratitude. As carefully as he could, Schlump untangled the boy, who'd got caught by two hooks in his cartridge belt, and carried him in such a way as to shield him from enemy fire. Then he climbed down very gently and laid the poor chap on the ground, the Tommies still firing away madly.

Schlump's young comrade had his eyes open and was still desperately clutching on to his insides. But he wasn't moving. He was dead.

Michael Quellmalz, who Schlump had played matchsticks with – the famous Michel, who crawled around the barbed wire every night and was freed from other duties – had found out that the Tommies had been relieved. There were Canadians over there now, he said. The colonel had instructed a patrol to bring back a British soldier, dead or alive, from the enemy trenches. Michel wanted to undertake the mission, but he needed another man to go with him. That would be perfect for me, Schlump thought. Michel didn't take just anybody with him, and Schlump was scared because he was still so young. But he went to see Michel and volunteered himself. Michel looked at him and said, 'Come tonight at half past one. Sap five, section five. You don't need a helmet, no spade, no rifle, nothing.' Schlump was mightily proud. He was relieved from guard duty for the whole day.

He set off just after one o'clock. As a precaution he put a few hand grenades into his pocket. It was pitch black, not a star in the sky. Just occasionally the moon shot some pale rays through the clouds. Michel arrived at half past one on the dot. As ever, he had no weapons on him except for a flare gun. 'Stay right behind me, always,' he ordered. They crept out of the trench. Michel knew every shell hole, every clump of dirt. They zigzagged their way across. In some places Michel had already cut through the barbed wire the night before so they could get through. At one point he stopped, dug a British helmet out of the ground with his hands, clamped it between his teeth, and continued crawling, Schlump behind him all the way. His hands were hot, so he cooled them on the frozen earth.

They stopped by a huge mud heap in front of a massive shell hole. With his fingers, Michel carefully bored a tiny hole in the mud and peered through. Then he beckoned Schlump over and made him look too. To the right you could see straight into the British trench. The guard was standing there, not moving. They stayed put for a while, then Michel made a sign. Schlump looked up. The guard was being relieved. The new guard took up position silently and the first man disappeared. They waited an age. Behind them everything was dark; the Germans had been ordered not to shoot flares. To the left the Tommies shot one of their own. Up it went with a whoosh, swaying one way then the other, providing a lengthy illumination of the area around. They didn't move a muscle, and to combat the tension Schlump bit into his own arm. Then everything was dark again. The thunder of cannon droned incessantly from the south. Down there the offensive had begun, and each night it was getting a little closer.

Michel grabbed Schlump and gestured to him not to move. Then he vanished. All alone Schlump lay there before the British trenches, waiting.

Suddenly he saw a Tommy appear in front of him in the trench, a helmet on his head and a short pipe in his mouth. Taking a closer look, he realised it was Michel! The false Tommy walked past him, over to the guard post. He leapt up, stood beside the guard and looked out. Neither man said a word. Schlump held his breath.

All of a sudden Michel swung round, smashing his fist into the Tommy's face. He sprang out and dragged the soldier by his coat tails. Schlump bounded over to help. The guard was a strong, heavy fellow. They hauled him as far as the barbed wire, where the Tommy came to and jerked himself free! Michel grabbed his flare gun and shot him in the body. The Tommy ran a couple more paces, then started to bellow like an ox. They threw themselves on the guard and took hold of him again. The flare continued to burn his body as they pulled him like crazy towards their trench. The Tommies had been alerted and now fired manically from all their machine guns, but their aim was wild. Flares shot into the air; their silhouettes became clearly visible and cast long shadows.

Now the bullets were whistling around Schlump's ears

and into the tangle of barbed wire, causing bright sparks to fly. One took the cap right off his head. If they attack now…he thought. Getting one hand free, he pulled a grenade from his pocket, yanked out the pin with his teeth, and threw it back to where he'd come from. He was in a state of incomparable excitement. The Tommy was yelling, the machine guns firing at full tilt, and Schlump gave a shrill, noisy laugh. Michel was expressionless; he still had the shag pipe in his mouth. He looked carefully in front of and behind him, avoiding all the deep holes and barbed-wire barriers.

The Tommy thrashed around in pain, and it required all their strength to keep hold of him. The barbed wire tore the clothes from their bodies, but Schlump felt nothing; he was sweating and mercilessly dragging the poor Tommy through the wire.

Finally they were back on their lines. The British had not attacked. They laid the Tommy down in the trench, but the flare had eaten away at his insides and he was no longer moving. He was dead.

'Shit,' Michel said, stomping off.

Spring had sprung – near the artillery at the rear a few daisies were in flower – and brought with it the offensive. In the days prior to this, the Tommies had regularly practised their barrage every morning from five till six. But one day the shelling didn't stop. The trenches were soon shot to pieces, the dugouts filled in, and the soldiers lay defenceless in the shell holes, which filled with blood and water. After a few days the Tommies switched their fire to the third line, and the German soldiers awaited their attack. The man who'd gone to fetch the food had been right: they weren't going to be relieved, they would have to hold on to the last man. But the attack didn't come, and instead the Tommies sprayed the front line with heavy shells and mortars, driving the soldiers to the point of madness.

Schlump sprang from one shell hole to another, always to the newest because that was where they thought they'd be safest. Behind the hill on the other side, the thunder of artillery was continuous, and at night they could see the bright flash of the shots. They soon got to know each one of the Tommies' batteries by its individual flash, and they knew whenever one stopped from time to time. They also had a rough idea of where each battery concentrated its fire. Supplies came only intermittently through the barrage, and the men suffered from severe thirst and hunger. Once some soldiers from another regiment came and brought them coffee in heavy steel pails. The poor fellows leapt from one shell hole to the next. Some of the men got swelling in their testicles, which made them howl with pain. It was horrible to watch. Schlump had become a bundle of nerves from the constant fear of the rotten shells. He wanted to get out of this mess at any price.

Finally his opportunity came.

The Tommies had broken into section A and sealed off the trench with sandbag barricades. On either side lay heaps of dead and critically injured soldiers over a metre high, forming a new barricade. The first and third companies had been completely wiped out. The rest were going to launch a counteroffensive. The assault troops were ready.

More volunteers were being sought from each company. Michel, of course, was one, and Schlump offered his services too.

They assembled in the limestone quarry to the rear. They'd had to cross a fallow field which the Tommies kept under constant fire. Rifles in hand, they raced across one by one with their kitbags, hotly pursued by shells. They were sweating like pigs by the time they made it. The quarry was a grisly sight. This was where they'd always come to fetch their food. It was full of blood, bandages, boots, bloody gas masks and broken rifles.

It was Sunday. The assault was to begin at five o'clock. Schlump fetched a few more hand grenades. They fell in at three o'clock. The lieutenant of the assault troops bid farewell to the adjutant of the third battalion, which was stationed back there. The lieutenant was wearing glasses, behind which a pair of good-natured blue eyes looked out. He was a secondary school teacher. They set off in the sun, which was warm and shining brightly. They sprang from shell hole to shell hole. They advanced and veered left. Here lay a multitude of corpses – Germans and British, all mixed together. At one point they'd collected in a heap, as if in death they were trying to warm themselves. All were lying on their stomachs, heads turned to the side, revealing their greenish faces, teeth glinting faintly between pairs of black lips. Rifles, gas masks, everything in a muddle, soaked in blood, everywhere blood and more blood. A section of trench wall was still standing, above which hung a telephone wire. They had to stoop. Schlump knocked into an officer's yellow legging. On the end was a shoe, and in it a leg. The flesh had been cut off clean with the legging. There was nothing else to be seen of the officer.

Four thirty.

The artillery was to start firing at four fifty and go on till five o'clock sharp, then stop at a stroke. At five the assault was to begin. In the meantime the Tommies were sending over at irregular intervals some seriously heavy ordnance, which exploded with a horrific din. Large stones flew around their heads and plugged in the mud. They crouched down. Schlump squatted in a fresh shell hole and smoked the last cigar his father had sent him.

Four fifty! Behind them the artillery burst into life. But what was happening? They were firing too short. It was all landing amongst their own infantry! Flares! Now the Tommies started shelling too. This was hell on earth! Without waiting for orders, they stormed forwards, the lieutenant at the head. He opened his mouth wide; he was about to shout something. But then his body jack-knifed, and his steel helmet rolled away in front of him. Dead, the first one. Schlump just kept running, beside him Michel. They yelled something without knowing what or why. There, about twenty paces in front of them, stood the Tommies, not moving. They were paralytic, shooting one rifle grenade after another. You couldn't hear them explode amidst the infernal racket.

Suddenly Schlump collapsed. He could feel pain, he didn't know where, but he couldn't get to his feet again. Beside him Michel stormed on. He wasn't hit by any bullets. Now he had reached the Tommies. With a skilful blow he knocked the rifle from the hands of one of them. But what was he doing? He tossed his own rifle away and grabbed the Tommy with both hands as if about to embark on a wrestling bout. The Tommy was a head taller than Michel and very broad. The two of them fought as the others blustered past. Michel must have superhuman strength. With his right arm he clamps the Tommy to his chest, freeing up his left hand. Grabbing a grenade from his belt, he rams it between himself and the enemy. He presses him more tightly to his chest. He pulls out the white pin with his teeth! Now! Now – both men are blown to bits!

Michel's head rolls where they've just been fighting, ending the right way up. Eyes wide open, it looks over at Schlump, appearing as if it is trying to smile.

Schlump lay unconscious amongst the corpses on the battlefield. Around him was blood, more blood, bloody scraps, human limbs and equipment stained dark by blood.

It was daytime when he woke up. The Tommies had switched their barrage back to the third line again, second position. But they were scattering the entire area with shells and shrapnel. Schlump felt an agonising pain in his left shoulder. He couldn't move his arm. His legs had slipped into a hole that led down into a caved-in dugout. He could feel blood trickling down his back and his right thigh was swollen, but he couldn't see an entry wound. Perhaps he'd been bruised by a stray sliver of a shell. Then something landed right next to him, stones flew about his head! He jolted in shock, forgot everything else, and scurried away. By the ruins of a concrete bunker he collapsed. But he quickly regained consciousness, and now the shelling was more intense. He stood up in indescribable pain and looked around for a stretcher-bearer. He was dreadfully thirsty. But he couldn't see anybody. No comrades, no stretcher-bearers, nor any sign of the Tommies. Only corpses lay around him, blood had turned the earth red or black, and the shells landing around him exploded with a hellish racket.

Frightened to death, he listened out for each and every shot. All his senses were on high alert, and his ears could distinguish every sound in spite of the crazy noise. His fingernails dug into the limestone; he was sweating with fear. Another shell landed near him, and again he leapt up and rushed away. He ran as far as the sandbag barricade, which was piled with corpses to the top.

All of a sudden he heard a voice. Four men were lying in a huge shell hole with a machine gun. With superhuman strength he crawled over to them and begged for water. But they had nothing; they'd been without rations for three days. Cutting up his coat, they clumsily gave him some rudimentary bandaging. At the bottom of the shell hole swilled a nauseating cocktail of blood, water and all sorts of other muck. Unable to stop himself, Schlump took a drink from the puddle. The others hauled him away. He started to rant and rave, and they had to hold him down.

Two men had gone off with mess tins. Maybe they'd be able to find something. Schlump sprang up and ran after them. There was a loud ringing in his head, and he felt as if he were blind drunk. Then, in front of him where the two men were walking, a shell landed right on an old dugout. Schlump saw the beams collapse, and stone and mud fly. He kept running towards a huge pile of rocks and limestone. As he hurried over, he heard terrible cries from beneath him: 'Comrade, help me, please, please help me!' Scourged, he moved on. He toppled, and felt as if he were plummeting into a deep dark abyss.

When he came to, the sun was on the horizon beneath a layer of grey-black cloud. He was lying on the steps to a dugout. Maybe there was something to drink down there! He crawled down, gritting his teeth against the unbearable pain. Below were some soldiers on slatted bunks. He touched them, but got no response; they were all dead. Rats scuttled past him. Horrified, he crawled out as quickly as he could, then lay down for a considerable while.

The enemy batteries were firing like fury on the second position. Schlump forced himself to his feet once more and ran away. He didn't care any more; he'd rather die in an instant than perish miserably here.

He raced through the feverish barrage, through the second position. All that remained were shell holes where soldiers he didn't know were crouched. Shells whistled past him, plugged in the ground and exploded, sending up stones, heavy rocks. Splinters hissed! *Crash! Bang! Wheeee!* Death howled blood red before his eyes, jets of flames sizzled green and yellow. Back, keep going back, past our artillery, on and on, as if chased by a thousand furies. Where was he getting his strength from? He didn't know what was driving him on.

At last he'd made it beyond the main bombardment, although the Tommies would send over the occasional large shell in the direction of where he was now. He wasn't looking for the field hospital any longer; he just kept running to the rear without any idea of where he was. He maintained a straight line, always eastwards. Then, in an instant, his strength vanished. He dragged himself forwards with great difficulty, stopping to lie down every metre or so.

Thus the hours passed, and the night. He didn't know where he'd gone, nor for how long. Before him, a dim light started to appear on the horizon. He came to a small wood and sat on a fallen tree.

There, from a bush not far away, he heard the most wonderful song. A nightingale was pouring out every ounce of joy from its tiny heart. So wistfully, so beautifully, so blissfully, as if things such as love and happiness really did still exist in the world. Now Schlump saw his home again; he saw his mother kissing him – he was sitting on her knee and she was singing him the songs she knew. The lights from the passing vehicles danced on his bedroom ceiling. It was cosily warm in the room and he fell asleep at her breast. Then he heard music; it was coming from the Reichsadler. He watched the girls dancing. One of them waved at him, and he went outside into the warm, sultry night, beneath the trees. There he held her in his arms. 'You're Johanna, aren't you?' he said. She whispered to him that they should dance together and then she'd like to go home with him.

Schlump lay on his stomach on the moss by the fallen tree. His head was turned to the side and his cheeks were glowing red; he was feverish. His bloody shirt and bandaging showed through his cut-up uniform.

When Schlump woke again, his head was nestled on white pillows and a white sheet covered his body. Some artillery troops had picked him up, the medical orderlies told him, and carried him on their wagon.

He was soon put on to a stretcher and taken to the operating theatre. On the steps he passed a lance corporal from the medical corps, carrying over his shoulder a bare leg as if it were a rifle, and making a joke of it. Schlump was laid out on the operating table and a nurse put a gas mask over his face. It wasn't long before he was dreaming again.

Once more Schlump was back home, but this time at the fair, where one carousel after another was turning round and round. The music was a jumble of burbling, gurgling and tinkling, with the occasional brash and throaty whistle of a traction engine. The girls were sitting on the wooden horses, holding their skirts above the knee, and laughing. All of a sudden Schlump saw Monsieur Doby beside him. They pushed and thrust their way through the throng of people and stopped outside a cinematographic theatre. The sun had just set, and the countless electric lamps shone in the clear dark blue sky. They were standing by the band – a delicate and friendly-looking gentleman made of wood, in buckled shoes and half-stockings, beat out time. Next to him massive placards had been erected, on which Schlump saw huge pictures of Michel, the famous Michel, removing the grenade pin with his teeth and blowing himself and the Tommy into the air.

Schlump took Monsieur Doby by the arm and guided him into the cinema. They sat on the front bench, where all the soldiers were sitting, and looked around. In the corner at the back he noticed sweet little Nelly, who gave him a smile and waved with her handkerchief. In front of the white screen sat the band, making a dreadful racket that sounded like bombs and shells going off. Beside the band stood a tall man in a black coat covered in stars. He was holding a baton and on his head was an incredibly tall pointed cone, on which the sun and the moon and all the constellations revolved. The man stared down his nose at Schlump through a pair of huge black spectacles. The lights went out and the screen started to flicker. Large writing appeared which Schlump couldn't read. Then he saw inside a house where a gaggle of pretty girls were rocking back and forth on soldiers' knees. And these soldiers wore expressions of bliss as they hugged their beauties. In the middle stood Michel, the famous Michel, playing the fiddle.

Now the buffoon in black next to the band started talking. Poking the screen with his baton, he spoke with a ridiculous trumpeting voice: 'Private Michael from the machine-gunners had a glint in his eye! He always seemed to be chewing a curse in his teeth. For six days the company rested up. For six days they brought him food in the girls' house, where he played his fiddle for six days and six nights. Sometimes it would sob, then all the girls would weep, indeed the entire house would weep.' The black figure tapped the screen with his baton, and Schlump could see Michel playing beautifully and all the girls weeping. The man in black continued: 'Occasionally his fiddle would flog the girls, then they would go wild, indeed the entire house would go wild. And flames would dart from his eyes.' He tapped the screen with his baton once more, and they saw the girls dancing in a frenzy, and the flames flickering from

Michel's eyes. The man in black continued: 'On the sixth night his fiddle came to life and the girls screamed blue murder. Michel tossed his bow into a corner, grabbed the girls, who were hanging on to him as if he were a deity, and danced with them.'

The man in black tapped the screen again. It grew light and Schlump looked around. Sweet little Nelly had vanished, the others too; it was just him and Monsieur Doby left. Schlump was keen to leave – he was starting to freeze – but the man in black knocked his baton yet again, the lights went out, and he carried on: 'The following evening they returned to the trenches. A cold wind blew from the darkness. No one said a word. Just the spades knocking against their legs. Coughing. Stumbling. Cursing. Shells exploded with great frequency, streaking red in the sky, mocking the soldiers. Artillery posts, black lumps, leaned against dead walls, silent. Machine guns barked in the distance. Suddenly cannons burst into fire behind them. Every one of them jumped in shock. Shells flew sighing into the distance. The company froze in cold holes. Michael wandered about the barbed-wire entanglements. Fear crept over the tormented clods of earth, choking the men beneath their steel helmets. The stars twinkled craftily and betrayed all the peoples on earth. Death lay in wait everywhere. Michael bent over the enemy trench and stared down. Dropped like a spider on to the double sentry post. Shot one of the guards in the stomach, strangled the other. Dragged the dying soldiers through the barbed wire, shrill screams piercing the night. Flares hissed into the sky, machine guns rattled, mortars boomed, shells, bombs, flames, yells, hisses, bangs, screams:

All hell has been let loose, all hell has been let loose! The earth rocked. Michael stood amongst the barbed wire, shaking his fist, laughing monstrously and viciously.

'Michael raged amongst the barbed wire for twelve days and twelve nights, then it was time to return to the girls' house. And Michael played his fiddle for six days and six nights. The following evening it was back to the trenches. Winter and summer, winter and summer, never ending.'

The nurse had not yet removed the mask. The gas poured into his blood, poisoning it. And his heart pumped the blood up to his brain, which was neatly coiled beneath his skull, sending the anaesthetic deep into his tiny cells. His soul freed itself from its fetters, and Schlump floated between life and death. His dream became deeper and stranger.

Schlump had been obliged to go through everything again, as if they wanted to torture him with it. Now the film broke and on the white screen a phrase appeared that he couldn't read. Then he saw a railway train rolling through the darkness. The windows were lit up and he could see soldiers asleep inside. The man in black knocked the screen with his baton again, and it resounded: 'The locomotive sent long piercing screams into the night. Then the silent roar of the darkness. The wheels kept rolling, onwards, onwards, ever onwards. The soldiers were wrapped in their coats and huddled together, snoring and moaning in their sleep. Michael woke up. Stared into the night. Dead towns drifted by, forgotten lights. Iron bridges slapped the wheels with a thunderous rhythm. Below, the alien river breathed gloomily with mysterious blue sparks. Pain hovered over the country, sucking up the plain and suffocating the silent forests. Michael grabbed his fiddle and, wielding the bow gently, played with such incredible delicacy that no one could hear. He played the song of suffering. His fiddle drew magical circles. The night sank slowly. People crawled down, far down like poor animals. And above stood the blue mountains, radiating eternal bliss, where the winds were like symphonies, where beauty dwelled in golden meadows, where joy was enthroned in temples, where sublime purity lived, where…'

Schlump stopped listening to the fool dressed in black and stared with shining eyes at these marvellous pictures. A wonderful landscape emerged between the blue mountains. In a colourful meadow, unbelievably beautiful young people played. An old man with magnificent shining eyes came up to him, took him by the hand, and led him affably into the golden meadow. It seemed as if the boys and girls were competing as to who could infuse the most beauty into their movements. 'You see,' the friendly old man said, 'only those souls who abhor evil are allowed here. And as we live off the air, none of us has any need to do another harm.' Schlump breathed in this wonderful air, spiced with the most splendid fragrances. Sometimes a light wind blew, bringing with it indescribably sweet music.

Schlump looked around and noticed, on top of a gentle hill, a temple built in a strange style, like nothing he'd ever seen on earth. 'That is the home of music; we are currently in the Vale of Beauty, where our souls practise refining their bodies, creating beautiful shapes and movements. Let us go on. That is where the artists live who magic the noblest figures from their materials.' And Schlump saw that they were working from the living models romping around the meadow. They passed the most magnificent gardens, where children were being taught. 'Here they learn how to think,' the old man said. 'We aim to educate the soul in three fields: goodness, beauty and knowledge. For if they wish to achieve harmony they must learn the laws of the world in which they live. There you see the adults' school. But I cannot take you there, for your eyes would never be able to stand the light.' Schlump couldn't get enough of the delightful flowers, the wonderful colours in the distance, and the young people's charming game. 'Well now I must take you back to your world,' the old man said, returning him to his bench.

Again Schlump saw the man in black standing by the screen and tapping with his baton. 'Slowly the visions sank, night came forth, and the magic fiddle softly faded out. Michael was allowed to look at the mountains his bow had conjured up...'

It was light once more. Schlump looked around. He was sitting all alone in the bare room. Even Monsieur Doby had gone from beside him.

Schlump continued to dream. In front of him an inscription appeared, then came a wild, heroic landscape. A wide river rushed past fertile fields. The far bank rose steeply, bearing a solid town that stooped down into the cliffs. Behind this stretched out a broad high plain where he could see German soldiers marching. In the far distance a rugged dark-blue mountain range loomed menacingly. The astrologer in black started to declaim once more: 'The iron rhythm of the wheels had died out, the final whistle stifled behind the city. The horses beat their tiny hooves against the hard earth. Company, halt! The horses panted. Soldiers lay on the road, in trenches, feet thudding. Onwards! March, march! The sun scorched with its flaming arrows. Heads bowed, the soldiers marched grimly on. The air roasted them unforgivingly, threatening to suffocate the poor men. The mountains on the left held their breath. A single cloud on the horizon! Nature threatening, stifling. The company bivouacked in shallow, pitiful tents on the high plain. The sky rapidly turned black. An eerie silence. Mysterious glowing shapes bubble up from the surface and lurk around the soldiers. And there, on the brightly smouldering horizon, trees bend, their tops lashing the earth, no sound … Suddenly a boom, thunder, the storm! Tents take off into the black sky, rain whistles down like bullets, lightning flashes, roaring thunder, hail, light, dark, light, dark, soldiers washed into the mud like fallen leaves, hailing, raging.

'Michael sped out, driven by the storm; yelling, whooping, laughing madly, he raced up and hid behind the mountains … There, where the weather is calm, he wanders freely, playing his fiddle. It sings with the birds in the green trees, and the weighty rocks gleam with happiness. Michael fiddles, the meadows bloom beneath his feet and the flowers shine. Far above, the sky is blue and bright little clouds flutter on the colourful rainbow. Michael continues to wander and night falls, singing with him its silent song. Morning comes and he wanders further. In the evening he descends into the valley, down to the large rivers below on the plain. Beside him wild spray splashes up from icy waters fleeing from the last valleys.

'Michael strode through the forest. Patches of jet-black burned his feet in the moss. The leaves interlocked without a sound, hatching mysterious blobs of moon that squinted as they inched up the fissured tree trunks. No chirping of birds sweetened the air, but snakes rattled venomous glances. Icy air stuck to his body, exhaling poisonous breaths into the tough foliage. His fiddle resounded only seldom. Behind him the forest vanished; before him the evening fled far towards the horizon. He trotted down into the village. Pointed gables thrust upwards into dark treetops, touching the sky, which stretched black and tight over the earth. Michael stood in the centre of the village, where the dark water was silent, beside the beech tree. He grabbed his bow, tore shrill notes from the night, hurled them at poisonous black walls, clawed the will-o'-the-wisp out of dark holes, dashed all the roofs with blue flames, where they blazed away as if possessed.

'Out of the gate stole a young woman, her eyes closed, her hands clasped behind her neck, and danced, danced in front of Michael, who fiddled wistfully.

'Slowly the night passed. The woman lay at Michael's feet. Slowly he stole out of the village, to move on...'

The light came on again. The mad actor toyed with the cone on his head. Schlump used the opportunity to tiptoe to the door. Outside he could hear the music from the fairground. The man in black leapt over to him, grabbed him by the scruff of the neck, and dragged him back to his bench. Then he picked up his baton and continued.

In his dream, Schlump was amazed that he was dreaming about such bizarre things; he was desperate to wake up so that he could escape this lunatic. But his eyelids pressed down too heavily, and he could not lift them. The man in black continued his lecture: 'The river bore his songs into the city. Michael loiters on the confused bridges, makes friends with the colourful lights that have been swimming in the river. His fiddle murmurs the dark melodies with the heavy water that gurgles in the canals. He thrusts himself down murky alleys, where the houses hang above his shoulders; he stoops down into cold, gloomy, mouldy cellars. He plays a note on the bottom string, low and sombre, creeps up the broken steps, crushes his bones, plays a note on the bottom string, low and sombre. Pitiful light flits wretchedly over horrendous filth. Moaning and groaning, a woman has given birth in the putrid straw. She stares at him with dying eyes. A naked worm slithers under the table, watching him with hollow eyes. Hunger sits cruelly by the dim lamp, licking out the stinking oil.

'Michael plays a note on the bottom string, low and sombre, crawls through the districts of misery; death perches on the steps, whoring with affliction. Michael lies in wait for the morning, which steals up, cold, dark and windy; he plays a note on the bottom string of his fiddle into the frightful whistling that announces work. It chases stooped figures out of hovels, large heads on weak torsos. The daily grind of the multitude echoes off the greenish walls, which crumble as they pass. Michael whips a sound from his fiddle on the bottom string, catching the momentum of the machines, playing in time with the wheels, on the bottom string, whipping it higher, whipping it through all the limbs, all the beams and walls of misery, playing it menacingly to the rich, who blanch at their tables, playing it in exquisitely gilded halls, letting it fall, jangling, into temples, playing it before the altars of love, frightening lust from its pillows, playing, playing, day and night into hissing lamps which burn horrific wounds into the nights, whipping a note on the top string, higher and higher. Everything screams from his fiddle, work, lamps, wheels, machines, gigantic heads on weak torsos, the naked worm with hollow eyes ... and they rush out, tearing out the stones from the streets, building up barricades with stones, ladders; lamps gyrate fiery wheels, walls collapse, bullets caterwaul, blood spatters on the ruins of houses, screaming, raging, Michael plays a note, hideous and hounding, women rip apart living bodies, destruction, destruction, bloody yarns, limbs and people. Michael steps on battered limbs, plays a note, plays a note, rafters, beams come crashing down, all-consuming fire ...

'A woman moves steadily amongst the rubble and flames, looking with her eyes for her beloved. Spying him, she sinks with joy, exhausted, into his arms. It's her, who danced before him in the village! Michael carries her away from the rubble and misery, steps through narrow gates, carries her out, towards the mountains that shine so blue in the distance.

'He holds his woman in his arms, enters the autumn burned with such ecstasy, drinks the colours of the joyful autumn; a blue sky smiles golden and shines. The two of them climb into the broad expanses, look far and wide at the thousand lands. She puts her arm around his waist; he fiddles blissfully... In the distance the blue mountains shine, and they descend into the valleys. They stop by the farm and pledge hard work and fidelity to each other.

'Michael kept to his promise. He didn't wait for the cock to wake him, but roused himself even before the morning dawned, led his horse through the cold fog, drove in stakes for the animal enclosures, swinging the hammer with both arms, while the sun ignited the mountains. His axe rang out through the forest as he felled the hard maple, waking the cuckoo. He dug with determination for the earth's blessing, he dammed the lively stream that gushed from the mountains, he heaved the enormous round stones, and watered the thirsty meadows.

'A commotion echoed from the farm, driving him back through the valley. The stalls were rattling: the bull is loose! It raged amongst cows and calves, which bellowed in fear. The woman wailed, holding her hand over her blessed belly. Michael laughed, strode into the stalls, grabbed the bull by the horns with Herculean strength, harnessed him under the yoke next to the ox, cracked the whip, hurtled out into the field, and ploughed the hissing clods of earth till evening. He drove the steaming beasts back to their rest and kissed his wife, who laughed with joy.

'Outside, the night sang, the fire cast flecks of red light on to the floor and ceiling, painting Michael's shirt with flickering colour, and pitching flames into the woman's hair. Michael stood by the stove, his trousers tied at the ankles and kept up by a belt, playing his fiddle, playing and pouring peace and joy over his wife, who swayed gently to the music...'

Schlump woke up. He was in the powerful arms of Sister Sophie, who was carrying him to his bed. She was as tall, as blonde and as powerful as Germania, and she put him to bed as a mother does a newborn after its first bath. 'Well now, my little boy,' she said, 'it's time you had a good sleep. You're a restless so-and-so, all that nonsense you were dreaming!'

Without replying, Schlump dropped off and slept for the first time in ages without being awoken after two hours. Without any dreams, he slept soundly, sleeping the happy sleep of youth.

BOOK THREE

The nurse brought him letters from home. Three of them. They had been sent first to his regiment and then followed him to the hospital. He looked for his mother's handwriting, opened the letter and read:

My dear child,

Three weeks have passed since I last heard from you. We live in terrible fear. I pray to God most days and nights that you may be spared. Dreadful rumours are circulating that our regiment has suffered heavy casualties. I wonder what you're going through at this very moment. I have no peace, I wake up at night and have to say a prayer for you. This makes me feel a little better. Hopefully you'll be out of danger soon, and then please write as soon as you can, my child. Oh, if only the war were over and you could work again, and I could see your happy, smiling face every day! The very thought of it fills me with joy. Father is still working in the factory. May the Lord protect you, my dear boy, and preserve you in the face of every danger. I hope we'll get a letter from you soon, and I hope the war is over soon.

With all our love,

Your mother

Schlump could feel his mother's heart; he sensed that she was trying her best to hide her fear, so as not to make his life any more difficult. He immediately requested some paper and ink, and wrote a letter:

Dear parents,

You need not worry. I'm in hospital but I'm fine. They've operated on me, but couldn't find the splinter from the shell, which is lodged somewhere in my right shoulder. The operation was fine. It didn't hurt, and I had the loveliest dreams. I hope I can come to see you soon, because it won't be long before I'm better again. The doctors have discovered a wonderful medicine called iodine. It cures you if you rub it all over your body. In the bed next to mine is a man with catarrh of the stomach and intestines. He'll be well again in three weeks, the doctor says. They paint this iodine on his belly. And on the other side of me is someone who developed consumption from a shot to his lung. His whole body is being pasted with iodine. The doctor says he'll be better in eight weeks. They're putting some iodine between my shoulders, but I still can't move my arm yet. Otherwise I'm fine, although I wish we didn't get soup every day.

Love to you both,
Schlump

Then he picked up the second letter, which was addressed in a wholly unfamiliar script. He opened it and read:

Dear Schlump,

You'll wonder who is writing you this letter, and yet you know who I am, because it's me you kissed beneath the chestnut trees when the war broke out. You said you'd dance with me in the Reichsadler, but you didn't come. But I haven't been able to forget you. I often came to the factory when you finished work and I would walk behind you. And when you signed up, I'd come to the barracks and peer through the fence where you were doing drill. I loved seeing you in uniform, and I wept when the band accompanied you to the railway station. Since then I've kept going back to the road where you live, to see your mother. I can tell from her expression if you're all right or not.

But for the last fortnight I've had no peace. I've a dreadful feeling that you're in serious danger, that you're going through hell. I've been up to your parents' house three times, and on each occasion I've had my hand on the door handle, but haven't dared go in. Terrified, I've gone back home and sobbed, because I'm at my wits' end. A few days ago I bumped into your mother, who looked so worried. Maybe she hasn't heard from you in a while. I couldn't stand it any longer so I got hold of the address (from the postman who brings your letters). Now I'm writing to you and I beg you just to let me know you're still alive, just a word to tell me you're all right. You don't need to write anything else. You can do what you want, just let me know you're alive, then I'll leave you in peace and you won't hear from me again.

Johanna

Below was her address. Her name was Johanna Schlicht.

Schlump could picture her clearly: her beautiful teeth, rosy cheeks and merry brown eyes. He was delighted by the letter, but was in a real dilemma as to what to reply. He put the letter away and decided to wait a few days. But then his conscience told him that she might be worried, so he wrote her a postcard, brief and to the point:

Dear Johanna,
    I'm well and in good spirits, and am in hospital.
    Yours,
    Schlump

The third letter came from sweet little Nelly, whose happy news has already been told. Straight away Schlump took pen and ink and congratulated her on her wedding and the child's christening. Then he gobbled down the package that she had made for him.

When his mother held his letter, her hands were shaking. She could barely tear open the envelope, and tears streamed down her cheeks as she read. Her knees started to wobble and she had to sit down. She laughed with joy and cried and prayed all at the same time, feeling as if she'd been gifted an inconceivable stroke of luck. Then she grabbed a scarf, threw it over her shoulders, and hurried out without locking up behind her. She ran through the streets to the factory where her husband worked. And it wasn't until she'd told him the good news that she was able to digest her happiness. She returned home in a state of calm, looking neither left nor right. She spoke quietly to herself:

'It can't be much longer now. He might be back in a fortnight. And the war must be over before he's fully recovered.'

When she arrived back home, she immediately took a brush and started scrubbing, brushing, washing and dusting, as if she'd be ashamed if her son didn't find every nook and cranny and curtain spanking clean. She got hold of a railway timetable and gave her husband a pencil and his spectacles, so that he could write down the times of every train on which her son might return from France. And then she went to the station every day, staying well into the evening, inspecting the brown face of every soldier who alighted, to check whether one of them might be the young man who was the dearest to her in the whole world. Each time she failed to discover what she was looking for, she was neither sad nor disappointed, because, she told herself, it can't be much longer now; he must come soon.

Schlump's right arm was in a sling. He was allowed to get up and walk around as he pleased. The hospital was overcrowded and every day he waited for his transport back home. And every day new casualties arrived in droves. His two neighbours had been taken away long ago. In one bed now lay a pilot wrapped head to toe in bandages, in which they'd left two holes for the eyes and a small opening for the mouth. On the other side was a drunken Tommy, whose face, hands and back had been badly disfigured by hand grenades. He only woke from his stupor on the second day and he moaned terribly. Soldiers suffering from gas poisoning were delivered with ashen faces and blue hands, wheezing and gasping for air in immense pain. Every day Schlump would ask several times whether there were any hospital trains to bring them home.

And then, early one morning, at five o'clock, came the order that anyone who could walk should get dressed, as a hospital train was coming with space for a few men. Schlump fetched his louse-ridden and filthy clothes from the closet; they had turned completely stiff from all the dirt and blood. The right sleeve was also missing from his jacket. But he didn't care any more. They fell in, around twenty men with bandaged heads and hands, clutching sticks and crutches, and marched to the station. There was no sign of the hospital train with the big red cross, however. They settled on the platform and waited, waited patiently, with gleaming eyes, for all of them could already see home. But the train didn't arrive. Noon came and went, but no large red crosses. Some of the soldiers had collapsed, and were taken to the station guard house, from where they were brought back to the hospital. They would not be permitted to see the Promised Land.

The afternoon passed. Finally, at six o'clock in the evening – they'd been waiting for twelve hours – the train arrived. But it was already full. They squeezed themselves on as best they could, and trembled whenever a medical orderly came past, for they didn't want to be thrown off again. The night orderlies cursed at them and threatened to call the chief doctor; the wounded soldiers begged, coaxed and cajoled. Then the locomotive whistled and the train rolled slowly out of the station, on its way home. It stopped frequently in the open countryside, then went on again, thundering over the Rhine, back to Westphalia, to the Weserbergland.

There they were unloaded and billeted in a school. Schlump was desperate to see his mother and father again. He begged the doctor, he wrote petitions, he gave the clerk money to be transferred to a hospital in his home town. And after four weeks, four eternally long weeks, success was his. He was handed his wages, one day's rations, and a railway ticket. Brimming with delight, he left and travelled home. As he got off the train and walked out of the station, his mother ran up and embraced him in the middle of the street. Then she walked proudly beside her son, with his arm in a sling, firing thousands of concerned questions at the boy, often without even listening to the answers.

They went up the steps and the door opened. A pale, tall, lanky girl of twelve offered him her hand. 'Who's this?' Schlump asked in surprise. 'This is Dorothee,' his mother said. And then he remembered that his mother had written to him about Dorothee. She was the daughter of his mother's sister, whose husband had been killed. A fortnight ago the child's mother had died too, of worry and starvation. All alone, the child had been taken in by Schlump's parents. While caring for her mother, the unfortunate girl had had to watch how hard it was for a woman to die and leave a child behind in the world. Schlump gave poor Dorothee his hand and said some friendly words to her.

When his father came back in the evening, Schlump was horrified by how old he'd grown. He walked with a stoop and had to stop frequently and hold on to the banister when climbing the stairs, because all his strength had gone. Schlump's mother was upset that she couldn't give her son meat or bread to celebrate his return. And she didn't mention that it had been a long time since they'd had enough potatoes to fill themselves up. But she set the table all the same, and brought him a small bowl of cauliflower that she'd put aside from her own meals. At that moment, however, Schlump took out the bread and tinned meat he'd been given, and they all sat at the table and dined.

The very next day Schlump had to report to the local military hospital. The medical orderly gave him a patient gown and slippers, and took away his uniform. Thus began his dull, unchanging existence in hospital. All day long they sat on the wall surrounding the place and watched the girls. They smoked and played games, but they could never banish the persistent torment of hunger. For all they were given was watery soup, and occasionally a few slices of bread, which were so thin you could see the moon shine through them. And the jam they spread on the bread was particularly tart. Schlump's healthy reddish-brown colour soon faded, and he lost weight at an alarming rate. He was desperate for a speedy discharge from the hospital. But his arm remained stiff and hurt whenever he moved it.

He was seldom granted leave to see his parents. The picture at home was a sad one. At lunch they ate swedes without any meat or fat, and in the evenings potatoes doused with black coffee. His mother was distressed that she couldn't give her son anything, that Dorothee was getting paler by the day, and that her husband was in rapid decline. She became a ghost of her former self, a very old woman. One day Schlump's father couldn't get out of bed. His anxious mother called for the doctor, who diagnosed typhus, hunger typhus. There was nothing they could give him to revitalise his weak body, and thus his condition worsened by the day. One morning Dorothee came to see Schlump at the military hospital with tears gushing down her face. His father had died. Schlump went to the funeral. He had to support his mother, who sobbed continually without being able to cry tears. Then the three of them went back home, sadly and in silence. That evening Schlump had to return to the hospital.

His wound was now fully healed, and they began to massage it to make the skin, flesh and muscle supple. Then they clamped him in a steel apparatus and let his arm swing free to make it flexible again. It was crucial he recover quickly; soldiers were needed in the trenches and the war was becoming ever nastier. But the swinging of his arm was a lengthy and painful process. His mother, at any rate, was glad to see her son stay in hospital rather than go to face the enemy again. She had suffered too much already, and doubted she could survive a third helping of worry. This would leave the two children on their own in the world, in this cruel world. Schlump had to promise her that he'd never return to the Front. There were plenty of others who were yet to risk their lives: all those hospital inspectors, paymasters and other plump gentlemen with officer insignia on their epaulettes. Schlump made the promise in order to comfort her, but of course it was not in his power to keep such a promise.

One morning Schlump woke early in his bed. He could hear someone cursing beside him. Opening his eyes very slightly, he squinted over. Someone was sitting on his neighbour's bed, talking excitedly. Schlump closed his eyes and listened.

'Yes,' said the man on the bed, 'I pretend to be out of my mind. If the doctor starts getting funny with me, I rant and rave, foam at the mouth, and smash everything to bits. And if anyone gets in my way, I try to punch their lights out. To begin with I was in the garrison hospital, and there I knocked the doctor flat. They transferred me here for observation. Christ, they're not going to get me back to the Front. Before they do that they'll have to round up all those overfed types who are still running around. You only have to wander through town, anywhere you like.'

'You're right,' said the man in bed. 'I'm playing a different game. I'm pretending I've got a grumbling appendix.'

'Really? How do you do that?'

'Well, it's not that simple. You need to have had a problem with your appendix in the past, because then you know precisely where it is. And you've got to make it feel hard beneath the skin, which isn't so difficult. And you need a temperature, but not too high. You know how to do that, don't you?'

'Yes. You rub the thermometer under your armpit.'

'That's right. But my game only lasts for about eight weeks.'

'So what'll you do afterwards?'

'Afterwards I'll be sent back to the garrison company, the home guard. I'll stay there a couple of weeks until things get unpleasant. You know, when the death-sentence committees start doing their rounds. Then I get shell shock. You know how to do that, don't you? The key is to get your heart pumping faster, which is perfectly feasible too. You need to concentrate on it the whole time, then the heart starts pounding of its own accord.'

'That's all well and good, but there's a snag. When a comrade of mine played the shell-shock card they sent him to Schkeuditz, which is somewhere near Leipzig. There's one in Homburg too, I believe, a torture chamber. They torture you by passing strong electrical currents through your body! Christ, it must be horrible! My comrade screamed the place down, he said; he begged the attendants not to strap him up. But they're butchers, that lot, and strong as oxen. They're entirely lacking in pity. If they ever thought of sending me somewhere like that, I'd rather kill someone and get locked up in prison.'

The two men fell silent and parted company. Schlump had heard every word they said, and their conversation lingered long in his mind.

Schlump was bored. He was sitting on the wall with his neighbour in the hospital, watching the girls.

'Fancy joining me in a little expedition?' his neighbour said. 'I'm going to slip out tonight. I know a really nice pub where there are women and food. All you've got to do is get your smarts this afternoon and hide them in the skittle alley.'

Schlump had his own uniform – his 'smarts', as the soldiers said – which his father had tailored for him while he was still a recruit. Schlump readily agreed to the plan and they discussed the necessary arrangements. It was Wednesday and he had leave to go into town. The corporal gave him his fatigues and Schlump went home. There he put on his smart trousers and coat beneath his fatigues, and smuggled them into the hospital. He got undressed by his bed, returned his fatigues to the corporal, and hid his smarts in the skittle alley.

That evening they went to bed as normal and waited until everyone was asleep. It took for ever. Eventually the other man gave the sign, and Schlump crept quietly and unnoticed to the lavatory. The other man, who was already there, pulled himself up and climbed through the ventilation window with a helping hand from Schlump. Once outside, he was able to balance on an iron railing and haul up Schlump, who could only hold on with one arm. Schlump had great difficulty squeezing through the window, but at last they were both out. In the skittle alley they removed their nightshirts and put on their uniforms and shoes (Schlump had long since learned how to knot his tie and do up his laces with one hand). Then they leapt over the wall, which was not without its risks, as Schlump had difficulty jumping down. But he managed, and wiped the sweat from his brow.

They sneaked through the park, through narrow lanes where somnolent gas lamps cast their yellow glow into the blue night. Dense shrubs hung drowsily over crooked walls, behind which houses slept. And the wind that was resting in the trees occasionally thrashed around in its dreams. They stole quietly along the walls, all the while listening out for the footsteps of patrols. For they had no exeat passes, nor any kind of identification on them. They crossed narrow bridges and climbed steep steps lined with iron railings that had been polished to a shine by all the hands using them in the daytime. Finally they turned into a particularly narrow alley and came to a square surrounded by low old houses. In the centre of this square was an ancient fountain between two lime trees, and on one side sat a squat tower that had once belonged to a church. But a pub now stood where the church had been. The windows were shut tight, with only a meagre amount of light slanting through a narrow crack. They stumbled over the bumpy ground and went inside.

In the thick smoke that greeted them, Schlump couldn't make out anything. Gradually he identified a powerful chap with infantry trousers and a sailor's blouse, who with his hoarse voice was drunkenly singing a song unsuitable for sensitive ears. At the tables sat broad, thickset men with raffish expressions. Some were wearing sailors' jackets and some field-grey coats. It was impossible to be sure whether they were soldiers or not.

Schlump's comrade guided him through the bar into a tiny room into which they'd squeezed a table. They'd even managed to put a sofa behind it, and accommodate a few stools and a gramophone besides. The two of them sat down and ordered some wine and fried rabbit. The door to the main bar had been taken off its hinges, and they could watch everything that was happening in there. Between the men sat women, a few of whom Schlump knew. Their husbands had all died or were fighting in the war. He was particularly struck by a strong, gorgeous-looking girl with rosy cheeks and beautiful arms. 'The landlord's daughter,' his comrade said. 'She's pregnant, as you can see. Her sweetheart is either in gaol or in a penal division. I don't know why. Beside her is the inspector from the vice unit. His job is to keep an eye on all the women here. But there's no need to worry; they're all in cahoots. My God, the man lives like a sultan here. He'd like to have his way with that pretty Katherine, too, but she's having none of it; she's staying faithful to her man, a rough, unruly type who's forever beating her. All the same, she remains as true to him as a girl could be. Him and the inspector, well they can't stand the sight of each other. But what do we care? The main thing is that we get something to eat.' And they ate like bears. There were potatoes on the side.

Someone started playing the gramophone, but it wasn't long before he'd broken it. Having finished his dinner, Schlump sat on the table and played the squeezebox he'd seen on the windowsill. He'd learned it as a boy, in the same way he'd learned the piano, by ear rather than reading music, having been given basic instruction by the foreman who lived below them. The people in the bar were delighted and started to dance. The inspector danced with the land-lord's pretty daughter. Out of gratitude for Schlump's playing, the men bought him schnapps and the women looked at him with curiosity and lust in their eyes. It was Schlump's turn to be delighted and he responded with a livelier tune.

The door to the kitchen opened and in came a person who could have been a young woman or a child – it was impossible to tell. She stood on the threshold and didn't move. Her body already had the shape of a woman, but her mouth didn't look as if it had enjoyed many kisses. Her eyes half closed, she brushed her raven hair from her forehead with the back of her hand. Her gaze shot from between long eyelashes, touching everyone in the bar, especially the men. She watched the girl dance with the inspector, but her gaze moved on indifferently. It stopped at Schlump; she opened her eyes fully – a pair of large jet-black eyes – and glanced at him briefly. By chance Schlump looked over at her and caught the glance, but her lids soon closed again to a narrow slit, and her whole body remained perfectly still as it stood there. Schlump got the feeling that she was watching him; he felt her stare run down the length of his body, as if she were trying to caress him with her senses. This fired him up, and he started playing something else, allowing those in the bar no peace. He kept looking past the girl, all the while thinking about her. Suddenly she left her place by the door and moved behind him – he was now standing in front of the table, half in the main bar – brushing him faintly with her dress and, he thought, her fingers too. Then she vanished and wasn't to be seen again for the rest of the evening.

Schlump kept playing for ages. He suspected the girl must be the sister of the landlord's beautiful daughter, but he didn't ask. He didn't say a single word as they stole back to their hospital beds.

The following day, Schlump went around like a man under a spell. Those black eyes followed him everywhere. And all the time he sensed that she was near him, within touching distance, or it felt as if she'd just wandered through the room and caressed him with the waft of her dress and hair. He often stood brooding in the same place for a while, before looking up in the expectation that she'd be standing there. Walking up the steps that led to the reading room, he stopped halfway and listened. It was as if she'd called his name. He waited there for an age, then turned around with excitement. He'd had the distinct feeling that she'd brushed past him. Then he leaned on the rail, pressing his cheek to the cool wood, before scurrying to the top of the stairs. He sat for a long time in the reading room, thinking of the pub, and unable to wait for evening to come back round. For he had it in mind to slip out again and return to the pub with the tower. His comrade didn't want to go, so Schlump would have to make the trip on his own.

It took a gargantuan effort to climb through the window. He ran through the night-time streets and played the squeezebox as he had the evening before. It continued like this for weeks, and it was a miracle that the corporal didn't get wind of it. By now they all knew Schlump in the pub. They'd got hold of a better squeezebox, and promised to pay his bill if he played. He didn't refuse, for he could play the instrument really well, and in return he enjoyed wine and fried rabbit. Whenever young Margret showed her face he was in ecstasy and played like the devil. She often came up close to watch him play, swaying her body in time to the music while fixing her gaze on him with her narrowed enchanting eyes. This drove him wild. Placing her slender hands on her hips, she moved like a gypsy girl. Several times Schlump was on the verge of tossing away the squeezebox and grabbing hold of her. But on each occasion she made a face of such indifference and mild disdain that he lost his nerve.

After evenings like that he snuck back to the hospital a very happy man. But his sorrow knew no limits if she failed to show up. The following day would seem an eternity to him, and he felt utterly helpless. He tried playing chess, but his absent-mindedness always spoiled the game for his opponent. He sat in the reading room, puffing away on cigarettes that the daughter of the hospital shopkeeper used to give him. She was a good, honest girl who he flirted with as a distraction. She pandered to his every wish, but usually he forgot to thank her.

One Saturday evening he went back to the pub with the tower. He picked up the squeezebox and started to play. Over in the main bar every seat was taken. They were talking excitedly with raised voices and seemed to have little appetite for dancing. The sturdy Katherine had two men sitting next to her: on one side the vice inspector, on the other a handsome, slim fellow with an energetic face. He wore his cap high up on his head, his hands were in his trouser pockets and he was smoking a cigarette. He was looking terribly angry, and had his back turned to the girl. The others were calling his name. He was her sweetheart, the handsome Max who'd just come out of prison. Katherine stroked him and served him food and drink, but he didn't budge. From the other tables, the rest of the crowd gave the three of them furtive looks. Schlump played and at last they did start to dance.

Katherine got up, wishing to dance with her Max, but he just shrugged, laughed out loud, and knocked back one schnapps after another. So she danced with the inspector. Handsome Max didn't appear to notice. But then, in a flash, he leapt up, pushed his way through the couples, and stood beside the two of them. Raising his fist, he punched the inspector square in the face, a blow of such fury that the man collapsed on to the floor like a sack. The women screamed, a few of the men tried to drag the inspector under the table, but handsome Max went for them … Chairs crashed to the ground, tables and beer glasses flew in the air, and Max bellowed like a bull, grabbing the leg of a chair and brandishing it around his head. A terrible rumpus followed, the petroleum lamp was swinging from side to side, then a woman's voice screamed as shrill as a whip: 'Patrol!'

The lamp smashed into smithereens and there was a frightful commotion in the dark. Schlump tossed away his instrument and dashed out through the kitchen into the yard. Outside it was pitch black and he had no idea where he was stepping. A small hand grabbed his shoulder, yanked him back with great force, up some narrow steps, through a dark corridor, more steps, across a floor, up a ladder, up to the loft where it smelled of the hay being stored there for the goats. Then Schlump felt a soft body, a pair of lips; it was raven-haired Margret. The two of them sank into the hay and forgot everything else.

It was already broad daylight when Schlump returned to the hospital. He felt like a mother fox who'd drunk her fill of blood in the chicken shed and returned intoxicated to her den. The corporal tore a strip off him and threatened him with every last punishment that existed in the German army. Schlump wasn't listening. He let them confiscate his smart uniform, which still had wisps of hay sticking to it. His thoughts were in quite another place.

.

★

The corporal had reported the incident and Schlump was sentenced to three days' confinement to barracks, which he would serve as soon as he'd been discharged from hospital. He was also relocated to another room, from which he couldn't escape at night, and was forbidden all leave, which was the worst sanction of all as it spelled the end of his fried rabbit and wine. You couldn't get full on a permanent diet of soup and jam with bread. Poor Schlump turned paler and paler, and lost a pound each day. And if the little shopkeeper's daughter hadn't slipped him something from time to time, he might have perished. It was like that for a number of them in the hospital; only the peasants, butchers and bakers had it better, because their supplies came from home.

Schlump had found a comrade of the same age, a recruit by the name of Friedrich August Mehle, who was also punished with permanent hunger. The two of them always sat together and tried to console each other. Schlump had to talk endlessly about life in the field, about Loffrande and the war, and Mehle couldn't wait for the day when he was better. He had stomach and intestinal catarrh from all the swedes the companies of recruits were fed on. He wished he'd been able to volunteer to go to France or Russia or Italy or Romania, maybe even to Thessaloniki or Palestine or Baghdad. He wanted to experience adventure and see different peoples. His mother was dead; all he had was an elderly father who was busy with his own affairs.

By now Schlump was able to move his arm a fair way to the side, but not backwards and only slightly forwards. But space had to be made in the hospital. A death-sentence committee of assertive military doctors turned up and declared them all fit. Schlump was discharged from the hospital and sent to the convalescent company. He ought to have been serving his confinement, but the cells were overcrowded so he had to wait a week for his turn.

The convalescent company, a sorry collection of individuals, was billeted in an old pub out of town. Schlump found himself a bed in the room where the peasant girls used to wash the dishes. He looked around. An old friend from his company in the field came and shook his hand, and made him acquainted with his new surroundings. Next to him was a man who was prone to the occasional fit of rage, upon which anyone in the vicinity had to scarper if they wanted to avoid being bludgeoned to death. For this reason all stools, benches and crutches had been removed from his reach. Further back, sitting up in bed, was a man who'd lost his marbles. From time to time he'd cry out, 'Mama, Mama!' and demand his milk bottle. He needed to be fed and changed like a little baby. But they couldn't always find men to perform these tasks and he was soon to be taken away. They were just waiting for a place to become free in the lunatic asylum, which was bursting at the seams too. In the bunk below him sat a man whose chin had been shot away. He looked like a vulture and was quite a chilling sight. In the corner lay a man all on his own. He'd suffered a shot to the stomach, and no one dared get close to him because he emitted the most revolting stench. He wasn't able to control his bowels. On the benches by the walls sat all manner of cripples, a horrific gallery of deformities in field-grey uniforms.

Schlump had fetched his rations, but ate with little gusto; he wasn't used to his new surroundings. Beside him sat a man who tapped his feet continually and hurriedly on the parquet floor while dribbling and shaking his head. At night Schlump dreamed of hell, terrible monsters and other horrific things.

Every man who was able was put to work. One day they had to harvest chestnuts (autumn had come round again, but Schlump hadn't even noticed), the next shift muck for the major's garden, and the day after that feed the garrison's pigs. As soon as he got some free time, Schlump hurried along to the pub with the tower to see his Margret again. But the door was locked, the windows covered; it looked as if the whole place had become extinct. A distraught Schlump made enquiries with the neighbours. 'They've all been locked up,' they said, 'and Margret sent to stay with relatives in Berlin.' Schlump trudged sadly away; he would never see Margret again.

His friend Friedrich August Mehle, who'd been discharged from the hospital at the same time, had meanwhile enjoyed a small slice of luck. Outside the barracks was an enormous potato clamp containing the potatoes for the troops. It had to be guarded at night, because the poor recruits would sacrifice the sleep they so badly needed to steal some of these vegetables. Friedrich August Mehle had the misfortune to be assigned to the potato guard. He performed his duty admirably, ensuring that the wretched fellows could go about their pilfering in peace. And whenever a sergeant came home late from visiting his girl, Mehle would warn his friends like the good comrade he was. In return they gave him a portion of their booty. On one occasion, however, when with great difficulty and caution they'd cooked the potatoes in their mess tins and were about to tuck in – after midnight, by the light of a tiny candle and with the windows blacked out – they were surprised by a nasty little corporal (all the other NCOs knew what was going on but turned a blind eye), who reported their offence. He was promoted, while the poor soldiers were punished, and Friedrich August Mehle was court-martialled for dereliction of duty. But his judges were sympathetic and he was only sentenced to six days' solitary confinement.

It transpired that Schlump was to serve his sentence at the same time. Thus the two friends, bread rations under their arms and military caps on their heads, strolled through town with their own guard of honour: a corporal and four men in helmets and with fixed bayonets.

Schlump had three days and three nights to ponder his life and the world in general. Once more he pictured himself as a young boy running away from his father to ascend the mountain behind which the sun set, and where the entrance to heaven must be. Then he saw himself in Loffrande, showing blonde Estelle the stars. Then he thought about his dream where he really had arrived in heaven… Out of the blue he thought of the letter the nurse had placed on his bed, the letter from Johanna, who had declared her love for him. He saw her standing before him on the occasion they'd met in the Reichsadler, when war broke out. He saw her dancing in the hall below, casting the odd smile up at him in the gallery. His reply to her had been so brusque. How could he have forgotten her altogether?

Schlump resolved to find her as soon as his confinement was over.

The three days passed more quickly than he'd anticipated, and he was allowed to report back to the convalescent company, the home guard. The following day he had some free time, so he went past Johanna's house; he knew her address – strange that he hadn't forgotten that. But he didn't see her. And because he didn't dare go in and ask after her, there was no other option but to leave again. He refused to give up, however; he walked past her house again and again. And on one occasion he struck lucky. She was just coming out of the baker's, a basket on her arm and a few bread coupons in her hand. He went up to her and all of a sudden his heart started pounding heavily. Looking up, she recognised him straight away, and her entire face turned a bright shade of red. At a loss as to what to do, he gave her his hand, and the two of them just stood there, awfully embarrassed but happy to have found each other. To him she seemed to be the kindest and most beautiful girl he'd ever met, and he was desperate to kiss her – on her hair, her dress or her beautiful hands. But he stayed put and didn't move. Eventually she asked, 'Are you better now, Herr Schlump?'

'Yes,' he said. 'I can move my arm again. At least I can move it to the side; forwards and backwards is still a problem.' He showed her everything he could and couldn't do with his arm. He was glad to have something he could talk to her about at length. But then he finished and she fell silent again.

Neither of them knew how long they stood there like that, but finally she offered him her hand and said, while averting her eyes, 'I hope you stay well.' Then she left.

Schlump watched her with a mixture of joy and sadness; his gaze worshipped her slender figure, which vanished behind a door. He turned around and returned to the barracks.

Once back, he heard the loud words, crude talk, commands, and bad jokes. Taking a deep breath, he shook himself and was soon back in the swing of things.

Once a week, and sometimes twice, the men were sent to the sick bay. The doctor, a stout fellow who reeked of pomade, treated all the convalescents like shirkers, even though he'd never been a soldier himself and had no idea what it was like to be ill or wounded amongst the shell holes. He declared them all fit for active service unless they'd lost a leg or came to see him with their head beneath their arm. When Schlump paid his first visit to the doctor, the latter grabbed his injured arm and wrenched it up with such force that Schlump collapsed on to the floor in pain. Before a livid Schlump had got to his feet to throttle the bastard, the doctor was already behind his desk declaring him fit for non-combat duty in the rear echelon.

Schlump remembered what he'd promised his mother, and decided to get away to the garrison as soon as possible. For he hoped that there he might be safer from the trenches than at home. If he hung around until the next inspection, he'd be declared fit for active duty, they'd give him a rifle and new boots, and send him to that hell-hole for the third time. This would go on and on until he finally copped it, after which the only place left was a mass grave.

He kept his eyes open and listened carefully to every announcement. It paid off. One day the sergeant read out: 'Anyone with a good command of French should report immediately to the battalion office.' Schlump wasn't going to wait to be asked a second time; he scampered off and put his name forward. The battalion clerk informed him that he should get himself ready; he would be leaving in three days' time for rear echelon headquarters in Maubeuge.

On a Monday evening around nine o'clock, a train pulled up which was transporting troops to France. It stopped especially for Schlump, who'd been given a railway pass on which was written: *Transport No. 1004. One man, no luggage, no horses.* This was followed by a mass of small print detailing regulations, orders and rules of conduct for the journey. Schlump was to report at every military headquarters along the line, starting with Engelsdorf near Leipzig. There he'd be told of his next supply point and headquarters. And so on.

His mother was glad to see him go. For she'd watched with horror as he got paler and thinner by the day, and was terrified that he'd die of hunger like her husband.

Schlump was squeezed into a carriage brimming with soldiers, rifles and kitbags. He barely managed to find space for himself and his own kit. He trod on recruits' feet and they cursed foully. He'd given away his helmet, cartridge belt and other superfluous items, for he was sure he wouldn't be needing those sorts of things any more. Travelling through the night in great discomfort, he decided to get off at the first available opportunity and make the journey under his own steam.

The first stop was Engelsdorf, at three o'clock in the morning. A trumpeter gave the mess call. They were given soup and a piece of bread. Schlump fetched his rations and afterwards reported to the military headquarters. Then he took his kitbag, crawled under the train, crossed to the other side of the station and wandered out into the night. In his opinion Leipzig main train station couldn't be far away, and surely there he'd be able to find a more comfortable way of travelling to France than with the troop transport. Stomping through the frosty grass, he headed for a light he saw shining in the distance.

It was a signalman's hut. Inside he could hear the merry voices of track workers, both men and women. They won't give me away, he told himself. I can spend the night here. He went inside, where there were two rooms. In one the workers were having fun with the girls; in the other, three soldiers were sitting around a stove. He joined the soldiers. They eyed him suspiciously without saying anything. But then, as if their inspection had finished, one of them said, 'Come on, comrade, there's enough space here,' and moved up.

They put on more wood and the flames danced on their faces, painting flickering figures on the wall. The infantryman who'd come back from the trenches in Italy looked like a right rogue. His eyebrows shot straight up towards the corner from where his black hair flowed on to his forehead. He fiddled with his belt, took out his canteen, and passed it around. It contained strong rum, which warmed the body and stirred the spirit. 'What about you, comrade?' the broad-shouldered artilleryman beside Schlump asked the infantryman. 'I bet there's a different billet on your railway pass, too.' The infantryman didn't answer immediately. Making himself comfortable, he said slowly, 'We've got time, all of us here. I can tell you the whole story, right from the beginning. Are you ready?' First he fortified himself with another swig, and then began.

'I'm an artiste by profession. And it's not an easy life. It's really hard work; you need persistence, and you must live respectably. Before the war we would move from one town to another, and just before it broke out we arrived in Schilda. You know, where the people are supposed to be simpletons. We soon put up our tent, evening came, and people came flooding in. Back then I had a really original routine. Made up as a negro, and half-naked, I took a chair up on to the tightrope, placed it right in the middle, and sat on it, but on the armrest, mind, with my feet braced against the seat. And up there I played my guitar and sang negro songs, you know, the mellow ones that people like. And all the while I noticed that beneath me was a pair of eyes staring at me as if they wanted to gobble me up. When the show was over, I stood at the entrance, as a negro, of course, scrutinising everyone as they filed out. Up comes this young, sturdy, powerful woman, unmarried, red cheeks, and her eyes – my goodness – what a woman! She stops next to me and secretly slips me a note. I go into the light and read it: "Come tonight, I'm alone." And below the message she's written her street and house number. Well, comrades, you can well imagine that I obeyed like a good child.

'The wonderful night was over, we're taking down our

tent and getting ready to put it up in the neighbouring town, and then bang! War's declared, and I'm to report on the first day of mobilisation!

'We go to France. I was unable to forget that beautiful Anni. Christmas comes and the war's not over as they said it would be. The first replacements arrive. One of them joins my group, and he's from Schilda! I ask him at once whether he knows Anni, Anni Birnhaupt, as she wrote. "Indeed I do," he says. "She's my wife." I was thunderstruck. Then I looked at the fellow: bandy legs, good-natured, but not so bright, a true simpleton, I thought. How on earth did Anni go for a man like that? I asked myself. Something's up here. So I decided to make friends with the simpleton, which wasn't too hard, and soon he'd told me the whole story of his love affair. He'd only met Anni three months after war had broken out, and because she was so nice to him they had a war wedding right away so she'd receive support. Both her parents were dead, you see, and she no longer had any work. After a fortnight she whispered to him that their union had been blessed. He was terribly proud.

'But now comes the good bit. Another fortnight passed, then one day she came home all agitated and in shock and half dead. "Franz," she cried. "Franz!" Then she sat on a chair and started sobbing and howling. Poor Franz was terrified. He stood before her with his kind bandy legs, at a complete loss as to what to do. He asked her questions, he grabbed her apron, but she shook him off. "Leave me alone," she cried, howling all the more. Finally it came out between the sobs and tears. She'd popped round the corner to the cigar shop, because he was waiting for his beer, and was frightened out of her skin when she saw the negro standing in the shop, a fat cigar between his white teeth. "Franz, what if it was a mistake to go to that shop? What if it means we get a negro baby now? I'll drown myself." Good-natured Franz said he wouldn't care; after all, it wasn't her fault. But he was going to tell the cigar seller to take that negro model out of his shop window, to prevent the women from getting a fright.

'Then he was called up. He'd seen active service and been transferred to railway duty. And now he was with me in the Argonne. Three months passed and one day he came up to me, a proud beam on his face, and a letter from Anni. "Look!" he said. "A boy! And no negro either! Just black hair and black eyes!" Franz was as blond as a bread roll, with blue eyes; Anni had beautiful golden hair and sky-blue eyes.

'One of the men in our group said, "So, Franz, how long have you two been married?"

'Franz counted on his fingers. "Four and a half months," he said. "We met five months ago, one Sunday outside the pub, and got married a fortnight later."

'"How much does the baby weigh, then? Ten pounds?"

'They all hooted with laughter, and Franz stood there angrily, not understanding a word, his face bright red. They explained everything to him, and he wrote a stroppy letter back home. He was hopping mad and wanted to kill poor Anni. But her reply came just a week later:

'"Dear Franz, You mustn't let your comrades tease you all the time. They've been pulling your leg and no mistake!

And now your poor wife's suffering for it. They're right, of course – you have to be married nine months before you have a baby. But isn't that the case with us? Just work it out. I've been married four and a half months, and so have you. Put them together and what do you get? We are together, aren't we? Just ignore your comrades. Keep quiet and wait till you get the chance to get your own back. The opportunity will come."

'Good old Anni. Franz came to see me in secret and showed me the letter. I said to him, "Your wife's quite right. Ignore the others; they're a crude bunch. Just write your wife a friendly letter and tell her you're sorry."

'A year later, when I was on leave, I went to visit his wife and his son, or rather my son. He's a dark, lively fellow, comrades, you should see him. I know already that he's going to be an artiste too.

'Then came the terrible battles at Verdun, and Franz and I always stuck together. When I was buried alive, he dug me out with his hands. You know what that entails. I shared my bread with him, and hunted down other stuff when he was starving. We became real comrades-in-arms. On one occasion I told him the true story. We were lying flat in a shell hole and I couldn't see his face. It took him a while to respond, then he said, "Fritz, we've become close friends. Either of us could die at any minute. The one who survives shall have Anni. If both of us do, we'll let her choose, but I want us to remain good friends." I'd never imagined he'd react like that. Nobody can tell me that Franz is stupid; he may be a little slow, it's true, but he's certainly not stupid.

'So now Anni has two husbands, and it's all going well. And that's how it's going to remain; it's no one else's business apart from us three. A few weeks ago she wrote to say that they – Anni and our boy, Friedrich – have nothing to eat. So we saved up and bought what we could in the mess, and then I stole some stuff from the kitchen while peeling potatoes. Then I absconded, taking leave of my own accord. Maybe Franz will come too, then the whole family will be together.'

Schlump ate his bread and joined in the conversation. They came from all possible fronts, one from Finland, another from Italy, and the artilleryman from Flanders, who now took his turn to speak.

'I left with the territorial army in 1914, and today it's the tenth of November 1917. To date I've yet to be given any leave. In our battery we've got nothing but peasants, and they need time off for the harvest every year. They have to go muck-spreading, and they come back with sides of bacon for the staff sergeant.' He paused, and then said bitterly, 'As if we didn't have women at home ourselves!'

He stuffed his pipe and lit it.

'I took leave of my own accord, too. My wife also wrote to tell me that she's got nothing to eat. The two little ones never get enough.' He spoke slowly and paused to think after every sentence.

'Then there are the two big ones. They're the real reason I absconded. The boy's sixteen years old. I'm a trained brewer, and I've earned good money all my life. But the boy earns more than I ever got. And he's never had any education. Straight from school to the factory, turning shells. He swaggers around the house as if he owns the place, never listening to a word my wife says. Recently he's been lighting his cigarettes with one-mark notes, my wife told me in her letter. When she gave him a clip round the ear, he fought back. And now he doesn't come home at all. At night he hangs around in bars or sleeps with war widows. She's ruining the boy, my wife is. It's time I came home and showed him the back of my hand, to let him know that we're in the middle of a war. Then there's Marianne; she was thirteen when I last saw her. She was a pretty, bright girl; I adored her. And now? Now she's got a Polish Jew around her neck, who was released from the camp where they keep civilian prisoners. He's acting as interpreter for Russians and Poles at the court, and on the side he's dealing in food, clothes and anything he can get his fists on. He's given my Marianne a few scraps of silk to put on, and now the creature wants to go away with the fellow and not come back home again, just like the big one.' After a long pause, he continued, 'I'm going home for four weeks to put my house in order. The little ones are going to be frightened; they don't know me any more. Then I'll return to my battery. They can do what they want with me.'

Schlump was tired and wrapped himself in his blanket. Resting his head on his kitbag, he listened to the service corps soldier's tale as he dozed off.

'Last autumn we were in the Ukraine. After a very long railway journey we were unloaded off the train and had a fortnight's continuous trek with our ponies, heading east on bad roads. At night we'd sleep in our wagons and tie the ponies together. Finally a few villages came into view. You won't believe the surprise we got; it was just like back home in Hesse. The houses were neat and tidy, with gardens at the front. And when we went up and talked to the people, they all answered in German. They were so friendly and delighted that we were there!

'We were divided up between the farms and then enjoyed a proper rest. All the peasants' horses had been taken away during mobilisation, so we were to help them out with their labour. My host was called Linsenmayer, and on his beautiful farm he only had a daughter called Marie. The three of us took care of the harvest. That Marie is some worker! I stayed by her side the whole time. Whenever she was cutting, or handing up sheaves – what a sight that was! And her eyes! I kept thinking of our horse, Liese, who also had such beautiful brown eyes, and looked so slender and elegant when she galloped. We tried to outdo each other in our work, and then we'd sit down together in the evening and drink wine from the same jug.

'Well, I'm sure you can guess the rest. One day it just happened, though neither of us knew how. We spent almost six months in the village. Towards the end there was no hiding it any more; one glance at Marie and you could see. She felt ashamed and wouldn't leave the house. Her mother ranted and raved, and kept giving me black looks. It was really miserable; the poor girl cried her eyes out, but there was nothing anyone could do.

'In the spring we got our marching orders. You can't begin to imagine the scene when we left. Marie hung around my neck and wouldn't let me go. She sobbed her heart out. Then she stood at the fence and watched me leave – with those eyes!

'We returned to the railway and were loaded on to the train. The journey took an eternity. Back to Galicia, through Poland, then up all the way to Finland. I never heard from her again. But I couldn't forget her. At night I'd be jolted awake, I'd see her eyes before me and I wouldn't be able to get back to sleep.

'In October I had some leave. Even at home she wouldn't let go of me; I had her eyes before me all the time.

'Secretly I took out all my savings from the Sparkasse. And when my leave was up I packed my civilian clothes and said my goodbyes. I wrote to tell them everything from the next station.

'She must have given birth by then. I got out at Leipzig. A railwayman told me that trains sometimes pass through there on their way to Galicia. I'm not going back to my group. I'll start by going to Romania or Galicia. I'll buy a horse and change into my civilian clothes. Then I'll ride off and look for my Marie. And I'll find her if it takes me ten years.'

Schlump was asleep. The others looked for their blankets and arranged their kitbags as pillows. The last one blew out the candle, and soon all of them were snoring together in the signalman's hut by the railway tracks.

When Schlump awoke the following morning, everyone had gone apart from the service corps soldier, who was still sitting in the corner, chewing away. Schlump unwrapped his blanket, rolled it up, and packed it away in his kitbag.

He stepped outside the hut. At that moment, a man in a railway uniform with officer's insignia was crossing the tracks. Schlump got a dreadful shock. Now you're for it, he thought. The man with the epaulettes called out, 'Where are you off to?' Schlump opted for what was always the best course in the army: he played dumb and looked at the officer with wide eyes. 'Aren't you the man who was going to Maubeuge? You were on your way through with the recruits last night.'

Schlump had a sinking feeling in his stomach. He played even dumber, and asked in very unmilitary fashion, 'How do you know that?' In spite of the epaulettes, he didn't take the railwayman for an officer.

'You don't have to worry about me,' the man said in his Saxon accent. 'I won't do anything. I can see your regiment number from the badge on your shoulder. But how do you plan to get there?'

Schlump told him that travelling with the recruits had been too boring. 'I wanted to get to France quicker. So now I'm heading for the main train station.' The other man warned him that the controls were so strict that he'd never even make it on to the train. There was a train leaving for Halle at ten o'clock; if possible, he should take that one. At midnight there was a direct connection to Liège. Then they discussed the war and the terrible hunger at home. The railwayman said that they had been going to strike last week, because they were having to work double time but weren't receiving enough pay, far less than the munitions workers. But it had gone wrong. The morning the strike was supposed to begin they'd been handed their army call-up papers. They were given their uniforms, placed under martial law, and now received even less money than before, especially the workers who just got their soldier's pay. As an official, he was in a better position, but there was ill feeling amongst the workers. And if the war weren't over soon, they'd have to bring it to a close whether they liked it or not.

Schlump's ears pricked up. If someone like him is saying things like that… he thought. Then Schlump asked the man the way and they said goodbye.

He trudged with his kitbag through the desolate suburbs, through the inner city, and arrived at the main station. He carefully avoided the patrols marching up and down in large numbers by the barriers. Then he chose the platform with the densest crowd and joined the queue. Soon there was a long line of people behind him, pushing forward. Schlump shoved along with the rest of them, and whenever the man in front, a civilian, looked round, he turned back to the man behind him with an equally indignant expression on his face. Eventually the girl in the conductor's uniform became worried, and when Schlump got to the front of the queue she just let him through. He was laboriously trying to uncrumple his huge railway pass, which he'd scrunched up into a ball. Then he ran for the fast train, stowed his kitbag away, and slipped into a discreet corner somewhere. It wasn't long before the train left and Schlump appeared again.

They were just leaving Schkeuditz when the door opened and the military control came in. 'Railway tickets, leave passes!' Schlump took his transport pass from his pocket and handed it over with a look of innocence. The sergeant

— behind him were two soldiers with rifles — slowly unfurled the document and read it. Then he turned it over and over again, finally saying, 'This isn't a legitimate ticket! Where is your leave pass?'

'I don't know,' Schlump said. 'I wasn't given one.'

The sergeant kept hold of his pass. 'Report in Halle!' Then he left the carriage. The two elderly women sitting opposite Schlump stared at him reproachfully. He pulled a cheeky face and looked out of the window.

He alighted with his kitbag in Halle. The sergeant was already by the steps, holding a fistful of white and red pieces of paper, and surrounded by a throng of soldiers. From the steps, Schlump edged his way towards the sergeant. He could see his document flapping right at the bottom. It was hanging down further than the others because it was the largest. With his left hand Schlump held on to the railing, and with his right made a swift grab, snatching his pass from the sergeant's grasp. He raced down the steps and heard voices calling behind him, but he'd already turned the corner and was dashing up the steps on the other side. In front of him he saw a sign that read *Station Command*. He went in — it was the last place they'd think of looking for him. Fortunately a mass of soldiers was inside, for he hadn't known what he was going to say. He saw a number of kitbags piled in one corner. He asked a clerk whether he could leave his kitbag there. The clerk nodded, gave him a red piece of paper, and Schlump left. With this red slip he could get past the barrier, and now he was free to do what he liked in Halle.

★

191

Schlump strolled around the angular streets of Halle. The icy wind blew stinging coal dust into his eyes, and he started to freeze. He was tormented by hunger too, so went into a café. The girl brought him coffee and a piece of cake that consisted of white foam with a paper-thin wafer on top. The coffee tasted bitter, and in the sugar bowl was nothing but a minuscule tablet of saccharin. His stomach was deeply insulted to receive such fare, and expressed its pronounced dissatisfaction. It was persecuting poor Schlump even more now; he had to look around for a remedy.

At the neighbouring table were some girls who'd caught the young soldier's attention. They were darting him friendly glances, and soon gave him the opportunity to strike up a conversation. Schlump sat at their table for a while, letting them feed him with the chocolate that they conjured from their bags. The girls worked at the chocolate factory and today was their day off. They stayed sitting there till the evening and then made a move. The dark-haired one next to Schlump with the pretty teeth and short nose invited him back to her place. Schlump could hardly refuse an invitation like that, and gladly followed her home. She had the sweetest little nest, a warm stove and a wonderful bed. She fed her soldier everything his heart desired. In astonishment he asked her where she'd got all these lovely things from. For in front of him was a plate on which plump yolks sat deliciously amongst the egg whites, gently bedded on roast ham. In addition to this, her dainty fingers served him cocoa, which had been boiled in milk, rather than having been insultingly paired with water. 'Money doesn't buy you anything,' the sweet girl said, 'but if you've got something to offer in exchange — such as chocolate — then you can have what you like.' After this festive supper she turned out the light and lit a small lamp by the stove, which cast a faint glow on to the low bed. Two days they stayed together in this paradise. Then it was time for Schlump to think about moving on. The friendly girl with her thick dark hair took him to the station late in the evening. She'd bought him an expensive bunch of flowers and cried bitterly when he took his leave of her.

At midnight, Schlump picked up his kitbag and climbed on to the fast train to Brussels. Two soldiers were sleeping in the compartment. Schlump unfastened his blanket, wrapped himself up, and soon he too was sleeping to the continual beating rhythm of the wheels.

The train was just pulling in to Liège when he awoke. It was midday and he hadn't been disturbed by any controls. He got out and went into the waiting room, which was stuffed full of soldiers in field-grey uniforms. They wouldn't be going on to Charleroi until the evening. He handed in his kitbag for safe keeping, to prevent it getting stolen, but they demanded he hand in his belt, too, which would stop him from going into town. He sat at a table; next to him were some strapping Pomeranians cutting huge hunks from a gigantic piece of bacon. They were holding pieces of bread thickly spread with butter and topped with generous slices of cheese. They ate and ate — enormous amounts — and seemed untroubled by the envious looks of others making hungry and bitter comments. After a few hours they got up, still chewing with their muscular jaws as they left.

In their place beside Schlump sat a posh type with a

high collar and lively mouth. He soon engaged Schlump in conversation, telling him that in civilian life he was a merchant, and that now he was being stationed at the Dutch border as a purchaser for the mess. There were a lot of opportunities, he added with a wink. Schlump was keen to know what sort of opportunities these were. He claimed to be a merchant too, and said that he was heading for rear echelon headquarters in Maubeuge. 'Goodness me!' the other man said. 'We're a perfect match. I mean, Maubeuge is not that small a place; there must be opportunities for deals there. Here in Belgium we're basically the government, and you can buy absolutely everything. I bring in soap from Holland. Maubeuge is part of the rear; things there are almost as bad as in Germany. I'm sure we can work together.' And in great detail he explained to Schlump how the profiteering worked. He could take advantage of the fact that he came to Liège every week by bringing a couple of quintals of soap as cargo. Schlump would then pick it up, or have it picked up, in return for cash, obviously. The best solution would be to have a railwayman collect the cargo. That way they could save on the freight from the Dutch border to Liège. The railwayman would get ten marks per crate. Schlump, of course, would have to find a mess that would buy the goods off him.

Schlump was amazed at the peculiar war that was going on here, but he concealed his surprise, said yes to everything, and made a raft of promises. Then his jaunty companion said, 'My God, there's nothing happening here, you can't even get a drink. Come into town with me, I know where to go.'

'I don't have my belt,' Schlump said.

'That doesn't matter. If the guard asks any questions, we'll say you're ill and I'm taking you to the doctor.'

The guard, a good Bavarian, was easily fooled. They went from one mess to another and finally it was time for the racketeer to leave. 'You'll find your own way back,' he said. 'Don't be caught without a belt.' Schlump took the tram, and whenever he saw an officer get on he moved to the other side. He marvelled at this beautiful city with all its bridges. As he passed butchers' shops full of meat and pies, he thought of home, where the shop would be empty save for a pink clay pig and the butcher sharpening his knife; where empty hooks hung sadly from beams; and where haggard women clutching their meat coupons thronged at the door. He passed bakeries giving off the sweet smell of fresh white bread, and thought of home, where his mother anxiously cut up the black bread into which potatoes, peel and all, had been milled.

At last he arrived at the station. The guard had changed; now there were Prussians standing there – Schlump didn't want to get mixed up with that lot. He found a good place to climb over the fence, and at six o'clock in the evening – it was dark already – he went on to Charleroi. There he had to spend the entire night in the waiting room, which was also full of soldiers sleeping at tables or under benches. The following morning they continued on to Maubeuge, where he reported to rear echelon headquarters.

Schlump was first assigned to the main currency exchange office, where he was to be trained to manage an exchange bureau. To begin with he had to fetch the post and carry out other important duties. One day the captain, who in civilian life was a director at the Reichsbank, sent him and a Frenchman to Hautmont by horse and cart. Schlump sat on the coach box and rode cheerfully along the Maubeuge ramparts to Sous-le-Bois, from where they could see Hautmont below. Chatting to the Frenchman, he asked him what was in the sacks they were carrying.

'Sugar, of course,' said the man with the black moustache, sounding surprised. 'Sugar for the *ravitaillement*,' which was the supply point for the civilian population. Schlump was amazed that no one had told him that the exchange bureau dealt with sugar too. But the Frenchman just clicked his tongue. Aha, thought Schlump, and fell silent. As the days and weeks passed, he realised that everyone here, if they weren't a complete idiot, was involved in deals of one sort or another.

After a month, shortly before Christmas, he was ordered to the exchange bureau in Maubeuge, which was right next to the main exchange office. He rarely saw the head of this exchange office; the man was permanently on the move, often travelling to Brussels, but there were also frequent trips to Cologne and Berlin. Mostly, however, you didn't know where he was. A particularly reserved fellow, he wore an elegant uniform and went around in a magnificent fur, even though he was just a common soldier like Schlump.

The exchange bureau was managed by another man, who had the lovely name Schabkow. He looked like a tadpole with his big round head and watery eyes. Anyone taller than him could comfortably stare into his nostrils. He came from

Breslau, but home was now Berlin, and when he laughed he revealed a cavernous mouth with a row of tiny pointed teeth, interrupted by plenty of gaps. He didn't talk much, but sometimes told jokes that Schlump had to think long and hard about. For all these gags originated from the stock exchange, where they'd been thought up by men who were experts on human weaknesses. Schabkow had the most extraordinary luck with women, even though he was as ugly as a toad. There was a barber's on the market square, where the barber's ravishing young wife and her niece, a beautiful, even younger creature, worked. The entire garrison had been lathered by these soft hands, but none of them had struck lucky. Apart from Schabkow. The two women quarrelled over him, and could have torn each other's eyes out, for both of them wanted to trim the toad's beard.

One day – it was in the first week of 1918 – Schabkow came into the office brimming with joy. He invited Schlump back to his quarters for the evening, telling him quietly that there would be sekt and oysters, and that he'd be delighted if he'd do him the honour. Schlump arrived punctually. He was astounded by Schabkow's comfortable quarters, and soon realised that a woman's hand must be behind this, a woman in love. They sat down at the table. Schabkow had laid on a magnificent supper, with all those delicacies to be found in Brussels at the time. The toad soon became more animated; the sekt was taking effect. He started talking.

'You see, young man, I haven't always had it so good. I've spent much of my life hungry' – he was about thirty years old. 'I travelled through Switzerland with a rumbling stomach and without any money – at the time your mother would have still been holding you up to stop you from peeing on your shoes. I went to the Somme and was badly wounded in the stomach. I've been through many schools, young man, but I always think of my father, who taught me more than all those schoolmasters put together. I was fourteen years old and the following day I was supposed to start an apprenticeship with a Jew who'd just emigrated from Galicia. My father – he's dead now – was a barber, but his shop was full of children, I was the tenth, and he couldn't make it a success.' He took a swig of sekt from the bottle.

'You seem to have a good head on you. Listen, boy, I'm going to let you know the precious advice that my father gave me.' He swallowed another dozen oysters and took a good gulp. 'There's only one thing in life worthy of your respect, my son, and that's money. Better to go into the world with a big bag of money than a big brain. The man who's born poor and dies rich dies honourably. For he's praised and eulogised, and the poor whisper his name in awe. Now listen carefully, I'm going to tell you the secret: All men are wretched. They'll all lick the hand that feeds them. It is more blessed to give than to receive. See to it, therefore, that you are sometimes a giver. Fear nobody. They're all worse than you, unless they're poor. Be suspicious of everyone, watch them like a hawk, but never let on that you know them. Always act as if you have no feelings. For death is to no avail. Good and evil are feelings too. Save up your feelings for the evening. Only the poor have pangs of conscience, which is why they're betrayed and sold.

'When you need the help of men, flatter them sincerely

and modestly, but never forget that you are lying... If someone is in your way, turn to his wife. Pay her a clear and direct compliment, but look her in the eye. Remember that every woman, even the ugliest, has one feature that is beautiful. You must find this feature. You must tell her. She'll know that you're not lying, and she'll be for ever grateful to you. She'll remove all the obstacles from your path and you will become a rich man. And when you have come into money, never forget to be pious and to give to the poor.'

That evening Schlump arrived back at his billet blind drunk.

It wasn't long before Schlump was getting in on deals too. He had a Frenchman who sold him bed sheets. This good man had hoodwinked his compatriots into believing that the Germans were about to start requisitioning all bedclothes because they were building new military hospitals, and the poor people gave him their last treasures for peanuts. He brought them by the dozen to Schlump, and Schlump shifted them on to the head waiter of the restaurant car that travelled every day between Cologne and Imperial Headquarters. They were large pieces of material, woven for French beds, in which nobody ever sleeps alone. They must not have been washed more than once. The head waiter gave him eight marks per sheet, and then had to tip the railwayman who delivered the stuff. He hid the sheets below the seats in second and first class, where officers sat with red stripes on their trouser legs, then passed them on to the big department stores in Germany. They were brightly coloured, and soon our good girls were proudly running around in their new fabrics without any idea that their clothes were already well acquainted with love.

Schlump dealt in schnapps that he got from the garrison mess and for which civilians would pay higher prices. He didn't touch the goods himself. They were delivered to him one day in return for cash, and the following day someone came to fetch them in return for cash. Little by little he accumulated money and lived a fine life. He bought flour, sugar and butter, and every week he sent a package home. One day, however, he had the chance to become a rich man at a stroke.

Schlump had in the meantime been transferred to Hautmont to run the exchange bureau there. One day a soldier appeared who'd crept straight out of the trenches. He unstrapped his kitbag and took out a large, heavy parcel. Unwrapping it carefully and laboriously, he placed a heap of beautifully neat and tight packages on the table containing brand-new locally issued banknotes. Staring at Schlump, the soldier slapped his thigh and let out a loud, triumphant laugh. 'I found it,' he said. 'Give me half a million of German money for it, then you can keep the stuff.'

Schlump was struck dumb. These really were the new banknotes that the French cities issued to pay for their citizens' wages and food. He picked up a note, marked five francs, and examined it. There was no doubt about it, this was genuine paper money. He abruptly put the note back down and said, 'You can take the whole lot away with you again. No one will give you anything for it.'

'What?' the other man shouted. 'Why ever not?'

'It's missing the mayor's signature and the town hall stamp.

Maybe the money was forgotten when the town was evacuated. It's not worth a bean; you might as well give it to the rag-and-bone man.'

The soldier picked up a note, looked at it closely, and threw it on the ground. Then he grabbed his kitbag, put it on his back, and left. At the door he turned round and exclaimed, 'You're crooks, the lot of you, damn it!'

Schlump picked up the banknote, gathered everything together, and put it at the back of his room. Then he started pondering the matter. Surely something could be done! The truth was that there were large quantities of money in circulation, issued by towns that had long vanished from the face of the earth. Schlump pondered and pondered. In the evening he went to see a friend of his, an architect in civilian life, who was supervising the foreign workers laying new railway track.

That night they started working feverishly. His friend made a stamp and Schlump focused on the facsimile of the mayor's signature. After a hundred attempts they finally got it right.

During the nights that followed they stamped and stamped until they sweated. The half-million had been stamped and signed! But how were they going to get the money in people's pockets?

In his exchange bureau, Schlump was to continue to take in German money and give out French, but keep back the falsified notes. It would have been dangerous to give out half a million of counterfeit money, especially new notes. Schlump's friend had a better idea. Every week he had to pay the workers laying track for the railway. The wages were paid in French local-issue notes, which he frequently obtained from Schlump at the bureau in exchange for German money. So Schlump was to give *him* the falsified notes and he'd receive genuine marks in return.

And that is what happened. They played this trick a few times until one day a report came from command headquarters that large quantities of falsified money were circulating in the district. The paper notes themselves were genuine; just the signature was fake.

Worried, they destroyed the remaining money and kept their heads down. A few days later a gendarme arrived, rifled through everything, but found nothing. He accepted a schnapps from Schlump and then vanished again.

The matter was forgotten. The two men had ten thousand marks each. Schlump put a few hundred-mark notes in an envelope and sent it home. The rest he sewed into his coat.

Schlump would often stand outside the door of his bureau, watching the comings and goings in this small town. He saw the clean, well-fed rear-echelon officers pass by with their shining gaiters, casually and elegantly greeting the poor wounded who leaned humbly against the walls. He recalled the words of his last German teacher, who had fought in the Franco–Prussian war. This ancient, white-bearded man had been called out of retirement because of a lack of teachers. Just before they were dismissed from their final German lesson, he had told them, 'Well, boys, I don't think you'll ever have to go to war. But just remember one thing: you will be called upon to be leaders of the German people. And being a leader means being a role model. If the leaders are diligent then the people will be diligent. Which spells progress for the nation. The prosperity or despair of a nation depends on the moral conduct of its leaders. A leader's responsibility is huge. And woe betide a nation whose leaders refuse to make greater sacrifices than the rank-and-file man. Just as the rider must first look after his horse, so the leader must first look after those who look up to him. The leader must go on even in hunger and adversity, for then the troops will die for him.' Shortly afterwards the old man died himself. Schlump felt a little uneasy when he thought of this, and started to whistle a soldiers' song.

Now the penal company marched past, the second-class soldiers without cockades on their caps. They looked pale and unkempt, and wore sad expressions. 'A cigarette, comrade, a cigarette!' they begged as they went past. Schlump always tossed them a few ciggies. One man stood out from the others, a wan lad with an innocent, childish face. Why is he here? Schlump wondered. Those poor devils were forced to work hard, and in return were given poor rations and no pay. They returned every evening exhausted and filthy, in tatty uniforms without any overcoats. Each time the wan boy was on the outside of the formation, so he always marched right past Schlump. Schlump often slipped him a roll or some salami. He would have loved to know what the poor lad had on his conscience.

One day he saw the wan boy huddled miserable and freezing by the sick bay, beside him a corporal with rifle and cartridge belt. Schlump went over and talked to the lad, who looked at him gratefully but said little. Schlump gave him some cigarettes and was keen to help. Gradually the boy warmed to him and told him of his misfortune. The words came out with difficulty; he often faltered, and Schlump had to work out a considerable portion of the story for himself. But he understood the boy, for his brown eyes talked more clearly than his ungainly mouth. And those eyes told him the following story.

'I was born in 1900 in a small village in Brandenburg. I never knew my mother, and my father died a few years ago. He had me apprenticed to a cobbler, who was very kind and did the best he could for me. We cobbled together, forever watching out for who passed by on the village street. Every morning the schoolmaster came with his daughter to fetch milk from the farm. The girl was my age and had gone to school with me. But she always sat on the front bench and I on the back one, and we seldom talked to one another. I just kept staring at her from my bench at the back. I always wanted to sit next to her. I went to church every Sunday, but never summoned up sufficient courage, and so stayed at the back where I could see her pigtails. Whenever she passed us in the morning I felt happy the whole day long. "Good morning, Ilse," I'd say (but nobody heard). "I hope you slept well. I dreamed of you last night. The two of us were angels and we played together."

'Once she brought us her shoes. I soled them. You can't imagine, comrade, how beautiful her shoes were. In the evening I took them up to my room, put them on the chest of drawers, sat in front of it and started talking. We played together like children. In the morning I took them back down so my master wouldn't notice. Later on, she came into our workshop and picked them up. "The boy repaired them," my master said. She looked at me, laughed and said something I didn't understand. I couldn't utter a word, and my ears were pounding as if I were in a mill. Then she was gone, as were the shoes. In the evening I sat all alone in my room and howled like a little child. Don't laugh at me, comrade, I wasn't spineless in any other way. I'd walk fearlessly through the forest in the middle of the night, and I'd have done anything for her. But she kept passing our window every morning, and that was a consolation. Then came winter. I went for my army medical and was conscripted into the infantry. But we weren't called up yet.

'I continued cobbling, and one morning the schoolmaster's maid came with Ilse's shoes, saying that Ilse was moving to the city, and that we were to put the buckles on her new shoes higher up. I was devastated. Ilse was moving to the city and she'd never pass our workshop again. She'd be taking her shoes to another cobbler! The master and I both adjusted her shoes, because it had to be a quick job. I took them up to my room again and couldn't sleep a wink that night. Early the following morning she'd collect her shoes and at noon she would ride to the city with the peasants. No one, comrade, can imagine how I suffered that night.

'At four o'clock I got up. It was pitch black and the windows had frozen. I packed up all my stuff, putting Ilse's shoes right at the bottom, and left in secret. I was going to start out as a journeyman. I took my military papers with me.

'I got work everywhere, because there was no one left to do those jobs. I wandered through Thuringia. Sometimes

I would take out the shoes and set them before me. I kissed them; comrade, you won't believe how I loved those shoes. Then I thought about how I'd wronged my master. He would have searched high and low for those shoes! I packed them away, beneath everything else. And I resolved never to take them out again. I made it to Hesse, and there I stuck it out with another master cobbler for a whole three months. The shoes remained at the bottom of my bundle; I didn't unpack them.

'But I always thought about the shoes. I thought about our village, I saw Ilse walking past. I saw the schoolmaster's house, I saw the maid collecting Ilse from the city because it was holiday time. I couldn't stand it any longer, comrade. I ran away again, at night and in the fog, those shoes in my hand. I begged my way, and weeks later, half-starved and in tatters, I came out of the spruce forest and steeled myself to go down into the village.

'That evening I knocked on my master's door, holding the pair of shoes. The storm raged through the pine trees, making them howl, and flayed the limes in the village, driving the withered leaves into my face. My master's wife opened up, and, Comrade, you can imagine the surprise she got when she saw me standing there at the door! She let me in; I put the stolen shoes on the table and looked at my master. He picked up the shoes, examined them all over, and put them back down. "Go to bed!" he said. I crept up to my room.

'I started working again, comrade, I worked as hard as I could so that the master would look kindly on me again.

'Ilse had returned from the city, and came past every

morning to fetch milk from the farm. My mistress delivered her shoes and everything was all right.

'November came, and one day the postman brought the red piece of paper. I was called up to the infantry. I really wanted to become a soldier and was looking forward to it. I ordered a soldier's crate from the carpenter, and my mistress knitted me some stockings.

'But at night I was unable to sleep. I couldn't stop thinking of Ilse. She was going to stay in the village and come to fetch her milk every morning from the farm, whereas I wouldn't be there any more, I wouldn't see her any more. I had nothing of hers, no souvenir. And she wouldn't notice my absence, either. I'd have to go to war and maybe I'd never look her in the face again. The day was approaching ever closer and I became increasingly unsettled and miserable.

'I had to leave the following morning. It was pitch black that last, unfortunate night. I sat on my bed, listening out for any sound. Perhaps there'd be a fire at the schoolmaster's house and I'd be able to save her. Then I'd get to see her one last time. I brooded over the matter and entertained the craziest thoughts. Then all of a sudden it clicked. I got dressed and slipped out. It was blowing a gale outside; my hair was dishevelled in an instant. But I made my way over as if driven. I sneaked around the schoolmaster's house I don't know how many times. Through the storm I heard the clock strike in the tower, but couldn't tell what time it was. I stood by the window and listened; maybe she talked in her sleep. But it was madness, for the trees were roaring like thunder and the roof tiles were rattling.

'I tried a window in the hallway – and was able to push it open! I climbed in. Once inside, I stood motionless, holding my breath for ages. Then I crept further. All of a sudden my foot hit something. With a fright, I stood there rigid and silent. It was a pair of shoes. Kneeling down, I reached for the shoes. Her shoes! My shoes, the ones I'd run away with! I wept for joy. I kissed them, comrade; don't laugh, I kissed them. How long was I kneeling there? I don't know. I wanted to take them with me as a souvenir. But I'd already stolen them once. I thought of my master and put them back down. I picked them up again and started to leave. But then I saw my master in my mind, I turned round, kneeled down, was just about to put them back when a door opened! A white figure appeared, holding a lamp! It was her! Now I'm beside myself with fear, I leap in the air, she screams out loud, the lamp goes out, I hear a hard bang. Comrade, I don't know how I got out of that house. I ran and ran, mindlessly, out on to the heath.

'The next morning I noticed that my face and fingers had been bleeding; I must have jumped through a window. I wandered around and about, comrade, just how many days and nights I do not know. One morning – it was still dark – I returned to the village. Collapsing by her fence, I fell asleep. I was woken by the gendarme. They led me away to the city. To gaol. Then I was put in front of a court. The schoolmaster was there, as was his wife, all dressed in black. My master and my mistress. None of them looked at me. The judge in his military uniform stood up. He read something out, it was very long. I understood none of it save for one thing: there had been a hole in Ilse's head! I grasped nothing. I didn't say anything. They kept asking me questions. I didn't utter a word. Then they led me away again. And now I'm here. Comrade, I didn't kill Ilse!'

Schlump asked him how many times he'd been beaten. He didn't know. Schlump gave him everything he had in his pockets and returned to his bureau.

Winter passed, the war got ever bloodier, and peace refused to come. But hope had revived: fighting had stopped in the east. The Russians were finished, in spite of the vast numbers of soldiers they'd had at their disposal. And now the troops were rolling in from the east, one train after another. The artillery was already being unloaded at the German border and heading westwards to the Front on the major roads. The soldiers in the rear echelon listened attentively; a good number of them had set out in 1914, almost four years ago. Recalling the mood back then, they sensed a fresh wave of something approaching enthusiasm in their disillusioned and withered hearts. People talked of numbers of armies that were scarcely credible. The seventeenth army was said to have arrived already, the eighteenth army was supposed to relieve the second, and things like that.

Sometimes when Schlump woke up at night he could hear a muffled rumbling and trundling from the hills around Haumont, from the masses of cannons, wagons and footsteps moving westwards. Even during the day they fancied they could hear the hum that seemed to come from the ground. There was talk of cannons that could fire from Péronne to Paris. They calculated the altitude the shells would have to reach and couldn't believe their findings. But everyone felt that something was in the air, maybe even something major. The infantrymen went around with a heightened sense of pride. They were looking forward to the advance, beyond the trenches to where there were provisions stores containing things they knew only from the fairy tale of peacetime. It was a fever that gripped them all, a different enthusiasm from 1914, which had been the enthusiasm of desperation. All that was needed was one general, one great idea, for these soldiers to perform a miracle the like of which had never been seen before. Schlump was close to volunteering for action again. But he'd been spoiled by his time at home and in the rear. Even if we win, he told himself, it's not going to be the filthy hero from the trenches who gets all the honours. No, those in sparkling uniforms will jump the queue. After all, most of those in the line of fire have disappeared anyway. He didn't volunteer.

They knew when the offensive was starting; they were told by the girls who worked for the high-ranking officers. They also knew precisely which army would have the honour of launching the first attack, and what the goal was. 'Don't you know?' said the pretty little Walloon girl who cleaned his room. 'Oh, *moi je sais tout* – I know everything.'

The day drew closer and everyone had lost interest in the dealings of the rear echelon. It was as if all ears were cocked westwards in an attempt to intercept the telegrams floating through the ether.

The day arrived, another night passed, and then the first report came through: a victory, yes, a victory – but they didn't hear the names they'd expected. The first offensive had come to a standstill; the supply line had been poorly organised, it was said. They'd relied on the power of the masses, and ignored the might of the brilliant idea!

A few days later came the confirmation of this terrible rumour. Schlump was still in bed; he was listening intently. He'd been woken by an odd tramping and clattering, similar to the sound of steady, unremitting rain when it hammers against the window pane and gutter. He got up and went to the window. They were passing in rows of eight, tightly packed together, without rifles, clothes in tatters, arms and heads bandaged, supported on crutches, in silence, tortured faces deadened from the strains and pains. And this procession was never-ending. Where were they all coming from? Schlump got dressed and went outside. 'It's been going on like this since midnight,' said his neighbour, the clerk in the supply depot. And it continued all day. Nobody could say with any certainty where they were all coming from.

That evening Schlump went up to Maubeuge. The same scene. The commandant of Maubeuge, Major Bock, had made no provision for any hospital facilities; he probably hadn't received any orders to that effect. All he knew was which of the conquered towns he was to make his way to: Epernay, home of the renowned champagne cellars. The poor devils lay in the church, the market square was jammed – they lay on the paving stones, blocking all the streets. Schlump thought of the French retreat from Russia a century before. We've lost the war, he said to himself.

He went into the soldiers' club, which was stuffed with wounded men. The hapless souls were pleased merely to have a roof over their heads. Schlump sat at the piano and played the tunes they all loved. Out of gratitude the soldiers plied him with schnapps, so much schnapps that he couldn't drink it all. The glasses lined up on top of the piano. 'Drink, comrade,' they said. 'Drink and play. We're delighted to be out of that nightmare – what a cock-up!' Schlump drank and played like a demon. As he became drunk, he turned into an automaton. They poured the schnapps down his throat and his hands played with such fury that the poor piano whimpered and moaned.

Hours passed amidst such noise, then at a stroke it fell silent. The commandant, a fat major, had entered. Schlump stood up – the others were already on their feet – and leaned against the piano. The fat major struck a table with his riding crop, causing the glasses to jump, then squawked through the fog of cigarette smoke with his shrill and sharp voice, 'Ten o'clock! The soldiers' club is closed! Everybody out!' When no one moved, the major turned as red as lobster and, with his eyes bulging alarmingly, lashed the table so hard that all the glasses fell to the floor and his voice cracked. 'Out!' he yelled again. No one moved, but at the back a few soldiers started muttering. The fat major raised his crop and whipped the face of the nearest man, who had a bandage around his head.

Schlump couldn't hold back any longer. 'Kill the fat bastard!' he screamed. Glasses started flying, followed by tables and chairs; raging and screaming to make the blood curdle.

When the men had regained their composure, the major was nowhere to be seen; he'd fled via a back door. They didn't know where his adjutant was, either. An hour later the guards arrived. The soldiers left obediently and lay down to sleep on the cold stones outside. Schlump pushed off back to Haumont. That night he froze. The following morning he wrote to his mother and told her that Germany had lost the war.

Schlump was back outside his bureau, watching the wounded men loitering in the street. Barracks had been hastily set up to accommodate them. A soldier from the trenches came tottering over, his legs apart. It was only when Schlump took a closer look that he realised from the silver tassel on the man's sword that he was a lieutenant. It would be impossible to make such a mix-up with the officers in the rear. A soldier from the artillery school, wearing tall boots and ringing spurs, came by and saluted. Stopping, the short lieutenant went red in the face and bawled out the poor cannon-cocker: 'Gunners! Bloody gunners! Off with you! March, march!' He must have gone insane. But Schlump was even more taken aback when the crazed lieutenant shouted at him, 'My God, it's you. What the devil are you doing here?' Then Schlump recognised him; it was his neighbour, Eger, who he'd mobilised with. The two of them had set off with their soldiers' chests and bags of enthusiasm. Eger was three years older than Schlump; he'd been immediately allocated to another regiment in the reserves and they hadn't seen each other since. 'I can't look at artillerymen any more,' he said. 'They make me fly into a rage.'

Schlump closed up his bureau and invited Eger into his room, where he offered him cocoa and American biscuits, which the handsome little lieutenant ate with relish. 'Tell me what you've been up to,' Schlump said, and the two of them prattled on for hours, before sharing a bed, even though the lieutenant had lice and scabies. In the morning they resumed their chit-chat.

'You know,' Eger said, 'how I was ordered back to the west from Krotoschin. I hadn't even located my regiment, for pity's sake! It took me ages to find the regimental dugout in a cellar in the cliffs. From there I was sent to the third battalion, which was meant to be on the right flank at the Front. The shelling over there was crazy – well, you know what I'm talking about; I don't need to go into any more detail. Anyway, I find my battalion chief behind a railway embankment. He's still got three officers with him and he sends me up front straight away. I'm to take over the eleventh company, even though I don't know the area at all. I race over the embankment, skipping along. No trenches, just shell holes. I finally find a few men at the very front, thrown together from all companies and several regiments. Crawling to my left, I make contact with the eighth company – eight or nine men at most. I crawl back in the other direction – nothing.

'The ground fell away sharply at that point, allowing me to survey a large stretch of land. And far in the distance I noticed columns of soldiers marching to the north-east. French. They must have broken through. In a few hours we were cut off. I had no idea what was in front of us. A small forest, badly damaged by shelling – the Frenchies must be behind that. I pass the order down the line, "Proceed slowly!" We move forwards. The artillery fire is now behind us. Not a single shot, nothing! I get to my feet, advance, rifle on my arm, just like at home on the freshly ploughed fields. The ninth company to the left joins up with us. All of a sudden: *tak-tak-tak-tak* from the right! Five, six men lie there, screaming for mercy. I am hit and go flying into the mud. A shot on the behind. Beside me lies a man whose jaw has been shot off, another one who's been hit in the privates. He's wailing in sheer agony. I ought to take him with me, but I can't. I patch him up as best I can and promise to come back for him.

'Crawling to my left, I tell the officer to take command of my few men. Then I drag myself back. Christ, what pain! The Frenchies are pounding the embankment, but there's no sign of our artillery. I wrench myself up and over the embankment. The battalion chief is still behind with his three officers, waving his hands furiously about in the air. I give my report and vanish, having told him to send for stretcher-bearers. An ensign runs in front of me, his upper arm badly wounded. He gives me a little support. "It's looking bad here. We'll be all cleaned up by the morning." We limp on towards the south-east and come to a railway crossing. About thirty men are sitting there, waiting for stretcher-bearers. I can't go on any further. We sit or lie down as best we can. And there it is – a shot from far behind us. Our artillery! *Whee-ee!* An incredibly heavy shell! Right on our bridge, on the upper edge. And then the whole payload comes down. The thirty men are rolling around and howling in agony. All of them have shots to the stomach. We were sitting on the other side, watching this gruesome scene. I think I had a fit, and ever since I've gone into a rage whenever I see an artilleryman.

'"Go on!" I say. "We're going on." Right next to the underpass behind the railway embankment I discover some dugouts. We creep in. Everything full, nothing but service corps! "For pity's sake, take these wounded men. The poor bastards are bleeding to death."

'"We've got no space, there's no room for anyone here."

'We go on, and the road bends further to the south. An ambulance comes up behind us. Driving in a hurry. "It's not stopping," the ensign says. "We'll see about that!" I say. I stand in the middle of the road and aim my revolver. "Stop!" I bellow as loudly as I can. And the driver does actually stop. The ambulance is empty! We drive like the clappers southwards. Suddenly we come to a halt. Field hospital; we get out.

'It was a shell-damaged church, full to the rafters with wounded men. One was being operated on in the sacristy by the light of a tallow candle. Not a medical orderly to be seen. The ensign bandaged me up as best he could. It was a flesh wound; the bullet had gone straight through, not perilous. A nurse came. "Be on your way now," she said. "We can't help you here, we don't have any bandages, we don't have any iodine, we don't have anything any more." The pain had subsided; I braced myself and we marched on. Eastwards.

'Night falls, we make slow progress. We see artillery on the retreat. Now we come across troops. A terrible crush. The poor infantry sinks into the sludge. Automobiles race past intermittently. We march between cursed artillerymen. I think I dozed off while marching. In the morning the guns are unlimbered. We walk a little way further to a field hospital with the American colours, which they must have abandoned during the course of our advance. Beside it a munitions depot with French munitions. A huge hospital! I get a bed, right at the top. The ensign is in the neighbouring bed. We are able to lie down, to sleep! Next to us and beneath, seriously wounded men are everywhere.

'We stay there a few days. What if aeroplanes fly across now and bomb the munitions depot? I ask the doctor about hospital trains; the railway is just next door. "Maybe tomorrow, maybe next week." He shrugs.

'And that night aeroplanes did fly over and bomb the munitions depot. It was full of mustard gas and blue-cross shells! Prussic acid and poisonous gases. Everyone makes a run for it. The seriously wounded with the shots to the stomach! Everyone save those without any legs, who are bleating with fear. My God, what a procession that was of half-dead men – in shirts or naked or with sheets around their shoulders in the moonlight. The shells start to explode, there is thunder and lightning and banging: a demonic spectacle! And these half-dead men begin to run, getting tangled up in their bandages. There is light behind us; the hospital is on fire! With every step some soldiers collapsed and moaned and bled. The roadside ditch was full. One man tore the bandages from his stomach and screamed like an imbecile; he'd gone insane. He ran around in front of us, screaming all the while. Then he collapsed and rolled on to his side. That's a sight I'll never forget.

'There must have been a few thousand men in that hospital. From all sides they came across the fields. Together we wandered down the road beside the railway embankment, a grisly, ghostly procession, with groans and screams. We became fewer and fewer. One man sat naked in the new grass and started weeping. "Mother," he wailed, "I have to die now." We moved on, leaving in our wake a conspicuous trail of blood and bandages. Like a gigantic torch the hospital still lit up the way. We became fewer and fewer. At the end there can only have been a few hundred men.

'Dawn comes. In the distance we see a station. It gives renewed hope. As we press on, field gendarmes approach on their horses and stop us in our tracks. Why? The village is already packed with wounded men. A gendarme officer comes and says, "You'll have to turn back, comrade." He recognises me by my cockade. For I'd managed to salvage my cap as well as my shirt. I'm unable to say anything. I'm seething with anger; I could scream out of sheer sorrow. The men sit numb in the grass and fall silent.

'The gendarmes have left. We go back over the embankment and make our way through. Me, the ensign and another man. We arrive at the station. And there it is — a hospital train! With a steaming locomotive! We charge into a carriage. What joy! Everything is forgotten. A few medical orderlies give us coy looks and scurry past. The beds are occupied, but there's still plenty of space between the rows of bunks. For all those at the edge of the village, who are sitting in the grass and bleeding. The chief doctor appears. "I'm afraid I can't take you, Lieutenant. I've already given the numbers to rear headquarters, and I can't exceed that figure." Well, that was just too much. Whipping out my revolver, I cry in desperation, "Anybody who tries to get us off this train will be shot dead."

'At that moment the locomotive pulled out of the station. We alighted here in Haumont.'

Schlump was not a born racketeer. Since his visit from the gendarme he'd lost all enthusiasm for wheeler-dealing. He reckoned, moreover, that with the ten thousand marks he'd sewn into the lining of his jacket he was rich enough. Now he planned to do something else in his spare time: he started reading. In a small stationer's he'd found a book that had been badly bound and printed on poor-quality paper. But he was captivated by its contents. It was a compilation of love letters that Mirabeau wrote from prison to his dear Sophie, on whose account he had been locked up. Schlump was spellbound by the French eloquence, with its indestructible belief in life, and felt as if he'd somehow been part of this love and its torments. He went for evening strolls on his own, behaving as if he were head over heels in love himself, although he had no idea who he was in love with, or what made him happy and unhappy.

Schlump was so caught up in himself that he didn't notice the sweet flowers blossoming around him, any of which would have been glad to offer him up their perfume. In his house lived a young Walloon girl with black hair and large brown eyes, fresh rosy cheeks and beautiful teeth. She had a strong but lovely body, and small feet with slender ankles. The girl came from a nearby village and attended to the inhabitants of the house: two elderly people and Schlump. Every Saturday he left four francs on the table for her, which she refused to accept to begin with, even though she was as poor as a church mouse.

The window in Schlump's bedroom gave on to a cramped, ugly courtyard, which the girl crossed back and forth as she went about her business. In the courtyard, a ladder against one wall reached up to his window, possibly because there was nowhere else to put it. Once, when Schlump was standing pensively by the window, she stopped and asked him if he was all right. He said he was, then enquired rather absent-mindedly but politely how she was. She shook her head sadly and left.

Schlump forgot to ask the girl why she was so unhappy. A few weeks later she came to his room and set about her chores. He was deep into the love letters and didn't even want to look up. Pointing at his book, she said with irritation, '*Toujours vos poésies!*' Schlump laughed and asked whether she didn't like love letters. She said no, and was about to leave, but stopped at the door. Keen to appear polite, Schlump asked her if she'd ever been in love herself. 'Oh yes!' she sighed.

'When?'

'Now.'

'I see. Am I right in thinking you have a sweetheart but you can't speak to him?'

'Yes, that's exactly the problem.'

'You're not even allowed to write to him?'

'No, I am. Every Sunday I go to the border of the military district and he comes. We chat for a while, then he gives me a letter, and I...'

'You give him a letter too?'

'The thing is, monsieur, I cannot write as well as he does, and I always feel ashamed when I give him my sorry letters.

Someone like you who reads so much, I'm sure you're very good at writing letters.'

'Oh, I don't know about that, but it wouldn't be of much use to you anyway. Or do you want me to write the letters for you?'

'Yes, monsieur, do that. Draft me a letter and I'll come and pick it up tomorrow morning.'

Schlump laughed; he thought it was hilarious to write love letters for a pretty young girl. But he relished the challenge. He felt that he ought to write something straight from the heart, something that would suffocate him if it weren't expressed. So that evening he sat down to compose the letter. He failed to notice that he was lifting material straight from Mirabeau, as if it were from the depths of his own soul. What Schlump found difficult was to strike the right tone. For he had to write as if all these glowing words were issuing from the coy heart of a very young and very pretty girl (he'd asked her to show him one of her sweetheart's letters so he could gauge just how much their hearts had become intertwined. But she didn't want to; she blushed and just said that they loved each other very much).

She picked up the letter the following day. That afternoon she thanked him and seemed quite happy. A few days later she came again, and after that she visited with increasing regularity. Schlump wondered how she found the time to keep going to the border of the military district. He challenged her, and she said her sweetheart was now at the pharmacy, but they couldn't talk to each other or people would start gossiping.

All this fervent writing was of little help to Schlump,

however. It offered no clue as to who *he* was actually in love with. On the contrary, it just stoked the fire even more, without showing him the water that could have extinguished this blaze. This was a blissful period, full of the feelings of love, and all Schlump was lacking was a loved one to make him immeasurably happy or unhappy.

For this reason sober reality never deserted him. One day the order came through that he was being relieved. He had to settle all his accounts and at four in the morning march to Bohain, where he was to report to the postal censor's office. This took Schlump by surprise. Maybe, he pondered, something's come to light about the falsified banknotes, or my act of heroism in the soldiers' club when we saw off that fat major.

Schlump's last few days were up. A paymaster from the head exchange bureau had come to settle up, and at three o'clock the following morning Schlump got up to set off on his march. With everything already packed, he took his kitbag and went downstairs. He had to pass through a small room to get into the street. Opening the door, he discovered Gabriele, the beautiful Walloon girl, in her nightdress. Out of the blue she embraced Schlump, kissed him and then started crying so intensely that he became worried. After what seemed like ages she eventually managed to utter a few words: '*Vous l'avez trouvée?* Have you found it?'

'Found what?'

'*La bague!* The ring!'

'No!' said Schlump in astonishment.

She dashed up to his room, as quietly as a cat, and brought something back down: a copper ring, finely worked, with a green heart. With tears in her eyes, Gabriele stood by the light, which shone through her nightdress, and smiled at him. All at once Schlump saw how beautiful she was. His kitbag clattered to the floor as he took her in his arms, and he was as sweet to her as one can imagine, thinking back to the ardour of one's youth, the ardour that was ablaze inside him.

'What about the love letters?' he asked a few hours later. 'Oh, I've kept all of them,' she whispered to his breast. The candle flickered slightly, casting inquisitive and wanton patterns of light on her body.

That morning Schlump couldn't march off before eight.

Schlump was travelling south-west. He was still full of longing as he thought about the beautiful Walloon girl, still able to feel her kisses. But he knew, too, that she was not the one he'd been longing for.

He chatted to comrades returning from the Front and those who were on their way there. Beside him sat a man who'd deserted from his company because he'd had enough of the endless squalor. This man was fed at the collection points that distributed the donations arriving from Germany, moving from one to the next. He'd sold all his equipment in Belgium, where each piece of kit had its fixed price. 'Now I'm going back to my company. I'll join in again for a while, I mean, I've eaten my fill several times and done nothing for a few weeks. The sergeant'll bite my head off, but nothing more will come of it. I mean, they're delighted if we come back at all. What could they do to us anyway? It doesn't get any worse than the trenches, does it?'

Schlump got out at Bohain. The postal censor's office was in a large red house not far from the station. He reported to the captain, who kept him standing to attention and didn't bother to turn round, but told him to report to Corporal Jolles. Jolles gave him a stack of postcards with red ten-pfennig stamps, and pointed to a room where two men were sitting with their own piles of cards. All the postcards were in French and in poor handwriting. They were from peasant women telling their sons or husbands at the Front that the red cow had come into milk again, that the calf was pregnant, and that everyone was in good health. They hoped this dreadful war, this catastrophe, would soon be over and that they could all be together again soon. Schlump read through his cards; each one said the same thing. He put his mark on them then passed them on.

He soon got used to his new surroundings. Corporal Jolles was a good-natured chap from Cologne, who became Schlump's friend. They led an easy, comfortable existence. In fine weather they could hear the rumble of cannon from the Front in the west, a reminder that every day thousands of young men were losing their lives in the most grisly ways. You had to train yourself to banish such thoughts.

Schlump got up at eight in the morning. He was billeted in one of those simple workers' houses which just had a parlour and a kitchen. In each of these two rooms was a bed. On the bed in the parlour was an elegant eiderdown. This was where Schlump slept. And in the kitchen, in the wide bed with its colourful cover, slept the dutiful, gentle married couple. The door between the rooms stayed open day and night. Around half past eight Jolles would pop in

– he lived a few doors up, just before the road led into the cemetery – and call out, 'Hey, Schlumpy old chap, let's have a coffee!' They would drink coffee or hot chocolate at Jolles's house, and at nine they'd walk to work through the little gardens behind the houses. At eleven o'clock Jolles came into his room (he'd arranged for Schlump to have his own tiny office) and sat on the table to consult about lunch. Schlump fetched a bottle of schnapps from a little wall-papered cupboard and offered his friend a cigar. At twelve they went off to eat. There was a small mess where the food was first-rate, for Jolles had excellent contacts. He knew the men who worked in the rear-echelon butcher's, he knew those who worked in the rear-echelon bakery, and the clerks in the stores. Everywhere he got his hands on the best things. A French woman cooked French cuisine for Jolles and Schlump; a German cook looked after the orderlies, the record office and the clerks. The captain ate in the officers' mess with another captain and an old major. The arrangement was perfect; the war could go on for as long as it liked.

After lunch they relaxed until three o'clock. Around this time they'd have a small snack – a cup of hot chocolate and fresh strawberries delivered by the cemetery gardener. Then they'd do another couple of hours' work in the office, after which came the most important part of the day: the evening. Supper took place at Jolles's house, consisting of all the delicacies that Jolles could rustle up, and which he often prepared himself with great culinary skill. All his suppliers had to part with their very best titbits for this special celebration. A small table was set up by the door, covered with a white tablecloth, club chairs were fetched, and an exquisite bottle of wine produced: a white Bordeaux or a red Burgundy. Sometimes they invited a few actors who were in the area making life more tolerable for the officers. These would be quite happy to come and clown around for the friends in return for a decent supper.

Jolles loved wine as much as life. He was around fifteen years older than Schlump, with red hair, and he had no luck with women. They'd often chat until late in the night and their paradise was lacking nothing – well, almost nothing. And Schlump would occasionally find the one tiny element that was lacking.

That is how they lived through the summer, without a care in the world.

Every morning when Schlump stepped out of the front door he said hello to Louise, the pretty girl who'd be sweeping the two steps in front of her house. Her mother was dead; her father left for work very early and came back home late in the evening. She'd billeted an ancillary worker in her front room, an old boy with a red face and a shag pipe in his mouth, who was hugely proud of his beautiful young landlady. He'd close one eye whenever he bragged about her to his aged colleagues. There was no doubt that they were all jealous of him on account of Louise.

Louise wore blue stockings and a terribly short skirt. She was as blonde as they came and had the most magnificent blue eyes, which matched her stockings. She thanked Schlump each day for his greeting, and whenever he looked into her eyes he was reminded of home. She'd often come over, browse his books and talk at length with his landlady, who was also blonde and not old, but very ugly.

Before he went over to Jolles's in the evening, Schlump used to chat with Louise. Then she'd stand for ages by her door and Schlump could see her white arms shimmering in the night as he drank wine outside Jolles's house.

One evening Schlump didn't go up to see Jolles. Pretty young Louise was showing him her lovely little garden that was behind the house and protected by a high wall. Then the two of them went into her tiny kitchen, which the delightful child had turned into a neat and cosy nest. She was as clean as a cat; her little white bed stood against the wall and smelled of fresh linen like a young girl. Her father was already asleep in the room upstairs; all was quiet. The door to the garden was open, allowing the dark-blue night to breathe in its intoxicating dreams. The crickets chirped noisily, as if trying to deafen any eavesdroppers; a soft, gentle wind picked up outside and breezed in, wafting her hair around his mouth.

Louise stood up, closed the door and turned on the light. The spell was broken. 'I wanted to show you my books,' she said, pointing to a row of lovely old leather-bound volumes with faded gold edges. They were tomes from Voltaire's time, the sort of books you can often buy cheaply on the banks of the Seine in Paris. Schlump picked out a volume and leafed through it: *Les Contes* by Lafontaine. There were brown marks all over the paper, betraying the book's age. The tales in rhyme were illustrated by engravings by Doré, who was peerless in picturing love. Schlump and Louise sat together on a chair and started reading.

They read the story of the girl whose greatest desire is to hear the nightingale sing through the night. Schlump had Louise explain the words he didn't understand or wanted to hear her utter. Then they looked at the wonderful illustration that Doré had put beside it: the mother looks in horror through the door at the balcony where the daughter is asleep; next to her, the father pacifies his wife, a mischievous expression of understanding on his face. For the wanton girl is lying there with her lover in broad daylight, and they've pushed back the covers to get some cool air. In the girl's hand is the nightingale she caught during the night.

Pretty young Louise gave a brief shudder then turned out the light, for she didn't want Schlump to see her blushing. But now the crickets outside were chirping so loudly that their noise filled the room, and the flowers had given off so much perfume that the two young people fancied they could hear the nightingales singing. Their hearts were thumping and their youth magicked them into a paradise created by sheer ecstasy, in which thousands of nightingales poured out their bittersweet love songs.

Around midnight, a deep, faint hum struck up far away to the west. It came ever closer, rising in volume, and finally the factory sirens in the town snarled into action, wailing like tortured devils. The two lovers awoke, and in her terror, young Louise let her nightingale fly away. '*Des aéroplanes anglais*, English planes!' The good child sprang out of bed and threw something over herself (for she had copied the lovers in the tale). Schlump gathered up his clothes and both of them hurried into the cellar. 'What if my father comes?' she exclaimed. 'And the old man!' Schlump stuttered. 'He's practically deaf, the old man, but my father… Oh God!' Poor Louise looked around in horror and helplessness. In the corner was a large chest, which must have been around two metres long. They'd brought it down so her father could sleep upstairs. They removed the heavy lid and Schlump climbed in.

Inside the chest was an eiderdown. Schlump felt warm and cosy. Through the gaps in the wood he could see Louise. She'd hidden his clothes and lit the candle that was always on hand in the cellar. She squatted beside the chest, holding the candle. But her father didn't come, the sirens lowered their shrill screams to a deep bass and eventually fell silent altogether. Pretty Louise began to stare vacantly into space. She blew out the light, opened the chest and climbed in to join Schlump, as daintily as a fairy. 'I'm not going up into the kitchen yet,' she said. 'The planes might come back.'

'But what if your father can't find you?'

'Oh, he'll think I'm with the neighbour. We bored a hole through the cellar wall, so you have to talk as quietly as possible.'

In the bedroom chest it was wonderful, and soon the tired lovers fell asleep. They slept soundly and long. Hours passed and the sun rose in the east. But it couldn't find a way into the cellar to wake the sleepers. And the sun rose higher and higher.

That morning Jolles looked for his friend in vain. He was worried, because he hadn't seen him the previous evening either. Schlump's neighbour, too, a young widow, took notice and joined in the hunt.

When the two sleepers woke in the chest, they could hear voices in the cellar next door. They didn't move and peered in horror through the chinks. 'I saw monsieur go over yesterday evening, but he can't have come back for I would have heard him for sure. I don't sleep well, you see,' the young widow said. Jolles muttered something under his breath. 'His slippers are upstairs, next to Mademoiselle Louise's slippers; they can't have run away barefoot,' the young widow added.

All of a sudden Jolles stood face to face with the widow and shouted in her ear, 'Madame, please don't go into that corner over there or you'll get a terrible fright. The two of them have hanged themselves!' Screaming, the widow fled. Jolles went over to the chest and said, 'Hurry! I'll stand guard by the door and make sure no one comes in.' A stocking poking out from beneath the lid had given good old Jolles the clue.

They hastily got dressed, then climbed over the garden wall that led out into the field, their paasage largely concealed by bushes. Schlump hurried into his office, and Louise to her deaf elderly aunt who lived at the other end of the village. A while later Jolles came into the office and laughed so much that tears ran down his face.

That evening Louise returned home as if nothing had happened.

The old boy with the shag pipe must have got wind of it, for he took Schlump aside and implored him to keep quiet like a true gentleman. 'Because she's a decent girl, that Louise,' he said.

From then on Schlump visited Louise every evening. But

he waited until the aeroplanes had passed over the town, always on the stroke of midnight, to drop their destructive loads on the station at Busigny, the neighbouring town. This always proved a stern test of his patience.

The Germans tried to change their fortune with a variety of offensives, which all had the same outcome. The brave infantrymen gained considerable ground. But back-up was lacking. This major enterprise had been ill thought through, and so innumerable young men met a terrible, horrific death.

Masses and masses of wounded men passed through Bohain — those who could still walk and were only lightly injured. The others had to perish forlornly or die on the way. Prisoners, too, were delivered to Bohain and assembled in large camps. The British and French were kept separate because they couldn't stand each other. Schlump was summoned to interpret for the French. The town's inhabitants had collected clothes and linen for their compatriot prisoners, even though they had scarcely enough to cover their own bodies. Schlump's job was to liaise between the prisoners and the townsfolk to ensure that no espionage took place.

The French soldiers looked just like our men at the Front; they were sick to death of the war and didn't say very much. They were desperate to go home immediately to earn their daily bread in peaceful ways. But one of them stood out. Dressed in fine clothes, he did all the talking, was clearly well nourished and didn't appear to have suffered too much exertion. He was the son of a silk manufacturer from Lyon, who had just been bringing a transport of rails to the Front when he'd been caught up in the offensive and taken prisoner. Full of patriotic enthusiasm, he pitied Schlump for clinging to his belief in a German victory. (Schlump was not absolutely convinced by this belief, but he wasn't going to let the big-mouth know that.) He spoke of the Americans, who were unloading huge volumes of guns, automobiles, munitions and soldiers by the day. 'They're in the process of laying a railway in a dead-straight line to the east: eight tracks side by side. You'll be rolled over in a few weeks,' he said.

'Oh, you brave Frenchies,' Schlump retorted. 'You have to mobilise the entire world to defeat the lone Germans. What's more, I think you have a particularly vivid imagination!'

Their argument went on for ages, touching subjects such as who had instigated the war in the first place, and what on earth they were fighting for. Eventually the Frenchman said, 'Listen, back home we tell a lovely fable that will make the causes and outcome of the war perfectly clear.' And he launched into his story with great eloquence and gesticulation.

'Two families of chickens lived on a large farm that belonged to a big landowner. They were separated by a high wire fence to prevent the breeds from getting crossed. One of the cocks lived peacefully with his hens, and would call them over whenever he found some corn. Each time they laid an egg he saluted them by scratching his claws and cackling loudly. The other cockerel was forever running up and down the fence, ruffling his feathers, flapping his wings, stretching out his neck and opening his beak as if he were about to kill off his honest neighbour.

'One day, when the sunshine was especially bright and pleasant, the wicked cock flew over the fence and attacked his peaceful brother. The ambushed cockerel, who'd just found an earthworm and whose mind was on anything but war, was given a severe beating. His comb was bleeding and one eye had been pecked out, allowing him to see only half of the world. "Right," he cried out rancorously, "now you'll see who's the stronger!" And he went at the invader fearlessly, striking him in the middle of the head and sending him to the ground. Then he put a foot on his body to prevent the vanquished cock from getting up again.

'After a while the wicked cockerel opened his eyes and said wearily, "Look, brother. Here I am, lying defencelessly in your power, with no strength left to fight. Goodness and love are the most wonderful gifts the Creator endowed us poor animals with to enable us to demonstrate that we are worthy of Him. Surely you're not going to show your contempt for these divine gifts; surely you will forgive your opponent who lies helplessly at your feet."

'"You're right," the victor replied. "Our Lord God gave us reason that we may allow our neighbour to live in peace. But he also gave us spurs and claws to defend ourselves from thieves and robbers." Whereupon he administered the death blow. "For what guarantee do I have that he won't attack me again tomorrow if I forgive him today?"'

The Frenchman looked around in triumph and took a seat.

'We're not so skilled at telling tales,' Schlump said, 'but

there is a story recounted in our country that I think is highly appropriate here. Listen – this is the story of poor Boch.

'In a village not far from my home town lived three peasants: Boch, Foch and Tim. Boch was a young man who with tireless hard work and great skill had managed to restore the inheritance his father had neglected. So it happened that on Sundays he would ride proudly through the village, cracking his whip perhaps a touch excessively. This annoyed Foch, his neighbour, to distraction, for he was a terribly vain man, and wanted to be the only one who could crack his whip that loudly. But the most noxious of the three was Tim, the rich mill owner. He was a proper crook who would have loved nothing more than to stuff all the peasants in his sack. He went to Foch and got him worked up into a lather over Boch. Boch had long since noticed that the two of them had been putting their heads together and were plotting against him, but he didn't worry about it.

'One Sunday, while out enjoying his habitual horse ride, he saw them standing at the entrance to the village. It didn't escape his attention that each of them had a stone in his hand. They're going to strike me dead from behind, he thought. To pre-empt them, he struck the nearest one in the face with his whip; the man collapsed in a bloody heap. But that was Foch. Tim, who'd been standing behind him, dropped his stone and ran through the village, shouting his head off. In disgust, he immediately gave an account of the terrible deed that the wicked Boch had done. Then he summoned all the peasants from the village, because each one of them was in debt to him. Some peasants even hurried over from the neighbouring farm, hoping to benefit from the misfortune. They all attacked poor Boch, who defended himself like a hero, striking in every direction with super-human strength. But there were too many of them. As he moved back, someone stuck out a leg. He stumbled and fell, and then all of them laid into him, plundering everything save for his shirt. Foch, who by now had recovered, put a foot on poor Boch's torso and struck a pose. He twirled his moustache and jangled his long spurs, as if trying to say, "I'm the mightiest fellow in the whole world." But Tim had already shared the spoils.

'Time passed and Boch was restored to full health. His livestock had been stolen from the stables and all his chests broken into. But once more he started to work tirelessly and with determination. And as he never lost heart, he regained his prosperity and respect within a few years. He no longer rode through the village cracking his whip, but people made way for him and greeted him, for they all harboured massive respect for this man, and every one of them felt somewhat in his debt. It is said that Foch and Tim were deeply ashamed.'

When Schlump had finished, nobody said a word. In the corner sat an old Breton in a tattered uniform, filling his pipe. He carefully gathered up the little crumbs of tobacco that littered his coat tails and trousers, and muttered to himself, 'What a bunch of liars!'

Summer was in full swing again and the cannons were still thundering away. Sometimes Schlump would go for a walk between the fields, past gardens in bloom, and sense the sorrow that weighed down on everyone he met. But he was a young man, and the song of the lark made him blissfully happy, stirring the old longing that had accompanied him from Haumont. He felt as if someone were walking behind him with light footsteps, calling his name softly and tenderly. When he stopped and turned to listen, the voice stopped calling out, but when he turned back he felt the presence behind him again, as if it were trying to play a trick on him. Schlump continued on his way, a faint smile on his lips, stroking the ripe corn with his fingers. He didn't tell anyone about this, and when he was together with friends he forgot it altogether.

Once on his way back he passed the church, where the door was open. The organ was bellowing out and Schlump stopped. A few children were playing nearby, and the sun warmed the large square. Large flies were sleeping on the white wall beneath the colourful church windows, and behind him the sparrows were bickering. Schlump went inside. It took a while to get used to the darkness. He sat on a small chair beside the alcove and looked around. He was all alone save for the organ booming around the tall interior. A powerful bundle of yellow sunrays slanted diagonally across the chancel, and countless sparks of light played on the shining gilded sword of the Archangel Michael.

On a wide pillar in front of Schlump stood Joan of Arc on a console with her white flag and helmet that bore a sparkling golden lily. Blonde locks flowed on to her shoulders. Schlump looked into her brown eyes and caressed her fine lips, her beautiful arms and her delicate slim fingers. He felt as if he'd seen her before, as if they'd once exchanged words, words from the heart that had deeply stirred his soul. Tired, he leaned his head against the rest of the prie-dieu. Above him the organ droned, filling everything with its earnest and uncanny chords, as if trying to talk to him about death and damnation. Schlump pictured himself back in the trenches, surrounded by dead soldiers in pools of their own blood. Lying on their stomachs, they turned their heads to look at him. As he fled, he came across ever more green faces staring into his eyes. He had to stumble over horrifically mutilated bodies, and everywhere before him the ground crumbled away, exposing mass graves where men rotted and decayed in their thousands. He waded through these bodies, some of which were still moving, having been buried alive. Worms crawled out of others and up his boots. Dying men staggered towards him with terrible injuries and lay down at his feet.

Schlump moaned. He wanted to escape, but the men hung on to him and so he had no choice but to drag them along. Thrashing about, he heard a delicate, soft voice calling out. He looked up. Joan of Arc had climbed down, leaned her flag against the pillar and removed her helmet. Smiling, she offered him her beautiful hand. It was then that he recognised her: Johanna, the girl he'd spoken to so bashfully back at home. 'I've often followed you and called out your name,' she said, 'but you've never recognised me. Do you remember when war broke out, you kissed me beneath the chestnut trees? But you didn't want to dance. And do you remember the letter I sent to the hospital? I was terribly worried about you. Do you remember we talked in the street? You see, I've been praying for you all the time, to protect you. I've often followed you and called out your name, but you've never recognised me.' St Joan leaned towards Schlump and gave him a kiss. Then she took away her hand, put on her helmet and picked up her flag.

And when Schlump woke up, she was standing back on the console. But, as in his dream, there seemed to be the hint of a smile on her lips.

The organ had stopped playing, and the organist came clattering down the stairs in his boots. He was a soldier in a grey uniform with a bandage around his head.

Schlump went outside; the sun had set. He strode home, still half dreaming like a child who's just been given their Christmas presents. That evening he sat down and wrote a letter to Johanna. He wrote late into the night. Beside him lay a heap of scrunched-up paper. Finally, seeming satisfied, he got up and read through his letter one last time:

Dear Johanna,
I can't stop thinking about you. Do you remember when we said goodbye to each other in the street, and I was unable to utter a word? If there's no other man in your life, if you still love me as much as you did when you wrote to me in hospital, dear Johanna, please write me another letter like that, without delay. I am longing to see you again; I can't stop thinking about you. But if you have another, then don't write to me for I'll be desperately unhappy.
    With warmest greetings,
    Schlump

From now on Schlump went regularly to the church and

sat in front of St Joan, who never failed to smile at him with her lovely eyes.

Only a few days later, a letter arrived from his home town, which made him the happiest soldier in the German army.

They took turns in manning the office and preparing reports for Imperial Headquarters and writing communiqués to rear-echelon headquarters. It was Schlump's turn. He was alone in the office, gazing out of the window. The door opened and in stepped a man in the uniform of the reserves, a very tall, scrawny and swarthy individual. His name was Gack; he was twenty-eight, from Schwaben, and a student in civilian life. He'd already studied his way through all the faculties, most recently philosophy, and after the war he wanted to become a priest.

'You're a lucky bugger being assigned to us, comrade,' Schlump said. 'You won't find a cushier job anywhere else. No one here has to go for inspection; we've all got insurance until the end of the war.'

The soldier looked cross and said, 'I haven't come here to take it easy; I'm going to do my duty just like those in the trenches.'

'The difference being that there's no gunfire here,' Schlump said drily. This one's a right nutter, he thought. He explained the man's duties and arranged his billet. He'd never come across anything like this in all his time as a soldier. If the man was such a good liar, why was he a mere private? He resolved to get to know the new arrival better. And the opportunity soon presented itself.

One day Schlump was crossing the marketplace when all of a sudden the sirens began wailing. At that moment there was a humming up above, too, and he dived into the nearest house. A loud, blood-curdling whistle pierced the air, followed by a bang. The cellar boomed, they all jumped and the French cried out, '*Mon Dieu, mon Dieu, seigneur!*' The humming stopped, the sirens fell silent and Schlump went back outside. A crowd of people had gathered in the street. A bomb had fallen in the middle of the marketplace, and a young woman had been hit by the shrapnel. It was the French girl who cooked for them; she'd been pregnant. What a horrible sight, impossible to look at. They covered the body and took her away. Schlump went to the office, where Gack was the only one present because it was still quite early. Still agitated, Schlump explained what had happened and cursed the British for pointlessly dropping their bombs on towns and cities. 'This entire war is nothing but the cruellest, vilest slaughter, and if mankind can put up with such an atrocity for years, or stand by and look on, well, it deserves nothing but contempt. But he who fashioned mankind, he ought to be thoroughly ashamed of himself, for his creation is an utter disgrace!'

Schlump was about to continue his tirade when Gack stood up, rolled his eyes and thundered, 'Stop right there! What you are saying is blasphemy! I will not tolerate such talk in my presence!'

'Come on, comrade, don't get so worked up. I didn't mean you,' Schlump said.

The lanky man had sat back down and now continued more calmly. 'I'm well aware that I'm not the Creator, but

I cannot permit you to blaspheme about things you do not understand.' Then he delivered a long philosophical speech that Schlump only grasped about half of. 'You see,' he concluded, 'one must differentiate between the longer and shorter point of view. From the shorter point of view all the war brings is sorrow, suffering and unbelievable torment. But seen from the longer perspective, one comes to a different conclusion. Just think about how many people have died over the course of the millennia. What do a few million more matter, who represent not even a handful in the endless sea of eternity? Are you trying to tell me that the individual counts for anything? The individual is nothing, he has no intrinsic value, he is just a part of a much larger totality, a nation. The individual has no soul, but a nation does. And the individual only has value when he is of use to his people.

'Do you think that the Greeks, who we esteem so highly, would have produced such wonderful works of art and such monumental ideas if the people had been worthless, if nothing but a handful of talented individuals had lived amongst them, while the masses were inept? No, the nation worked together as a whole, generation after generation, to accumulate such talent in the figures of Plato, Phidias and Homer. For this reason it is wrong to eulogise these men for having given us such works of genius; rather we ought to eulogise the nation that gave birth to such men. Indeed, it would be better if we forgot the names of these men altogether. And so it is *not* pointless when a war like this occurs. Many · have to die; the entire people must suffer terribly.

'But know this: greatness comes only from suffering! Did the Greeks not suffer? And can there be greater suffering than war? We must all suffer now, and our people should be happy to enjoy the privilege of suffering more than any other in this war. This suffering is the price we have to pay to ensure that men will arise from our midst who will tower above the rest of us and guarantee the honour and glory of our nation for all time. There is but one thing to consider, my friend: on your own you are nothing, but the honour and greatness of your people is everything.'

Schlump said nothing, for he realised that the swarthy soldier meant what he said. But as he sat there in silence, he wondered why this man who'd talked so big had opted for a soft job here rather than heading straight for the trenches, where surely he'd be able to experience far greater suffering for his nation. Looking at him frankly, Schlump posed this very question. The philosopher answered, 'I am here because my captain ordered me here. I will go at once to the trenches, and with a joyful heart, if he so commands. But I also know,' he added, lowering his voice, 'I also know why providence led me to a place where I have a lot of time on my hands. Look, I know that we are going to win the war' – at this Schlump gave a look of astonishment – 'and after the war there will be a great united Europe in which the soul of every people will be free to unfold itself. Its leader will be a man with a superhuman soul, a man from our nation, which has suffered more than any other.'

He spoke increasingly softly. 'Friend, I have been called upon to create a language for this united Europe, with whose help all nations will be able to live side by side in harmony, working happily, in peaceful competition. The name of this language is Europarozn. I need to work on it for another five years at most; the war is going to last that long.' He showed Schlump a huge stack of paper that he carried around in his kitbag. He'd written it all at night, when he was undisturbed. 'To make room in my kitbag,' he whispered, 'I ate my iron rations.'

Schlump left the room shaking his head, flabbergasted at the peculiar madness of Gack the philosopher.

The captain in charge of the postal censor's office came from Breslau and was a refined gentleman. He'd been summoned from home directly to Imperial Headquarters, where he was awarded the Iron Cross, second class. He won the Iron Cross, first class during his time in Maubeuge when two women were killed in the course of an air attack. Unable to retreat to the safety of the cellar in time, the captain had been wounded by a small splinter in the thumb, which had then bled. For this he also received the black Wound Badge. He'd been transferred to the postal censor's office because he could speak Polish, but he never monitored the Polish post.

He presided over the office with great skill by signing his name three times a day. This lasted from eleven in the morning till twenty to twelve, at which time his duties were complete for the day. He had two orderlies whose tasks were to feed his pigs and send large packages back home.

One day he called Jolles into his office. 'Now, Jolles,' he said, 'let me tell you what happened to me today. I was coming out of the officers' mess when I caught sight of the following lines daubed on a wall: "With equal rations and equal pay, the war would be over any day!" Are you acquainted with this little rhyme, Jolles?'

'Yes, sir.'

'I see. Well, it's quite new to me. Utter nonsense, of course. Anyway, on I go a little further and bump into a chap who's clearly straight out of the trenches. Uniform in an appalling state. Jumps down from the pavement and stands to attention. But his deportment! Belly out, head to one side, hollow back. I stop him. "Don't you know that you salute an officer by putting your hand up to your cap?"

"'Sorry, Captain," the fellow grins, "I thought that because the uniform was so fine I had a general in front of me!" What do you think, Jolles, how am I to interpret that?'

'Well, Captain,' Jolles said with a serious face, 'there's no doubt about it; that was sheer mockery. Those fellows have no respect for officers any more. Let's hope it doesn't get any worse,' he added with a smile. Then Jolles went to see Schlump and gleefully related the story.

But his prophecy had been right: it got much worse that evening. A theatre had been set up in Bohain, in a former dance hall. The performance was scheduled to begin at eight o'clock. The officers sat downstairs in the stalls. In the first rows were the rear-echelon officers and the ladies, behind them the front officers, but not many, then a few rear-echelon sergeants. Upstairs in the gallery, facing the stage, sat the soldiers, mostly wounded men from the hospitals. Schlump was upstairs too, with his friend Jolles.

It was long past eight o'clock, but the curtain had not yet been raised. The soldiers were getting restless and cracking jokes. In the front row one of them stood up, took off his coat, turned it inside out and put it back on with the lining showing. He hung his cap on his nose and started larking about. The soldiers were delighted by his clowning and applauded heartily.

The commanding officer, however, who was sitting downstairs in the front row between two St John's nurses, was not at all pleased. He shuffled edgily on his chair, taking out his monocle and sticking it back into his pathetically daft face. When applause broke out upstairs, he leapt up and screeched to the soldiers in an irate voice, 'I demand silence!' At a stroke they went quiet. The clown, however, turned around and looked down in astonishment. Then he turned to his comrades and shouted, very audibly, 'The colonel is right. You shouldn't make jokes in front of these fine gentlemen. Instead, let's sing a song together about the war. Ready?

> 'Who has his fill of women and wine,
> Whose bed is creaking all of the time?'

And the chorus of soldiers joined in:

> 'It's that bastard behind the line.'

The commandant leapt up, as red as a lobster, and was so irate that his voice cracked when he yelled, 'Quiet!'

But the clown was not to be interrupted. He sang to the attentive audience:

'Who has to starve, who has to sweat,
Who has to live in the filth and the wet?'
Chorus: 'We do.'

'Who's nice to your face, who raises a glass,
But behind your back calls you an arse?'
Chorus: 'The top brass.'

'Who eats with the rats, who shits in the mud,
Before dying a nobody in his own blood?'
Chorus: 'We do.'

The clown was about to continue but the commandant screamed like a lunatic, 'Gendarme! Bring that man down now!'

There is nothing more odious to a front-line soldier than the sight of a military gendarme with the metal badge on his chest. They all started jeering and hooting and yelling: 'Come up! Come up here!' Then, all that could be heard amidst the rumpus were odd, scattered words: 'Mincemeat … pulp … lights out … knives out … three men to stir the blood!' The unfortunate gendarme had to obey his orders. Full of trepidation, he went upstairs; the jangling of his spurs could be heard through the racket. But upstairs it got quieter. They let him make his way past the front row to the middle. Then hundreds of fists laid into him, knocking the man over the railings. He lay motionless on the floor below; his neck was broken.

Two medical orderlies came forward and took him away. Downstairs, the ladies had jumped up from their seats in horror, and the officers formed a protective ring around them. A terrible scrum ensued, and within moments the entire hall was empty.

But a large pool of blood shimmered below the gallery.

As the communiqués said, our troops had been withdrawn to entrenched positions. The rear of the eighteenth army had long since retreated a considerable distance. First to Avesnes, but then further back to Belgium, to Charleroi. Not far from there, in one of those industrial villages on the Maas, the heroes of the postal censor's office were to set up their headquarters. The whole of Belgium resembled a vast military camp, the railway stations were clogged with soldiers looking for their units, the rear was flooding back-wards, and a covert excitement had taken hold of everyone. Strong words were hurled directly at officers, and it felt as if the end was near.

Schlump was lodging with Jolles in a splendid villa, where everything lay exactly as its owners had left it when they'd fled four years earlier. The servants still lived in their quarters on the ground floor, loyally looking after their master's property.

You could buy anything you wanted in Belgium; Schlump and Jolles thought they were in paradise. They got hold of the tastiest titbits and lived even better than in Bohain. The caretaker's wife cooked for them, and everything was as good as it could be.

But this charmed life was short-lived. One day the news came through that our troops had to leave their fixed positions, and that both Lille and Tournai were now under threat. Belgian territory was no longer regarded as safe; it was time to move on again. The postal censor's office was in an old house beside the garden of a wonderful little castle, in which the officers of some rear unit had set up a mess. One morning Schlump went over and said hello to the cook standing by the gate. 'Comrade,' the cook called out. 'Listen to this – last night all my officers did a runner, in secret, without saying a word!'

'What!' Schlump exclaimed. 'Crikey! That's not good.' He hurried back to Jolles and told him the news. Jolles became deadly serious. 'It's high time we made ourselves scarce too,' he said.

A few minutes later the soldiers at the postal censor's office were discussing what to do. They came to the following conclusions:

One: There wasn't a moment to lose.

Two: Schlump was in charge of provisions. To this end he had to get the cook to join forces with them and bring all his supplies.

Three: Jolles had to negotiate with the railwaymen to secure a carriage.

Four: The orderlies were to negotiate with the captain.

Each of them went about their task. Schlump soon won the cook over. It transpired that he had the most amazing supplies, which would last for a month at least. The captain agreed to everything. Jolles, on the other hand, was having trouble. The freight yard was full of trains, which were all ready to be sent eastwards. But there was a lack of loco-motives. Jolles reported back and got them all to give him money, whatever they had left, so he could persuade some railwaymen to hook up one more carriage to the first train scheduled to leave. Its locomotive had been in steam for two days and was waiting for a clear track.

It worked. All day long they toiled to load their carriage with supplies: huge quantities of conserves, bread, fat, cigarettes by the thousand, schnapps and large bottles of rum. In addition there were mattresses to sleep on, blankets, and a little stove, which they set up immediately. That evening they moved into their carriage. The captain sat in one corner, looking troubled. Beside him stood Gack the philosopher, equipped for action with his kitbag and rifle, keeping watch. They waited the whole of the following day and night, eventually getting bored by the delay.

On the afternoon of the third day, Schlump and Jolles left the train. They went to Charleroi to say goodbye to the war and the rear echelon over a bottle of wine. The city felt like it did during the annual fair. Soldiers streamed out of every alley; wherever you looked, you saw field-grey uniforms. They went into a bar which until then had been out of bounds to soldiers. Every table was full of officers, who were surprised to see the two of them come in, but they didn't say anything. Jolles ordered the best wine he knew from his considerable experience, and they celebrated a wonderful quiet hour. They moved on to a cabaret theatre where the Belgians went to drink their absinthe. The locals sat at small round tables, hats on their heads, and some danced between the chairs to the music. They were all very excited. On the podium beside the band stood a beautiful girl with a wooden leg, singing a wonderful selection of songs, the audience joining in occasionally.

All of a sudden a surprised voice shouted out Schlump's name. It was the architect he'd made the counterfeit money with. They celebrated their reunion, drinking greater volumes at greater speed.

Eventually Schlump could only see the world through a fog. He could just about make out that all the tables and chairs had been overturned, and that the pretty girl with the wooden leg seemed to be rolling around with someone on the podium. They left around midnight. Jolles had disappeared and Schlump staggered back with the architect to his billet in Rue du Mont, where he had a large room with two beds. They lay down. The cool air had sobered them up slightly. 'Look,' the architect said, 'I'm on my way home with a civilian and a wagon with two horses. In the end I worked in an exchange bureau like you, and now I've got to take the coffers to Germany. With my horse and the Frenchman who's been my agent; he's got to decamp with me, obviously. We've got around a million and a half in the till. Recently the French have been coming to give us masses of German money. They want their own local-issue money back.' Schlump had already fallen asleep and couldn't hear the architect.

But then, at four in the morning, he woke with a start, as if someone had called his name. Still tipsy, he swiftly got dressed and crashed down the stairs. He hurried through streets he'd never seen. He was hit by blasts of cold air, and ravenous-looking workers shuffled past. A tram packed with people rattled down the street, and on one corner a half-naked, freezing girl called out in a weak, timorous voice, 'Gazette, Gazette!' Schlump took in all of this as if in a dream, but the girl's voice penetrated deep into his soul and he would often think about it later on. He passed through unfamiliar suburbs; at some point he roamed across a temporary bridge over the Maas, and then all of a sudden he heard Jolles calling his name. He was standing beside their carriage. He stumbled in without thinking, and as he dozed off, he could hear the wheels squealing and the carriage rumbling. They were on the move. He'd arrived just in time.

When he awoke, they'd stopped outside Namur. It was afternoon and the train was making slow progress, often having to remain stationary for hours at a time. In Namur they stopped again for hours. Beside them was another train which had arrived before them and was also trying to head eastwards. Here they found out the latest news: a convoy of elegant automobiles had driven through Belgium and fled to Holland. Apparently the Kaiser had been amongst the passengers.

Gack, the tall philosopher, stood up and rolled his eyes. Raising his hand as if to take an oath, he said clearly and solemnly, 'The Kaiser will never abandon his people. You will see, Comrades,' he continued in an exalted and prophetic voice, 'you will see that the holy war is just beginning. The Kaiser will rally around an elite of noble officers, placing himself at its head, and then march west. Dagger in hand, he will charge the enemy, and be joined by ever more groups comprising the noblest elements of our people. They will follow the white banner that the Crown Prince, his ensign, will unfurl. He will stop those who flee and he will terrify the enemy. He will breach the lines with his very body. He will fall in battle, but his body will accompany the offensive as a holy symbol of the holy war. It will be a majestic battle; the enemy will be petrified and the world will acclaim the heroes. We will conclude a noble peace in which revenge will have no place. We will plant the white banner in the earth, around which the very best of our people will henceforth assemble. Their names will never be known, for they will call themselves Germans. The entire people will emulate them in tireless labour, and they will be a model for all nations!'

He paused. The others stared at him in mockery. 'He's quite mad!' Jolles said.

They stopped for ages in A., a small town between Namur and Liège. Suddenly Jolles came running in and said that the locomotive was moving off with the front half of the train. They leapt out and saw that he'd been telling the truth. They cursed furiously, but there was nothing they could do other than stay where they were. Schlump and Jolles headed into town to look for somewhere to stay; the others cleared out.

When the two friends arrived in the town, they got a shock. Flags were draped from all the houses; everywhere they saw the black, yellow and red Belgian colours: armistice! The civilians were wandering around looking proud and confident.

It was hard to find quarters. Everywhere was full of soldiers, no matter where they went, in every street, in every house – field-grey soldiers. They finally stumbled across an empty room where they could lodge with their supplies.

All afternoon they hauled their goodies from the station and moved in. In the evening they went for a wander around the town. Jolles had found the rear headquarters and managed to obtain pay for all of them, including their arrears. Schlump was handed a fifty-mark note, which he slipped into his back trouser pocket. That money was going to come in handy. All the coffee houses and pubs were packed; on the pavements and squares the soldiers stood in groups chatting animatedly to each other. The most extraordinary rumours were voiced. One group claimed that revolution had broken out across the world, the British had deposed their king, the French were mutinying, and back home all the officers had been shot. They stopped French prisoners-of-war who had somehow escaped and were still wearing their red trousers, and jabbered on to them about world revolution. The Frenchmen just smiled, at a loss as to what to say. Others reported that the British had ignored the armistice and were advancing, destroying everything in their path. On the market square were service corps soldiers, each with a cow on the end of a rope, which they were selling for eight marks. A company of recruits had sold its machine guns to the civilians at two marks apiece.

That night there was shooting, and the following morning dead soldiers were found in the streets. It was high time they pushed on. But how? They could hardly carry their supplies on their backs!

They were standing by the main road that led from west to east, watching intently the scene being played out before them: the retreat of the rear echelon! It had been going on all day, one column after another – service corps wagons, hours-long processions of lorries, flocks of sheep, ox-drawn carts that had come from the Ukraine in spring, in between a single soldier pushing his kitbag in a perambulator, a huge herd of mares, each with an adorable filly at her side, more lorries, and behind a reservist with a pipe in his mouth, slightly tipsy, humming a soldier's song. He gave everyone a friendly wave with his walking stick and seemed to be without a care in the world. Then came more columns, automobiles, foot artillery, sappers, service corps columns, engineers – everything and everyone that makes up an army's vast retinue. As time went on, the procession became ever more densely packed, and it was no longer possible to get from one side of the road to the other.

They were standing there all together – Jolles, Schlump, the orderlies, the cook, the captain – and no one knew what to do. The philosopher Gack stood apart from the rest, looking gloomy and muttering to himself. The captain wanted to contact rear command for some orders. But they knew that wouldn't be of any help either. Jolles got chatting with some bridge engineers who'd sent their officers packing. Their plan was to use their pontoons to get home by river, but they were out of supplies. Jolles didn't trust them as they were drunk and lacking any discipline. Eventually he managed to find a service corps unit which was also without a commander. They were haggling with a driver who was standing with his two ponies. He was prepared to take them in return for provisions for him and the horses until they got to the border.

They were out of bread. They'd found plenty of preserves,

cigars and delicacies in the mess, but not enough bread. Jolles, their jack of all trades, came to the rescue once more. He'd discovered that there was a supply train in the freight yard, which must have bread too. They crossed the bridge over the Maas and ran back to the station. A supply train was indeed there, but plundering was already well under way. If they were going to get anything they'd have to wait their turn. They watched Belgian civilians roll out enormous cheeses as large as mill wheels. French prisoners were looting a carriage laden with sekt. They were smashing the tops off the bottles and necking the contents, cutting their lips in the process. Next to them service corps soldiers and automobile drivers were fighting over a carriage crammed with furs for the drivers and officers. Infantrymen were at loggerheads over a carriage full of bread.

Jolles sprang forward and shouted out, 'Comrades, stop! Comrades! There's enough for everybody!' They did stop. He jumped up into the carriage and tossed out the loaves. Each man took away whatever he could carry. The philosopher had stayed behind in their quarters to guard their supplies and had lent his rifle to the cook, to whom the other men brought all their booty.

Another carriage contained infantry uniforms. Four men were throwing out coats and trousers. Beside the carriage, soldiers stood in their underwear, helping themselves to new clothes. Schlump, who was fed up with his shabby coat, went over and grabbed an elegant new *Litewka*. He put it on and threw the old one away. Jolles had also rustled up a bicycle from somewhere. Packing everything on to their backs, they headed into town.

Near the bridge they heard shots and sharp commands. Jolles, who was in front on his bicycle, got off, turned around and yelled to them, 'Back! Looters are being shot!' They gave him a puzzled look, then understood. Turning swiftly on their heels, they darted through a house and hid their booty in a stable. 'That could have gone pear-shaped,' Jolles said. They waited a few hours, by which time the company of recruits – the only one still obeying its commanding officer – had disappeared.

Arriving back at their billet, they sat down wearily on their kitbags. Out of the blue Schlump leapt up, slapped his palm against his forehead and shouted, 'I don't believe it! What an idiot I am!'

He'd thrown away his old coat into which the ten thousand marks had been sewn. He ran back to the freight yard as fast as he could, but the Belgians had already squirrelled everything away, including his coat. Schlump was a poor man once again.

They left very early the next morning, but the retreat on the old military road was already in full swing and they had to wait for hours before there was a break in the procession and they could join the throng. Overnight people had stuck up pieces of white paper signed by Hindenburg on their houses. The text called for level-headedness and asked the troops to form soldiers' councils and obey their orders. Schlump could sense just how difficult this decision must have been for an old field commander who would never abandon his troops; later he realised that by issuing this order the ancient Hindenburg had spared his people no end of misery. The soldiers' councils felt they bore responsibility, they negotiated with the officers, and so a terrible danger was averted: chaos.

When they finally took their place on the road, they were part of a never-ending line that slowly twisted and turned its way through the whole of Belgium back to Germany. Following the River Maas, they passed magnificent castles that were reflected in the green water of this wide, proud river. But on both sides of the road they saw the first victims of the retreat: corpses, automobiles, dying horses kicking with their back feet as if trying to drive away death that was squatting on their bellies. Belgian peasants had come bearing neat little baskets, offering the soldiers butter at the most exorbitant prices.

When they reached Huy, they left the beautiful valley and the majestic river, and turned right to climb the steep road that led up to the high plateau. The heavy wagons, the large automobiles and the foot artillery continued on the lower road to Liège, which they'd conquered four years previously. Huy is an old nest clinging to the rocks that descend in a sheer drop to the Maas. From the top they had a wonderful view. The sun was shining, and in the distance blue forests were gleaming. Jolles rode ahead on his bike, the captain had got hold of a walking stick and strode alongside the horses; behind him were the two orderlies. Schlump sat on the wagon, singing a song. Behind trotted Gack the philosopher, kitbag on his back and rifle over his shoulder. He was wearing a sombre expression and muttering to himself. They passed through silent forests, where the autumn had left a few flashes of gold. The sky, however, had preserved all the colours of autumn, and the men were caressed by a soft, cool breeze.

Schlump stopped singing and started to dream. He thought of when the war began, that summer's night when he'd been allowed to kiss Johanna, of poor Michel, of the nightingale that had enchanted him, of his strange, long dream. He felt as if he could now go on with the dream, as if Michel were wandering next to him, invisibly with his wife, as if he were pointing to the blue mountains that Schlump had seen in his dream and which he was now heading towards. He was filled with a wonderful sense of bliss, delightfully certain that everything would turn out all right in the end. He thought of Joan of Arc in the church, who was the same person as his Johanna back home – the girl he'd soon be able to embrace again. He saw the world and the future in a thousand marvellous colours. He would work like the dear departed Michel; he was determined to make something of his life, because surely there would be peace again now, soon, peace! Peace and decency – how lovely life would be! What a golden era was beginning now! All of a sudden he started laughing out loud for sheer joy; the shocked carriage driver turned round. Schlump was back to his cheerful self, and he sang again, a bright and joyful tune.

He noticed the swarthy philosopher walking behind him. 'Hey, what are you doing?' Schlump laughed. 'Are you scoffing acorns?'

The philosopher rolled his eyes and gave him a wild look. 'I finished the last of my bread yesterday.'

'But look, there's plenty more bread here, and meat, and whatever you fancy!'

'Are you saying,' the philosopher thundered, 'are you saying that I'm a thief, a robber, a plunderer? What you're offering me are stolen goods, aren't they? Do none of you feel any shame?'

Schlump gazed at him in absolute astonishment and said nothing. They were already some way into the uplands of the Belgian Eifel; the road snaked from one peak to the next. They crossed a narrow valley and climbed back up the steep road on the other side. In front of them and behind them they could see the endless procession advancing slowly. It looked as if the road had come to life and was heading eastwards with them, back home.

Evening came and they looked for somewhere to stay and keep their horses. They would be on their way again very early the next morning. When the captain complained about having to sleep on straw, they laughed, and Jolles said, 'Well, Captain, just be glad you never had to go to war; sometimes we had to sleep in shit.'

They passed through Stavelot and arrived in Malmedy, the first town in Germany: home. Here they learned that revolution really had broken out in Berlin and other cities. Near the station they stopped for ages. Supposedly a train was ready to leave. Jolles said, 'Our supplies are running low, so I think it's best if everyone tries to get home as soon as possible.' They packed their kitbags and handed out the bread and tinned meat. The captain was chatting with a group of officers. The philosopher said he'd look after the captain's share; the others shook his hand and left.

The station was a horrific sight. A supply train carrying flour had derailed, strewing flour knee-high between the tracks. There *was* a train ready to depart; the locomotive was already steaming and soldiers were running back and forth excitedly. But there was no room; all the carriages were jam-packed and the windows had been smashed, as if there'd been a fight for every place.

Suddenly Jolles whistled; he'd found an empty brakeman's cab. He and Schlump piled in; the others, the orderlies and the cook, had vanished. More and more soldiers appeared. Russian prisoners in their dark-yellow uniforms squatted on the buffers and roofs. An entire detachment of recruits, really young lads who'd run away from their officers, were still racing up and down the platform. They perched on the running boards and steps leading up to the brakeman's cab. 'Hold on tight, boys, when the train leaves,' said Schlump, who was peering out of the window.

Out of nowhere the swarthy philosopher Gack appeared with his kitbag and rifle. He went searching all the way down the train until he spied Schlump. He looked alarmingly feral; his beard had grown over the past few days, his eyes were sat deep in their sockets, and his voice sounded desperately sad.

'Schlump, I beseech you, both of you, think of the soldier's oath you swore and return to your captain!'

He spoke so loudly that the entire train could hear. Men stared at him from every window, and when he'd finished he was met by resounding laughter from all quarters. One man called out in a shrill and scornful voice, 'Keep your hair on, old chap! After all, the Kaiser himself has done a runner!'

The swarthy philosopher shrugged when he heard the Kaiser mentioned. He rolled his eyes before taking a large army pistol from his belt, which he must have found some-where, and shooting himself in the chest. He cast Schlump a final glance before collapsing to the ground. The kitbag slid over his head, the straps had come loose and countless sheets of draft paper, filled with writing, billowed over his face.

At that moment the locomotive pulled away and the train started moving.

They headed into the rough peaks of the Eifel. At night the train stopped somewhere. Jolles got out; he wanted to continue on foot to Aachen, where he had a sister. It was icily cold. The poor boys on the runner boards had vanished and the Russians on the buffers were nowhere to be seen either. There were a few left on the roofs; they'd frozen to death. Jolles disappeared into the darkness. It was a brief farewell and they never saw each other again.

The train stopped in Jingerrath. It wasn't going any further. Schlump went down into the waiting room to warm himself up. He was on his own now. A few soldiers were asleep beside him. He came back out a few hours later. Up on the platform – like a vast block – was a column of soldiers. They waited in formation, in rows of twenty, silent and still on the endless platform. There must have been in excess of a thousand men, waiting for a fast train from Strasbourg which was going on to Cologne. Schlump knew there was going to be a terrific struggle, and he was right. When a rumbling sounded in the rails, the soldiers tensed in anticipation like a huge beast crouching for the kill. A pair of white lights appeared in the night. They approached, but then stopped a fair distance from the station. The beast set itself in motion, charging at speed towards the lights. Schlump ran behind. A fierce battle ensued for every window. They crawled on top of the locomotive and the coal wagon, screams and cries pierced the night, glass shattered. Then all was quiet and the lights went on their way.

Schlump went back down to the waiting room. He was hungry. Unpacking his supplies, he ate in peace. Another train pulled in above; he went on eating. After a few hours he went out and saw a long passenger train. He walked the length of the platform. Everything was dark and quiet, then he heard someone speak.

'Any room in there?' Schlump asked.

No answer. Someone laughed and he knew that it was hopeless. He headed back towards the locomotive, where he'd seen a slim crack of light. It was the baggage car. Schlump took the fifty-mark note from his back trouser pocket and waited. Waited a long time until finally someone came out. A postal official. Schlump went up to him and offered his hand with the fifty-mark note. 'Do you think you might find some space for me, comrade?' The man inspected the note with his pocket lamp, then said, 'Come on.' He led a delighted Schlump into the warm baggage car; it was very cosy. A few drivers and service corps soldiers were sitting playing cards. 'Got any cigarettes?' they asked. 'You'll get schnapps in return!' Schlump had some packets in his coat, from the officers' mess in Charleroi. The train pulled out of the station and he fell asleep, comfortably stretched out on a soft bale.

They alighted in Cologne, where there were sailors with rifles slung over their shoulders, muzzles pointing down. In the underpass, rifles were piled high to the ceiling. The officers were not wearing epaulettes.

Schlump caught a local train to Kassel, and once there found a train ready to leave for Halle which had room. But they had to wait in an unheated carriage until six in the evening. At four o'clock a locomotive arrived, steaming, puffing, screeching and wheezing. But the train didn't move; only a shudder quivered down its spine. At six o'clock another locomotive appeared and it took them twelve hours to get to Halle, where Schlump had a connection straight away. He was amazed that everything was still running so smoothly. His journey took another twelve hours. And when, in the evening, he got out in his small home town, the guard asked him for his ticket. Schlump looked at him blankly. 'A ticket?' he asked. 'Well you see, comrade, we didn't really have time to sort that out.' He left the station as a simple soldier, just as on the day he'd embarked from there.

Someone was standing on the steps by the exit: Johanna – St Joan. Schlump rushed towards her. 'How did you know?'

She gazed at him, her eyes radiating happiness. 'I've been waiting for you every day,' she said. He took her in his arms and kissed her in front of all the other people there.

Then the two of them went to his mother, who at that moment could not have dreamed that the happiest moment in her whole life had just arrived.

AFTERWORD

A pale wall in the living room of a grey house with a pointed roof in the thousand-year-old Thuringian town of Altenburg. The sun is shining through the large windows. Against one wall is a blue sofa, at the other end of the room a grand piano, while a colourful Bauhaus carpet adorns the floor. Cups and small porcelain plates sit on a round coffee table. A closer look at the pale wall reveals a fine crack in the plaster. Here, on this wall, in this house, a strange German fairy tale began. Or is this where it ended?

The house, with its large fir trees in the garden and white bench beside the front door, was built at the beginning of the 1930s by doctor of philosophy and schoolmaster Hans Herbert Grimm. Some of the money to finance the house came from a book he'd written, although nobody here in Altenburg nor anyone anywhere else was to know he was its author. *Schlump – Tales and adventures from the life of the anonymous soldier Emil Schulz, known as 'Schlump'. Narrated by himself*: the book of his life. Grimm was worried that he wouldn't be able to go on living normally if it became known that he'd written the novel. It would spell the end of his career as a teacher, and of his peaceful existence in his beloved Altenburg, if word got out that he was the author of a book that described the German soldiers of the Great War as less than heroic, German military strategy as misguided, senseless and foolish, the Kaiser as a coward, and the entire war as a cruel, bad joke.

Hans Herbert Grimm wanted to remain unidentified. But of course he wanted his book to be a success, too, with lots of readers. This was not easy from a position of anonymity. Kurt Wolff, who published *Schlump*, made great efforts to publicise the book, spending considerable amounts of money on the promotional literature. 'Schlump!' was written in large type, followed by the question 'Have you read *Schlump* yet?' and the invitation 'If not, then make sure to do so as soon as possible. You'll be glad you did as you won't have laughed so much in a long time. Here is a book which every German man must read.' According to the text of the advertisement, the novel was politically neutral and unbiased, but every war veteran would be able to recognise themselves and their experiences in it. *Schlump*, it continued, represented a turning point in popular and truthful depictions of the war. It was nothing like the conventional, rather dry war stories. Below this, the urgent question was posed again: 'Have you read *Schlump* yet?' Followed by the prediction: 'This question will soon be on men's lips everywhere.'

Today, this exuberant leaflet can be found on a desk on the second floor of the house with a crack in the wall. Here was Hans Herbert Grimm's study. The desk is still by the window with a view of the Thuringian countryside. Beside the leaflet are manuscripts, diaries and letters. At the top of the pile is a letter written by Grimm on 3 March 1929 to his lifelong friend Alfred. By now *Schlump* had been in bookshops for a few months, but had sold only 5,500 copies. The author's mood alternates between disenchantment and hope, tending more towards the former. For only a few weeks beforehand, a book had appeared on the market that attracted everyone's attention, a book that Ullstein-Verlag was doing its utmost to turn into the biggest literary success in the Weimar Republic, a book that was selling 10,000 copies per day, a book that also had as its subject the Great War: Erich Maria Remarque's *All Quiet on the Western Front.*

Remarque's novel was talked about with enthusiasm, but also angrily denounced by war veterans and 'Stahlhelm' activists. And this was just the beginning of the triumphant and unparalleled success it would achieve both in Germany and across the globe. It soon became the German anti-war novel par excellence, stirring discussion about the whole intellectual and moral foundation of the new German republic. A documentary work, a quintessential work in clear language and with a clear message. A book that would dominate the market and debate for a long time to come. Grimm no doubt suspected this and hoped for a different outcome. He wrote to Alfred about Remarque's novel and about another book that appeared at the same time on a similar subject, Ludwig Renn's *War:* 'Once you get beyond the sensation of the material, neither of these works is in competition with *Schlump*, in my opinion. For now, the need for realistic depictions of the central event in our entire generation's lives swamps any artistic aspirations as far as this material is concerned. I personally think that the time is ripe for *Schlump*, but I know it's going to take longer than my patience would like.'

The 'sensation of the material' endured, however. There was still much to tell of the story of the Great War. The majority of war-related books that appeared at the beginning of the 1920s were heroic accounts of the fighting, – heroic, clinical accounts of the deeds of German soldiers in the field, beginning with Ernst Jünger's *Storm of Steel* in 1920.

Many others followed. The shock of defeat was still fresh; readers and no doubt authors, too, needed to make sense of the heavy losses, the pain and the deprivations of the four-year conflict. It is not until the second half of the 1920s that we see the first proper literary engagement with World War I: the questions of everyday life during the war, heroism and futility. Arnold Zweig began this process with his 1927 novel *The Case of Sergeant Grischa*. After this came Ludwig Renn's *War* in 1928, Oskar Wöhrle's *Querschläger. Das Bumserbuch. Aufzeichnungen eines Kanoniers (Ricochets. The Gunner's Book. The Account of an Artilleryman)*, Alexander Moritz Frey's *Die Pflasterkästen* (*The Stretcher-Bearers*), Edlef Köppen's *Heeresbericht* (*Army Report*) (all 1929), and Adrienne Thomas's 1930 *Katrin Becomes a Soldier*. Most of these novels were documentary in character; their portrayal of the war and military action was stripped bare, unadorned and unheroic. This style came as a shock to the reader and was a provocation to many who wished to preserve the heroic memory of their own deeds or those of fallen relatives.

When, just a few years later, the books of so-called

un-German authors started to be burned, it is not surprising that most of these anti-war novels were at the top of the list for the bonfire. *Schlump* burned along with them, the book whose authorship was known to practically nobody, and which had not received the attention from an anti-war readership that it deserved. It *had* come to the attention of the National Socialist students, however, who hadn't forgotten just how explosive in nature these pages were.

Schlump is different from all the other war books of its time. It is a fairy tale with an emphasis on the truth, a sort of docu-fable. A book in which the hero goes through hell, almost losing his belief in the goodness of the world along the way, but then returns at the end to a sort of idyll. Schlump's heroism is a heroism of resistance to hostility, misanthropy and disillusionment. He is an illusionist. He has experienced the worst a human being can experience here on earth, but he wants to go on living, wants to walk tall again in the world, and for that he needs a belief in humanity. Without that, we can infer from the book, there can be no Schlump, no Schlump alive in this world.

What kind of a young man is Schlump, the optimist who sets out into the world by going to war? A fairy-tale hero, somewhere between Tom Thumb, the Valiant Little Tailor and Hans in Luck. A boy who is saddled with the daft nickname given to him by a policeman; he's known as Schlump his entire life.

He goes to war with all the hopes and dreams harboured by his comrades before him. Only all his dreams actually come true. Having arrived in France, he's put in charge of a small commune at the age of only seventeen, the girls fall in love with him, and he tries to administer justice in his little world. He does administer justice. No prison in Loffrande? Never mind, the ruler of the commune will organise one at the other end of the town. What is going on here? What are we to make of this ridiculous, implausible idyll in the middle of the war? Or is it reality?

It is a stage, an initial stage on Schlump's journey through the world. At this point the war is still just a rattling of the window panes, a distant thunder of cannon. As everyone here knows, only fools end up in the trenches. And Schlump is certainly no fool; perhaps just a little over-optimistic, a little naïve, a little too philanthropic. It is odd that in this wartime world there appears to be no place for chauvinism and nationalistic hatred. And when later, as a recruit moving around France, Schlump is surprised by the hostile looks from the French standing at the roadside, he thinks, Oh, I see; they don't know me here yet.

It is easy to underestimate this novel; indeed the reader is even invited to do this. Schlump progresses through the war as if in a dream, floating from girl to girl and from adventure to adventure. When he finally arrives at the Front – the real war – he is treated by his superiors like a sack of peas. Then the war explodes before his very eyes. The description and depiction of sheer horror runs to no more than a few pages, but they are all the more devastating for that, branding themselves more deeply and intensely on the memory when juxtaposed against the idyllic background of the wandering tailor. The limbs of the two British soldiers flying above the heads of the Germans. The brain on top of the skull, served up as if in a restaurant. The German soldier calling out for his mother and stuck in the barbed wire, who Schlump can only rescue dead. The trumpeter with a death wish. The flare exploding in the belly of the British soldier – the gory version of a cancelled pregnancy and birth, or a child of the war: death. And then that completely surreal scene illustrating the utter madness of war: Michael in combat with the British soldier. Holding the Tommy tight to his chest, Michael grabs a grenade from his belt, stuffs it between himself and the Brit, pulls out the pin, and the two of them, still firmly entwined, are blown to bits together. A brutal love scene, a rape that ends in death. 'Michel's head rolls where they've just been fighting, ending the right way up. Eyes wide open, it looks over at Schlump, appearing as if it is trying to smile.'

What about Schlump? Does he remain cheerful, unaffected, an eternal Schlump in Luck? It seems as if he's wearing an impregnable coat against the war, as if he's protected by an invisible skin. Only twice do we see holes appear in this skin. The first occasion, shortly after Michel's dance of death, is when he briefly becomes enraged by the appetising smell of frying coming from the officers' tents: 'Schlump talked himself deeper and deeper into this bitterness; all of a sudden he saw everything with new eyes. He worked himself up and felt unhappy for the first time in his life. It was as if he'd awoken from a deep sleep; for the first time in his life he was thinking seriously about himself and the world.'

Seeing everything with new eyes. It is the eyes of the reader through which Schlump momentarily looks on from the sidelines. A reality shock for the novel's hero. For Schlump, the episode seems to have no significant effect. For the reader, however, it is a decisive moment in which our suspicions are confirmed that this is no fairy tale, but a report from a world totally out of joint. Immediately afterwards, Schlump shows his vulnerability a second time in another brief outburst of awareness: 'For a moment he lost his golden childish innocence. But it didn't last long.'

Schlump is an anti-coming-of-age novel from a world in freefall. Everything collapses; one man walks on. Like an astronaut in zero gravity. Brief moments of lucidity are dwarfed into irrelevance by the dreamlike life surrounding everything. It truly is madness. What is reality? In all seriousness, is it when an innocent young pregnant girl crosses a market square only to be blown to bits by a bomb? And when a Joan of Arc figure calls out to our hero on the opening page of the novel, chooses him and then regularly encounters him in endlessly different guises, wrapping him in a protective cloak – is that unreality? Is that the fairy tale? The docu-fable *Schlump* repeatedly challenges the reader to establish what is fable and what documentary. The rule here is that the unlikely is always the documentary part, the part that depicts so-called reality.

Following the scene in the market square where the girl is blown sky high, Schlump lays a curse on the world: 'This entire war is nothing but the cruellest, vilest slaughter, and if mankind can put up with such an atrocity for years, or stand by and look on, well, it deserves nothing but contempt. But he who fashioned mankind, he ought to be thoroughly ashamed of himself, for his creation is an utter disgrace!' Schlump voices his outrage in the presence of a newly arrived character, a messenger from the world of reality, who in a nutshell outlines the value of the war, using his historical analysis to dismiss the human sacrifice as irrelevant and statistically insignificant. The philosopher Gack, with his rational yet utopian visions of a peacefully united Europe after the war, is mad. A crazed man. Not someone the future will listen to.

Then the war is over – over and lost. Everything has disintegrated, producing the craziest, worst outcome, and yet the Schlump idyll remains as unaffected as before. 'He was filled with a wonderful sense of bliss, delightfully certain that everything would turn out all right in the end.' This wonderful certainty is the thing that even *Schlump*'s author cannot comprehend. He attributes it to his hero because that is the magical power of the author, because he knows that without this belief there cannot be an optimist like Schlump in this world. Belief, belief, belief. Despite all probability. Despite everything that has happened during the war years. When Schlump returns to Germany, he is amazed that 'everything was still running so smoothly'. His surprise is short-lived. More than anything over these years he has learned how to be amazed. The world has not changed and will not change. The crucial thing is to survive.

This Schlumpian sunny optimism is the triumph of a resounding 'nevertheless'. The sunniness of the will, in defiance of a mighty darkness. Even reading *Schlump* today, we find this darkness present everywhere. It is a book balancing on the edge of the abyss. Down below, where the hero refuses to look, darkness, despair and oblivion lie in wait.

We are back in the room in Altenburg, at the desk with

the diaries and letters. Letters from the field, too, from France, where not only Schlump but his creator, Hans Herbert Grimm, experienced the war. Grimm wrote countless letters from the Front. To his mother, and especially to his friend Alfred, his soulmate, with whom he enjoyed a literary, philosophical and intellectual friendship. Both men experienced the war similarly, as an inner phenomenon. In March 1918, Grimm wrote to his friend from Maubeuge:

Dear Alfred,

Where are you? Outside the weir is rushing. Will we ever succeed in escaping from the yoke of human beings? We're suffering at the hands of people, irrespective of who these are. Human beings are tormenting us. Where are you now? I'm worried about you.

What else is there to say? I'm no longer alone. What happened to those secret evenings when a thousand little nothings came to life? In which direction are we going?

Yours,

Hans

There are many other letters here. A good number of these speak of solitude and the desire for solitude, of perseverance, and of admiration for France and the French. When God created the French, he drank a bottle of Burgundy beforehand, Grimm writes to his mother. And 'The French boys are the smartest of all. They stand in the middle of the street and laugh at everyone.'

We can hear Schlump in this voice, Schlump's wisdom and Schlump's desperation. Just laugh at everyone, everyone and everything, the entire ridiculous world. 'The enthusiasm of desperation' is how *Schlump* describes it, and at another point surprise is expressed at 'the peculiar war…going on here'. Peculiar war – *drôle de guerre*, as the French themselves would call the coming conflict against Germany, those quiet months following the declaration of war in autumn 1939, when these countries were at war again, but a war without hostilities. A peculiar war. What war isn't peculiar?

Hans Herbert Grimm returned from the Front to begin his middle-class existence. He married Elisabeth, with whom he had a son, Frank, got his PhD, became an English, French and Spanish teacher, and wrote in his spare time. A short story, 'Schlafittelchen', appeared in *Vivos Voco*, the journal published by Herman Hesse. And then came *Schlump* with Kurt Wolff, the publisher of Franz Kafka, Arnold Zweig, René Schickele, Georg Trakl and many others.

Schlump never became a great success. Remarque's novel dominated discussion and the market. And when the fuss had died down, *Schlump* had almost been forgotten. The book was translated, appearing in both Britain and America. The English novelist J. B. Priestley wrote in *The Times* that it was 'the best of German war books so far (excluding Grischa)'. But major success was elusive. And as the author didn't want to lose his anonymity, there was little he could do about it.

He remained a teacher. In Germany the National Socialists came to power, *Schlump* was burned and banned, and at home Hans Herbert Grimm bricked up his book in the wall. He was afraid, afraid of being discovered, afraid of imprisonment and persecution. His wife advised him to flee; she said she was prepared for it, and also prepared to give piano lessons to feed the family. But he wanted to stay. Wanted to stay in his beloved Altenburg and keep teaching for as long as possible. He joined the NSDAP so he could live in safety. According to his pupils, he taught tolerance in his lessons – so far as this was possible – recommending books written by banned authors whose works had been burned, and getting the girls he taught to read them. He hated being photographed. But in the few pictures that do exist from the time, he looks terribly happy amongst his pupils, with a round face, round glasses and thin hair.

Then he had to go to war again, working as an interpreter on the Western Front. During his second war he kept a sort of diary for his son, later having it bound in red linen. Here it is before me on the desk, a pressed clover leaf on the first page, followed by the dedication 'To my son, not actually for reading – for that would be asking too much – but as a crazy souvenir from my second time at war. 1942.' This is how it begins:

Dear Frank,
If one wishes to live life sincerely and gracefully – surely the most useful form of this great art – one must be generous, letting others express their opinions first, listening to them and not contradicting until the following day, and only if one is sure that they no longer know their own minds. If they do still know their own minds, then one must leave them to it, and yet do what one must according to one's convictions.

For it is impossible that two people can agree completely

(and profoundly) on everything... Ultimately we are all alone, enclosed in a fixed shell with no exits. And each of us leads his life more or less inertly, more or less conscious and awake. This is a salutary realisation that makes life easier and spares one failure. Which is why it's in equal measures cheerful, colourful, wonderful and thrilling. One must never let oneself be troubled by this pleasure in colourfulness and incomprehensible beauty, which is offered up at every turn. Rather one must be grateful for it anywhere and at any time, sure in the knowledge that it is the inexhaustible outpouring of a secret harmony flowing through everything. And one must connect with this secret reality, the harmony of the universe, which one finds in the smallest and largest things. Then it flows into you, fills you, flows through you, shines from within you, finding you secret allies who will strengthen your soul with their power and make you lissom and flexible when life is tempestuous, felling and splitting mighty boughs.

The letter to his son goes on like this for many pages, on thin paper and in black type.

When the war was over, Grimm returned home to Altenburg. A new political system was established. On account of his NSDAP membership, he was prevented from resuming his career as a teacher, in spite of the fact that his former pupils were willing to vouch for him. It didn't even help that he finally revealed himself to be the author of the anti-war novel *Schlump*, and that his claim received official confirmation. This document is on the coffee table too, the letterhead reading 'Mayor of Altenburg'. Below this: 'I confirm that Herr Grimm, the schoolmaster resident at Braugartenweg 9, Altenburg, is the author of the well-known anti-war novel *Schlump*, published by Kurt-Wolff-Verlag in Munich. This novel also fell victim to the Nazi auto-da-fé in 1933. Knittel. Head of the Cultural Department.' The head of the district authority, too, penned an official letter in which, besides highlighting the 'anti-fascist and anti-militaristic leaning' of *Schlump*, he wrote, 'Moreover, I know from my daughter – a pupil of Dr Grimm – that he made no secret of his anti-fascist stance at school. In my opinion Dr Grimm cannot be regarded as a Nazi.'

To no avail. Hans Herbert Grimm was no longer allowed to teach. But he could work in the theatre, which he did for a season as a dramaturg. He compiled lists of plays he wanted to see on the stage in Altenburg, including Borchert's *The Man Outside* and Max Frisch's *Nun singen sie wieder* (*Now They're Singing Again*). He put ticks beside the plays that the administration approved for theatrical performance. There aren't many ticks on his list.

After eighteen months the theatre was finished too. He'd staged two plays by J. B. Priestley. Cultural policy became stricter. Grimm was forced to go and work in a sand mine. He was prohibited from working in schools or the theatre for an unspecified period. But his situation could get worse at any time. In April 1946, his good friend, fellow teacher and later headmaster of the Karolinum, Friedrich Wilhelm Uhlig, was arrested, imprisoned and then interned in Buchenwald, near Weimar, which the Soviet occupiers had continued to run as a camp. On 24 May 1948 he died there from starvation.

In summer 1950, Hans Herbert Grimm was summoned to Weimar by the authorities of the newly established GDR. He never told anybody what was discussed at this meeting. Did they make it clear to him that he'd never again be able to work as a teacher? Did they impose conditions such as obligatory membership of the SED (Socialist Unity Party), or help in founding a new block party? Would he again have to play along with a party he despised?

On 5 July, 1950 Hans Herbert Grimm went back to his family in Altenburg. Two days later, while his wife was out shopping, he killed himself in his own house.

A small crack remains in the wall.

Grimm's name is not recorded in literary histories.

In the letter to Alfred in which he expressed his concerns that Remarque's success could completely swamp his book, Grimm also wrote, 'My publisher hopes that one day someone will come along and rediscover *Schlump*.'

It is a peculiar but major stroke of fortune that today, more than a hundred years after the beginning of the war it describes, many new readers can now do exactly that.

—VOLKER WEIDERMANN
2014

OTHER NEW YORK REVIEW CLASSICS

For a complete list of titles, visit www.nyrb.com or write to:
Catalog Requests, NYRB, 435 Hudson Street, New York, NY 10014

Also available as an electronic book.